THE ROSE ARCH

THE ROSE ARCH

Linda Sole

Severn House Large Print
London & New York

This first large print edition published in Great Britain 2002 by
SEVERN HOUSE LARGE PRINT BOOKS LTD of
9-15, High Street, Sutton, Surrey, SM1 1DF.
First world regular print edition published 2001 by
Severn House Publishers, London and New York.
This first large print edition published in the USA 2002 by
SEVERN HOUSE PUBLISHERS INC., of
595 Madison Avenue, New York, NY 10022

British Library Cataloguing in Publication Data

Sole, Linda
    The rose arch - Large print ed.
    1. Female friendship - Fiction
    2. Love stories
    3. Large type books
    I. Title
    823.9'14 [F]

    ISBN 0-7278-7179-X

Printed and bound in Great Britain by
MPG Books Ltd, Bodmin, Cornwall.

Prologue

Tears cannot change it. I can never return to those sunlit, carefree days of childhood ... the days of innocence, when loving was uncomplicated, wholesome and free of shadows. Yet would I if I could? Would I wipe the slate clean as if none of it had ever happened?

It hurts to remember now, but perhaps in these last few, short weeks I have known something precious, something few are lucky enough to experience.

Sometimes, I think life is like a tapestry. The picture is beautiful, full of light and shade and wondrous colours – but when you look beneath the surface a web of threads is revealed, crossing back and forth in an ugly tangle.

Sitting here now in my room in Paris, looking out at the street below and reflecting on the future, I have tried to make some sense of what has happened to me. Why did it all go so terribly wrong – and how did it begin?

Perhaps it would help me to think if I wrote it all down. I need to clear my mind, to decide what I must do now – but where to start?

Not with my childhood, for it seems to me now that I lived a dream. Nothing was as it appeared on the surface – or perhaps it was simply that I was too innocent, too naive to see the truth? Yet I was loved and I was happy, that was true enough. My home was a secure, warm nest from which I seldom strayed until ... Yes, I see that it all began after the kiss.

One

Ours was just a small village somewhere between Boulogne and Paris, not particularly pretty or interesting, with a church, a tiny school, several small farms that flourished on the fertile soil of the region – and the vineyards of Monsieur Bertrand.

They were not grand vineyards and the wine made there was not like the rich red wines of Bordeaux or the fine crisp sparkling wines of Champagne country, but the treading of the grapes was always an important part of our lives. Yet I could not have guessed how important it was to be this particular year for me.

Without the grape-treading there might never have been a kiss and had it not been for the kiss ... who can say?

But I must begin my story by telling something of myself.

My name is Jenny Heron, though some call me by other names. I was born in London but brought to France as a child of just a few weeks by my mother, who was known locally as Madame Heron but was in fact English.

At the time my story begins, I was fifteen and a half years of age and had lived on the farm with Tante Marthe for as long as I could remember. My childhood was perhaps unusual in that I grew up a little apart from the other children, because I was not a Catholic. When I went to worship it was to the English church with my mother and in the town some distance away, and though I attended the village school I was allowed to miss prayers.

I was also different because I had a very special mother. She was extremely beautiful and she lived in Paris. When she came to visit me – which was at least once a month, and sometimes more – it was in an elegant carriage, and her clothes were stylish, more expensive than those worn by the mothers of the other children. I had special clothes I wore for her visits, which were much finer than my everyday ones.

My mother designed and made the special clothes herself. She was a skilled seamstress and she made gowns for the fashionable ladies of Paris; I had been told she was successful and very much sought after, and that was why she had to live in Paris. And because she was too busy to look after me, I had to live with Tante Marthe.

It had all been carefully explained to me as

a very small child. I understood the situation, because my mother had told me, and she was so beautiful, so loving and generous, that I always believed her.

'You are not here because I do not love you, Jenny,' she had said, kissing me tenderly as I sat on her knee and looked up at her in childish wonder. 'It is only that I have to work so hard to support us – and one day, when you are older, you will come to live with me.'

'Poor Maman to work so hard,' I said, patting her face with hands that had been scrupulously cleaned by Marthe in preparation for my mother's visit. 'One day I shall look after you and you will not need to work.'

'My darling Jenny,' she said. 'All I do is for you, my precious. You are my own sweet baby.'

So I understood that I was loved, but it was an unusual arrangement – and made me different from the other girls in the village.

Perhaps it was this difference that made André Bertrand notice me. I had often seen him as I passed the entrance to his father's vineyards on my way to school. He was tall, dark-haired and dark-eyed, a handsome man of almost twenty at that time. We had never said more than a few words in passing – until the grape-treading that year.

The warm summer had followed a wet spring and the grapes were full of juice, sweet and heavy on the vines. Most of the village folk had gathered at the vineyard for the harvesting and then the treading: it had been a good crop and the atmosphere was one of excitement and gaiety that fateful day in 1895, because many of the men looked to Monsieur Bertrand for their living and a poor harvest could mean lean times for all.

The air was heavy with the scents of the grapes, sweet and musky. It was a day to stay in the memory, a scene of bright colours and laughing, chattering voices as the workers called out to each other, their faces expectant, eyes bright as they waited for the treading to begin.

I took my place amongst the other girls of my age, who were being helped into the large wooden vats by young men, many of them already sweethearts. It was a tradition in our village that if a man helped you into the vats you would eat supper with him that night – and it was often a sign that a marriage was being arranged. So I was surprised when André came to lift me into the vat with the others; it was usually Pierre who did that for me, Tante Marthe's husband.

'Tread well little, Jenni,' André said with a smile. I liked the way he pronounced my name in the French way. Mama always called me Jenny, though I had been christened Jennifer and at school I was usually known as Jeanette – but André called me Jenni. 'My father has promised me a house of my own if the wine is good this year.'

A house of his own? That must mean he was thinking of taking a wife in the near future ... and he had chosen me from all the village girls as his partner for the supper that night.

What foolish thoughts went chasing through my mind at that moment! I giggled as young girls will, feeling flattered that he had singled me out for attention, and went to my work with a good heart. I was not sure that I wanted to marry André – my head was full of foolish, romantic dreams, that could never have been anything other than dreams – yet it was pleasant to be picked out by the son of the vineyard owner.

I was too young to think of marriage, too young to understand what love might mean, but not too young to dream of a handsome lover like the heroes I read of in the fables and legends of long ago. My head was full of the romantic stories of Charlemagne, of Napoleon, of Sir Lancelot, and the brave knights who lived for me through the poems of John Keats, rescuing damsels in distress or dying from broken hearts.

My mother had given me the book after discovering me once with my nose inside a rather tattered volume of one of Moliére's farces, which Pierre had found somewhere and given to me without even realising what it was.

'It is not that I do not like you to read the great French writers,' Mama explained, 'but I do not want you to forget your heritage. You live in France, Jenny, and it is right that you should respect the country of your adoption, but always remember you are English. It is right that you should know and love English writers.'

If my mother wanted me to remember my heritage, why would she never tell me anything of her family and her home? I knew that England had a Queen called Victoria, who was also the ruler of a large empire, that London was a vast city, that it was a land of many heroes – like Sir Francis Drake and St George – but I knew nothing of what it was really like apart from what I read in my school books.

I did know that asking questions made my mother sad, and so I did not ask the things I longed to know. Instead, I made up stories in my head to satisfy myself.

I was at this time a dreamer, an innocent, living inside my world of shining glass, untouched by the cruel hand of reality. Perhaps I should have demanded answers, been aware of the tangled threads beneath the surface, but there was no reason to seek for more than I had, because it was so good.

Treading the grapes that day was hard work, but fun. I loved to feel them squashing beneath my bare feet as they gradually changed into a sweet, sticky pulp. This was my life, and life was sweet.

I was amongst friends. We sang as we worked – songs that had been sung by people like us for centuries past: ballads, patriotic songs – and also the latest risqué ditties that came from the cafés of Paris.

The early morning was cool, with a slight breeze and a misty haze over the land, but as the day wore on it became hotter and hotter. My legs ached and my stomach turned as the smell of the grapes became overpowering.

I began to think that supper time would never come, but of course it did – and so did André, to claim me.

He smiled at me as he helped me out of the vat, and his hands were firm about my waist. I was aware of him walking tall and proud beside me as we made our way through the vineyard in the fading light.

The supper tables were set out in the orchard at the back of his father's house. They were laden with all kinds of food: huge, soft cheeses, quiches and pies, cold meats and fowl, jugs of rich sauces and platters of delicious fruits. And jugs of wine made from the treading of previous years.

André brought me wine, cheese, cold meat, fruit and bread, which we ate together in the shade of an apple tree. I was hungry and I ate everything he gave me, then I stole a ripe peach from his platter, the sweet juice spurting as I sank my teeth into it. I wiped my mouth with the back of my hand and laughed.

'You have a good appetite,' he said, his eyes bright with amusement as he passed me a cup of wine. 'Drink this, Jenni – and then we shall show the others how to dance.'

The fiddlers had struck up a tune and the young men and women had begun to dance. We ought all have been too tired after our long hard day in the vats, but the food and the cool of the evening had revived us. André seized my hands, pulling me to my feet and into that whirling, laughing throng.

Round and round and round we went, until my head was spinning. André gave me more wine and a moment to rest, then dragged me back for another wild fling.

It was quite dark when he drew me away from the lights and the music into the shadows of the shrubs. The night air was warm and seductive with the scents of the grapes and flowering shrubs.

'You're so pretty, little Jenni,' he murmured. 'I want to kiss you.'

'Then why don't you?'

There were a thousand reasons why he

14

should not have done so and we both knew them, but we had become drunk on the strong rough wine and the excitement of the occasion. My heart was beating wildly as André drew me to him there in the dusk of that glorious summer evening, his mouth closing softly and tenderly over mine.

My very first kiss.

It was just a kiss, innocent and sweet, nothing more. I do not believe that André intended any harm – nor would it have mattered had we not been seen by someone who stood in the shadows and watched.

'Where are you, Jeanette?' I heard Tante Marthe's call as she came out to the barn where I was hiding some ten days later. 'Come down, you naughty girl. Why do you not answer me? Your maman will soon be here and you not washed and ready for her...'

I watched consideringly from my vantage point. Hidden securely in the sweet-smelling, dry hay, I could see her but knew she would not find me unless I wanted to be found. She was far too stout to climb the rickety ladder that led to my loft, and far too sensible to attempt it: she was also too kind for her own good. When I was forced to answer her call I would receive nothing harsher than a scolding.

Tante Marthe was not truly my aunt nor

any blood relation of mine. I had been told many times that my father had been an English gentleman, who died in a carriage accident just after I was born, leaving my beautiful, clever mother alone in France with very little money and a small child to bring up alone.

'Marthe was my maid but more than that, a true friend,' Mama had told me over and over again, explaining why I spent so much of my life with the good woman and not with her. 'If it had not been for Marthe I think I should have died of grief and despair.'

I knew the story by heart. After my father's sudden demise, Marthe had taken my mother and me to her family home. She had given us a bed to sleep in and food to eat, and for that Mama was eternally grateful. Later, when my mother began to work in Paris, as a seamstress for the quality, Marthe shouldered the task of caring for me – and when she married Pierre Dubois, she brought me to live with them at the farm.

I knew all this because my mother told me, and naturally I believed every word she said, because she was so special. She was generous, warm and loving towards me. I would never have believed she could lie – why should I?

The farm was my home. I was sheltered,

protected and loved – what more could I want?

Pierre was twenty years older than his wife, a thick-set, harsh-featured man who spoke little in my presence. I had never been sure how he felt about being saddled with the daughter of an Englishwoman but he never complained – or not in my hearing – so perhaps he did not mind so very much.

He was sitting by the fireplace when I finally went into the kitchen that morning, and he looked at me with a smile, knocking his pipe against the fender.

'Here she is,' he said. 'Where were you? We were worried about you.'

'In the hayloft. You shouldn't have worried. You knew I would come back when I was ready.'

'You're too old to be hiding in haylofts,' Tante Marthe scolded.

I glanced round the comfortable, slightly shabby kitchen that was always redolent of herbs and cooking, then perched on a stool near the table, stealing a piece of pastry from the pie she had just taken from the oven.

'Whatever would your maman say if she could see you now?'

'That I looked like a scarecrow,' I answered truthfully. One glance in the mirror of the large, ugly sideboard had told me that there was dirt on my face and straw in my hair. I grimaced at my reflection. 'Forgive me for being so much trouble to you, dear Marthe. I'm sorry I hid from you; I shouldn't have.'

I scuffed my stout boots, which were the only sensible wear for life on a farm, and looked ashamed, as I ought. It was wrong of me to tease and plague her the way I did, because I loved her dearly. It was her arms that had held me when I suffered from childhood ailments, she who had comforted me when I woke from a nightmare. Next to Mama she was the person I cared for most in the world, and I knew that she loved me. I was the child she and Pierre had never had themselves.

I was not sure why I had hidden from Marthe, except that I had felt nervous and uneasy when I woke that morning and remembered that it was the day my mother was coming to fetch me.

'Take those boots off before you go upstairs,' Marthe said in a scolding tone that was meant to hide her own emotion. 'Not that there's any mud for you to bring in; it's been dry as a bone for two weeks or more now. Hurry and change, Jeanette. We don't want your maman here before you are ready. She will think I have traded you for a changeling.'

I bent to unlace my boots and place them beside the newly blacked range, which threw out a fierce heat despite the glaring sunshine out in the yard behind the house. Walking barefoot across worn stone flags to the dark passageway beyond the kitchen, I hurried upstairs to my own small bed room and changed into the latest pretty dress Mama had sent for me.

Most of the clothes Mama sent were far too good to wear on the farm. Tante Marthe often shook her head over them, insisting that I keep them for Sundays or my mother's visits.

That morning, as I lowered the froth of petticoats and fine blue muslin skirts over my head, then wriggled into the tight-fitting bodice, I began to feel excited. Mama's visits were always pleasurable, but this one was different because she was taking me back to stay with her at her house in Paris. Her letter had explained:

Dearest Jenny,
    How often we have spoken of you coming to stay at my little house. I am usually so busy that it cannot be managed, but now, my darling, things have changed. I have come into a little money. Not a fortune, but enough to make it possible for me to have some time to myself this summer ...

I stared at my reflection in the clouded, rather spotty dressing-mirror as I dragged a comb through my unruly curls. My hair was the bane of my life; dark red and so thick and strong that it had a will of its own and would not be tamed unless Tante Marthe dragged it back with her strong, callused hands and fastened it with a ribbon. Even then it had a habit of escaping as I started to move around, hanging about my face in wayward tendrils.

'You look like a gypsy, Jenny Heron,' I told myself as I wrestled with the wild curls, finally managing to achieve a reasonable result. 'You must take after your Papa – whoever he was.'

My father was a mystery, an unknown, shadowy figure of whom Mama was reluctant to speak.

'Do not ask me, dearest Jenny,' she would say whenever I mentioned him, her lovely eyes misty with tears. 'Do not make me remember that sad time, I beg you. We have each other and dear Marthe – is that not enough?'

Whenever she looked at me in that way I was overcome with love and pity for her. Poor Mama. She had been so young to be left alone with a child; she had struggled bravely to make a living for us, and I was an ungrateful wretch to plague her with my questions.

My papa had been a gentleman, well bred and kind, but of little fortune. That was why Mama had had to leave me in Tante Marthe's care and go to Paris to make our living.

If in my secret heart I longed to know more of my father and of my mother's family in England, I had learned not to ask. In my mind I saw Papa as a tall, bewhiskered, handsome fellow: perhaps destined for a scholarly life, he had fallen desperately in love and abandoned the cloisters of some ancient college to run away with Mama to Paris; or perhaps he was the scion of some noble family who had cast him out because he had married beneath himself ... Or perhaps I was a foolish child, my head stuffed with dreams.

It was not because I was unhappy or neglected that I dreamed of the life that might have been mine had my papa lived. My childhood years had been good ones. Mama's visits were less frequent than I might have wished, but perhaps all the more exciting for that, and I was sure no child had ever been more dearly loved.

No, my dreams were merely the sign of a lively mind. The teacher at our village school had told Tante Marthe that I was of above average intelligence – hence the scholarly father of my dreams – with rather too much imagination.

21

Recently, my teacher had written a harsh letter to Marthe.

Jeanette needs the company of others of her own standard. If she were a boy I should advise a university, but in this case I believe she needs to be set to a trade. The Devil makes work for idle hands, Madame Dubois. Sorry as I am to say it, Jeanette stands in some moral danger, unless she can be given adequate employment.

Tante Marthe had read the letter with growing distress.

'Whatever have you been doing that your teacher should write me such a letter?' she cried. 'Tell me, child, for I shall know if you lie.'

She had always been able to shame me into the truth and I could not lie to her. I told her exactly what had happened.

A few days after the grape-treading I had met my teacher at the school gate. It was he who had stood in the shadows watching as André kissed me that night, and he had been scandalised. Tall and thin in his dusty black gown, Monsieur Bartoli looked like a scavenging crow, his eyes hooded, his mouth white with righteous anger.

'Such wanton behaviour cannot – will not! – be tolerated in a girl of your age,' he had thundered at me. 'I shall inform Madame Dubois at once.'

'It was only a little kiss...'

'Be quiet, girl! Your wickedness shall not go unpunished.'

He had never liked me. I was different, too spirited to be cowed by him as his other pupils often were. He thought me a rebel because I asked questions in class and looked at him without fear – and perhaps he was right. Even now when he glared at me and called me names, I lifted my eyes and met his gaze without flinching.

He could not frighten me, so he had written to Marthe and she, after hearing my confession without comment or punishment, to Mama. Because of the letters Mama was coming to take me back to Paris with her. I had often longed to visit with her, but there was always some reason why it could not happen: she was too busy, her house was too small or her customers too demanding. Now she was coming to fetch me because of that kiss.

And so my excitement that morning was mixed with apprehension. Would Mama be very angry because André had kissed me? Her own letter to me had not seemed angry, but I'd sensed that my life was about to change and that was why I had run away to hide in the hayloft.

Why was Mama taking me to stay with her

in Paris – and what did she intend to do about my future?

'You are sending me to a convent school near Paris?' I stared at my mother as she sat in Marthe's front parlour, my eyes wide with dismay. 'But why? What have I done that was so wicked?'

It was just an innocent kiss. Why was everyone acting as though I'd committed a terrible sin?

'You've done nothing wrong.' Mama's hand reached for mine. 'You must not think of this as a punishment, my darling. Perhaps I ought to have sent you to the nuns when you were younger, but you were so happy here with Marthe...'

'I am happy here. I do not want to be sent away!'

I looked at my mother sitting there in her fashionable clothes that were too smart for Marthe's cottage. She was so pretty, so elegant, and she smelt of a delicate perfume, but for a moment I felt as though she were a stranger.

How could she do this to me? How could she take me from my home and the people I loved? If she had taken me to live with her it might have been different – but she was sending me to live with strangers! I felt the tightness in my throat and tears stung behind my eyes, though I would not cry.

'It is for your own good, Jeanette,' Tante Marthe said, looking at me sadly. 'You have outgrown me, my love. You need more than I can give you. The nuns will teach you things that a young lady should properly know.'

'No, that's not true! I have not outgrown you.' I wanted to run to her, throw myself against her bosom as I had so often in childhood, and weep. Yet I could see that this was already painful for her, so I held back. 'I love you. I do not want to leave you.'

She said nothing, merely turning her face away lest I see her tears.

My chest felt as if it were being crushed by the pain; I knew that Tante Marthe was suffering as badly over this as I and that made me wretched with guilt. If only I had not let André kiss me! It had not meant anything to either of us – we had been swept away by the excitement and the wine we had drunk.

'I do not want to leave you. Please – please let me come back to you after my visit with Mama.'

'If you go to the convent school you will be able to see more of your mama,' Marthe said huskily. 'You are the daughter of a gentleman, Jeanette, and you need to complete your education accordingly. If you stay here you will end by marrying beneath you. Think, child – would you really wish to marry someone like my Pierre? Not that I'm denying he's a good, decent man...'

'Pierre has always been kind to me – as you have.'

'But he is not your equal,' Marthe said. 'Nor is André Bertrand ... handsome as he is.'

'His father owns a fine vineyard.'

'André is promised to a girl from the next village. Their fathers arranged it when she was born. André will marry her – he has no choice. He might flirt with you, Jeanette – but you could never marry. His father would not permit him to marry anyone who was not a Catholic, nor would he think of it himself.'

'Oh ... I did not know.' I gazed into Marthe's kindly eyes. 'I do not want to marry André! I promise never to speak to him again – if you will only let me stay here.'

'You can visit Marthe sometimes.' My mother took my hand in hers and made me look at her. 'This is my fault, Jenny. I had not realised you were almost a young woman. I always meant you to have a better education one day. Your father would have seen to it long ago, but I...' Her voice trailed away and she looked sad.

I was smitten with remorse. The pain in her eyes at that moment was so intense that I could have wept for shame. What a wretch I was to cause her so much trouble!

'Forgive me,' I said. 'I shall do as you wish, of course I will – but you will let me visit Tante Marthe?'

'We shall come together,' Mama said and kissed my cheek. 'Do not look so upset, my darling. Before you go to the new school I shall show you the delights of Paris. We are going to have a wonderful time together, I promise you.'

I nodded and smiled at her tremulously. I had often wished to stay with her in Paris and a part of me longed for new adventures, but there was an ache about my heart that would not be banished.

Because of one foolish kiss that meant nothing I was being sent away from my home, and I knew that things would never be the same again.

Two

'So here we are, my love. What do you think of my home?' Mama asked when we arrived that morning. 'I hope you will enjoy your visit with me; I have longed for it so often.'

I was surprised by Mama's house. Although quite tiny by the standards of the *hotels particuliers*, which had sprung up in the Marais after Henri IV built the nearby Place Royale, it was a beautiful (if slightly neglected, like the rest of the area now) seventeenth-century building constructed around a private courtyard and garden.

Inside, however, the house was far from shabby. Mama had decorated it tastefully with small, exquisite pieces of eighteenth-century furniture, pretty pictures, one or two of them by Renoir and the other Impressionists who had become so popular now, and good china and glass. The windows of her salon frothed with lace and velvet drapes, the shades of restful blues and greens blending into each other perfectly.

It was the house of a lady. I suppose I had

expected something more in keeping with Mama's profession as a seamstress ... and yet it suited her. She had of course been born a gentlewoman, and was accustomed to living in comfortable surroundings, forced to work only because of her awkward circumstances after my father was killed.

I knew she was successful in her profession, for she had told me so. Looking at her house that day, I thought that the fashionable ladies she made dresses for must pay a great deal of money for the privilege.

'It is wonderful,' I breathed. 'Quite lovely.'

I gasped with pleasure when she showed me the bedroom I would be using; it seemed to have been recently refurbished in delicate pinks and creams, and besides the bed there was an elegant sofa, a desk, chair and a large armoire to hold my clothes.

'It's lovely,' I said, turning to her excitedly. 'So pretty.'

'I'm glad you like it, my darling. I chose everything specially for you. It will be your room whenever you stay with me.'

'You must have spent a great deal of money?'

I looked at her doubtfully. I had grown up in Marthe's comfortable, ugly old farmhouse, but I was not completely ignorant of the world. I did wonder how Mama could have earned sufficient money from her sewing to live in such luxury. She had often told me how little time she had to herself, how hard she had to work to provide for us both – so how could she afford to do all this for me now?

'I told you in my letter...' Her cheeks were flushed, and she seemed awkward, unable to meet my eyes. For one moment I suspected she was not telling me the truth, but then I was ashamed of my wicked suspicions. 'I have come into a little money.'

'From your family? Was it a legacy, Mama?'

'Of sorts,' she replied and frowned, sensing my doubts. 'I have done nothing wrong, Jenny. This house ... the furniture ... it was owed to me. I have nothing to be ashamed for – nor shall I be!' She finished on a note of defiance, her eyes angry.

'Of course not. Why should you be ashamed?' I asked, looking at her curiously.

'There are things I have never told you.' Her eyes darkened as though she were remembering something that hurt her. 'You may have wondered why I did not return to my own family when ... I was left alone with a small child?'

I nodded, saying nothing as I watched the play of emotions on her face: grief, sadness and a wistfulness that lingered longer than the rest. What was she thinking? What memories had brought that look to her eyes?

Slim, elegant, graceful, my mother, Adele, was an exceptionally beautiful woman. Now in her mid-thirties, she looked much younger, especially when she laughed and her eyes lit up: they were a deep blue and very clear. Her hair was a rich honey-gold, her skin soft and downy.

'I was very unhappy as a young woman. There are things of which I cannot speak even today.' Her voice broke on a sob of distress. 'I was only just eighteen when you were born, Jenny. I had scarcely begun to live and perhaps I should have done things differently...'

'Do not upset yourself, Mama.' I hastened to reassure her. 'I need no explanations.'

'One day I shall tell you – at least a part of it,' she promised. 'For the time being I ask only that you trust me. Whatever I do now, my darling, is for your sake – because I love you. Because I want the best for you.' She touched my cheek with the tips of her fingers and I was aware of some deep emotion she was struggling to hide. 'You do believe me, don't you?'

'Of course, Mama.'

I would have believed anything she told me. She was my mother and I adored her. If she said the money was owed her it must be so. I would not question her since that might cause her pain.

There would come a time in my life when

31

I would bitterly regret this wasted opportunity to discover the secrets of my mother's past, but on that sunny morning in the summer of 1895 I could know nothing of that future time.

'I have never regretted having you, Jenny.'

Her words, and the passion with which they were spoken, startled me. It had never occurred to me until then that she might have had cause to regret my birth.

'Mama...?'

'No matter what – I have always loved you.'

I frowned, unsure of her meaning.

'Papa – did you love him?'

'Of course. Why do you ask?' There was a shadow in her eyes then and she turned her face from me, as if trying to hide her emotions. 'Why do you question it, Jenny?'

I was not sure, except that there was something about her then that made me wonder. What was she keeping from me? What secrets lay hidden in her past? I tried to decipher her odd expression, but she had regained control as she began to tidy her hair in front of the long, gilt-framed mirror on the wall. And when she turned to face me, she was herself again.

'This evening we shall go for a cruise on the river,' she said, tucking a wisp of hair behind her ear. 'One of the best ways to see Paris is from the river. At night it looks so mysterious and exciting. Tomorrow we can explore on foot.' She was smiling now as she looked at me and caught my hand in hers. 'I am so happy to have you here at last, my darling. I want to show you everything.'

That strange, almost haunted expression had gone. Perhaps I had imagined it.

Why should she have regretted having a child? It had been tragic for her, being widowed at such a young age, but she had never been tied to me. Marthe had been there to care for me. Marthe had nursed me through my childhood ills ... she had bathed my bruised knees and wiped away my tears.

Had the existence of a child spoiled my mother's life in some way? I sensed a mystery and was a little hurt. Why should she say that she had not regretted my birth – unless there was some reason that might cause her to feel regret?

'I'm going to spoil you, Jenny,' she said, almost as though she could read my thoughts. 'I've wanted to have you with me all these years, but it wasn't possible – until now.'

'I was happy with Marthe.'

'Marthe loves you – but I love you, too. Please don't be angry with me, Jenny. Life has not been easy for me. If I could have done things differently I would. Believe me.'

Her eyes pleaded with me for understanding. My doubts melted away. How could I question her? She had always done what she could for me. I had lacked for nothing. If my mother had her secrets, she was entitled to keep them.

'I love you, Maman.'

'Oh, my darling.' She opened her arms to me. 'My sweet, innocent Jenny. Nothing shall hurt you. I won't let you suffer as I did. I shall protect you. Always.'

As she clung to me I felt the shudder run through her and knew that some deep emotion had her in its grip. I suspected then that something terrible must have happened to her in the past, but when she released me she was smiling serenely.

'Paris is a beautiful city,' she said. 'Some people say that between them Monsieur Eiffel and Baron Haussmann have done their best to destroy it – and it is true that the Baron has swept away much that had an ancient charm about it in his efforts to bring us into modern times – but I believe there is still much to celebrate. Tomorrow I shall take you to the top of Monsieur Eiffel's tower, my darling – and then we shall see what you think of Paris.'

Those first few weeks I spent in Paris with Maman would always remain with me, enshrined in my memory as a very special time in my life.

She took me everywhere. We walked in

beautiful gardens beside the river, promenaded in the Bois de Boulogne, explored the narrow winding lanes of the older parts of the city, ate delicious ices at pavement cafés and visited various museums. We often visited the art galleries, with which Paris seemed to abound, especially those showing the pictures of Manet, Cézanne and Renoir – my mother had a passion for the Impressionists, as I had already discovered. Maman was determined to fill in the gaps in my cultural education, to broaden my mind.

There were other times, however, when we simply went shopping. Oh, those wonderful shops! After living for so long in the country I was overwhelmed by the array of treasures to be found: perfumes and lotions, scarves, silk lingerie, hats, pretty beaded purses, gloves and kerchiefs – such a bewildering choice that I should never have been able to make up my mind if Mama had not been there to advise me.

'You should have this scarf, Jenny,' she would say when I could only stand and stare at a profusion of spangled trifles. 'Look how well the green goes with your colouring. You have such glorious hair, my darling. You are going to be a beauty one day.'

'Oh Mama!' I disclaimed with a blush, but we purchased the scarf, just as we purchased all the pretty things she thought were right for me.

'You must have those beads, and this fur muff is so smart. Those ankle boots are charming but so are the black suede ones...' And with a clap of her hands, 'We shall have both!'

She seemed like an excited girl at a fair; so extravagant was she in her purchases for me that at last I protested.

'You are spending so much money on me, Mama. Do you think you ought?'

'Your papa would not want you to shame him at your new school.'

'My papa?' I had such an odd feeling at that moment. I gazed at her in bewilderment. 'But...'

'Don't you sometimes feel that he is there in the background, looking after you?' Mama's smile was a little strange. 'Besides, I am very much alive, and I want you to have everything the other girls have. You will be mixing with young ladies from good families at your new school, Jenny. You would feel very uncomfortable if I did not provide you with the things you need.'

Her words made me think about the new school to which I was soon to be sent and the girls I would meet there. Would they think me very much a country girl? I supposed they must, for I knew myself to be ignorant of the world, though I was a good scholar and had read everything that came my way.

Mama liked to tell me little bits of history as we wandered about the streets of Paris during those sunlit days. She had a lively mind. She told me stories about the way the Franks cleared the Romans out of Paris and converted its people to Christianity, of the twelfth century, when the city became the centre of a wonderful renaissance with a flourishing trade, of the building of Notre-Dame, of the suppression of the order of the Templars, the persecution of the Huguenots, the fall of the Bastille and the bloody revolutions that had marked its turbulent history.

'Paris has seen such terrible times,' she told me, pointing out various buildings to illustrate her stories. 'Rebellion and sieges, riots and massacres ... but now we live in happier days, Jenny. Paris is the centre of the art world, for it is here that Manet, Degas and Cézanne began their new school of painting.'

She made me see it all in a way my teachers never had. It was as if I were there, watching the struggles she described, feeling the terror and the fear of the people she brought to vivid life for me.

I had always thought Maman beautiful, but now I began to realise that she was much, much more. It was as if a flame burned within her – a flame of pure light that was so bright it almost blinded me when it flared out of her. She was an exceptional woman – the kind of woman that men had died for throughout history. She might have been a Helen of Troy or a Queen of Sheba.

It made me wonder why she had never married again.

It was at the end of the first week that we met them as we were walking by the Seine – the Comte Laurent de Arnay and his wife's cousin, Madame Henriette Rossi, who was young, very beautiful and already, I soon learned, a widow with a small son.

'Adele!' The voice that called to us was deep and husky for a woman. 'How wonderful that we should meet like this. I was just saying to Laurent that I intended to call on you later this afternoon.'

'Madame.'

The man tipped his hat. He was speaking to my mother but looking at me. He was smiling. I was aware of warmth and interest in his eyes. He had nice eyes, a bluish grey, very intent. I thought him handsome. A tall man with good bone structure and fair hair. Well dressed, of course, he was perhaps in his late forties, lean almost to the point of being thin, but with a wiry strength and a look of alertness that made him seem younger than his years – altogether a very distinguished man: an aristocrat of the old school.

'Monsieur le comte.' Maman looked as if she had lit up from inside, her skin and eyes glowing. 'May I present my daughter – Jenny, this is the Comte de Arnay and Madame Rossi, who is a cousin of Madame la Comtesse.'

'Mademoiselle Heron,' the comte said. He took my hand, holding it for a moment. His hand was large and cool with long fingers. 'I have heard much about you, mademoiselle. It is a pleasure for me to meet you at last.'

'I sometimes make gowns for Madame Rossi...'

I turned to look at my mother as she spoke. Her cheeks were flushed and I sensed she was a little flustered by this meeting, though I had no idea why she should be.

'Henriette,' Madame Rossi said chidingly and I turned to look at her. She was very elegant, her gown obviously expensive. She was wearing short black lace gloves and carried a cream and black lace parasol. Her gown was blue, but trimmed at the hem with more black lace, and her jacket was nipped in at the waist with black braiding. 'Why so formal, Adele?' She laughed. It was a wonderful sound, warm and inviting, her smile seeming to draw us in. 'So this is your lovely Jenny. She is going to outshine us both in a few years, Adele – wouldn't you agree, Laurent?'

'You are making Mademoiselle Heron

blush,' the comte said with a lift of his brows. 'But yes, I do agree. Charming ... your daughter is charming, madame.'

'I knew you would think so,' Mama murmured. A look passed between them – an intimate, understanding look, as if they were good friends. 'We have been buying Jenny all the things she needs for her new school.'

'Ah yes, the school.' Those intent, passionate eyes came to rest on me again. 'You are soon to be a pupil of the good Sisters of Mercy, is that not so?'

'Yes, monsieur.'

'Adele's daughter is going to the sisters?' Madame Rossi was immediately interested. 'I spent three years at the school myself, Jenny. You will find them stern disciplinarians but fair minded and kind. My time there certainly did me no harm.'

'You might have done better had you been longer in their care, my dear Henriette,' the comte said.

Madame Rossi's infectious laughter rang out as he teased her.

'How unkind you are, Laurent,' she cried. 'Would you have me hide myself from the world and wear sackcloth and ashes? My poor Raoul would not have expected it of me.' She looked at me directly, her eyes bright with amusement. 'I have been widowed for almost eighteen months, Jenny. My

40

husband was much older than I and lived long enough to see his son born. I miss Raoul, who was my dearest friend; my cousin-in-law would have me still in deepest black but it does not become me. Grey or lilac – or the blue you see me in today – but not black. You will agree with me, won't you?'

'I think you would be beautiful whatever you wore.'

'You sweet girl!' She darted at me, kissing my cheek. She smelled of a fresh light perfume. 'We shall be friends, Jenny – and you shall call me Henriette, as all my friends do.'

'Thank you, madame.'

'No, no: Henriette!' She wagged her finger at me scoldingly. 'I insist. I am not so very much older than you, Jenny. Even though I have been married and have my sweet Charles.'

'We must go, Henriette.' The comte laid a gloved hand on her arm. 'We are delaying Madame Heron.'

'Men are always so impatient.' She pulled a face at him. 'Very well, we shall go – but may I call on you later, Adele? I want to discuss some new gowns.'

'Jenny is staying with me for another week. I shall not take on any work until after that.'

'In a week, then,' Henriette agreed. 'But may I not call as a friend before that – to become better acquainted with your lovely Jenny?'

'We are out most days,' Mama replied. I sensed she was flustered again ... or reluctant. 'But perhaps tea – next Thursday?'

'Thursday?' Henriette frowned. 'Oh, I am already engaged with friends. What a shame!'

'There will be other times,' my mother replied, smiling easily now. 'Jenny will spend some of her school holidays with me.'

'Then we shall meet again.' Henriette gave me a brilliant smile. 'Until next time, Jenny.'

'Madame – Mademoiselle Heron. Excuse us, please.'

The comte tipped his hat to us and they walked on.

Mama was quiet for several minutes afterwards. I glanced at her curiously. She seemed thoughtful ... a little annoyed.

'Do you not like Madame Rossi, Mama?'

'Why do you ask, Jenny?'

'We could have been at home to her any day had you wished.'

'Henriette Rossi is pleasant enough in her own way. A little flighty, perhaps, but generous.'

Her tone was guarded, reserved. She suddenly looked at me and smiled.

'You will think me selfish, Jenny. I want you all to myself. Just for this one time. You don't mind, do you?'

'No, of course not. I would rather it was that way.'

I had liked Madame Rossi, but Mama was right. Our time together would be all too short: we did not want to be bothered with other people.

We wanted to make the most of our precious time together. Every day we went somewhere. I remember particularly the morning we had our portraits drawn by one of the artists who earned his living on the Left Bank by making quick sketches of anyone who would pay.

We had been wandering at leisure in the sunshine. Mama was carrying several packages and I had an armful of flowers we had purchased from one of the street sellers.

'We shall have coffee at that little café over there,' my mother said as I stopped to admire some pictures. 'Are you hungry, Jenny?'

I thought of the mouth-watering cakes the patisserie sold and nodded, but I could not take my eyes from the artist who was sketching passers-by. He noticed my interest and beckoned, showing me pictures of myself and my mother.

'Oh, they are so clever,' I said, calling my mother's attention to them. 'How much are they, monsieur?'

'I have already been paid,' he replied. 'By

that gentleman over there. He asked me to draw you, mademoiselle – and he took the first two sketches with him.'

'Who was he?' my mother asked and frowned as she looked in the direction he had indicated.

I looked too and saw the figure of a gentleman walking away. I was almost too late and received only an impression of a youngish man with dark hair dressed in a blue cloth coat and grey riding breeches.

'Why did he ask you to draw us?' I asked curiously. 'Do you have a sketch of him?'

'No, mademoiselle,' the artist replied, 'but I can sketch something from memory if you wish?'

'No, that will not be necessary,' my mother said, a sharp note in her voice. She looked annoyed about something. 'We shall pay you for these ourselves.'

She dropped a few coins into his hand, and gave the sketches to me. I looked at her curiously as we walked away.

'Did you know that gentleman, Mama? The one who asked for our likenesses?'

She looked at me oddly for a moment before she shook her head. 'No, of course not. It was just a foolish whim on the part of a stranger, that's all. We shall forget about it.'

I sensed that the incident had annoyed her and I wondered why. It hardly mattered, but

I should have liked to know why a stranger had wanted the artist to sketch us.

It was our last day together. I was due to leave for the convent school the next morning. We had decided to spend the day at home.

'We must help Marie with the packing,' Mama said. 'Besides, I want to make the most of our last few hours.'

I was busy upstairs for most of the morning. Mama's maid was quite young – much younger than her mistress – a pert, pretty girl with dark hair and a rather secretive manner. I was not altogether sure that I liked her, though she did her best to be helpful and friendly towards me, and I sensed that she was very loyal to my mother.

'Madame will be sad when you leave,' she said as we checked the contents of my trunk before locking it. 'She works too hard – and has too few friends.'

'Is Maman lonely?' I glanced at Marie in surprise. I had never thought of my mother in that way.

'Not exactly.' Marie looked conscious of her *faux pas*, as if she wished she had not made the remark. 'She has one or two good friends she can rely on, but...'

'Like Madame Rossi?' I asked as she hesitated.

'I would not call that one a friend.' Marie

frowned. 'You've met Madame Bruge and her husband, haven't you? And Madame Leconte?'

I nodded. Several ladies had spoken to us when we were entering or leaving the house, but no one had actually come to visit while I was staying. I had thought this a little odd because, as busy as Marthe was, a day seldom passed without one of her friends popping in for a gossip and a glass of her delicious wine. So it seemed strange that none of Maman's friends had called – unless she had made it clear to them that she wished to have her daughter to herself?

I left Marie when the packing was finished and went downstairs to find my mother. As I reached the hallway I heard a man's deep voice coming from the front parlour and hesitated. I had not realised there was a visitor.

The door from the parlour opened as I lingered and, without wishing to eavesdrop on their conversation, I heard the man speak.

'You are being very foolish and selfish,' he said in an angry tone. 'She has made a reasonable request to see her. Surely you could allow a short visit?'

'No, never!' Mama's voice was charged with emotion. 'Never while I live. I thought I had made this clear – neither of us will ever set foot in that accursed house.'

At that moment the man became aware of me. He was quite young, not much above twenty-three or so, with black hair, cold, chiselled features and stormy grey eyes. He stared at me hard and a chill seemed to spread throughout my body. I had a feeling of apprehension – of danger – and I believed he wanted to say something to me, something important or disturbing.

For a moment I felt there was something familiar about him, but I could not imagine what. I was trying to recall if I had seen him somewhere else, quite recently, but my mother had followed him out into the hall and he turned to look at her, as if asking her a question.

'Please leave us, Mr Allington,' she said. 'Say nothing more. Just go. Go now!'

The expression on her face at that moment was a mixture of fear, anger and ... was it guilt? I could not be sure.

He turned his gaze on me once more, nodded to himself, then walked to the front door and looked back at us once before going out. The door was closed with more force than necessary and the resulting bang echoed through the house.

'Who was that?' I asked, shocked. 'What did he want, Maman?'

'Nothing ... nothing important.' She sounded distressed. I glanced at her and saw that her face was very pale.

'Maman?'

As I moved towards her she swayed a little. I reached out to catch her arm, leading her to a chair and urging her to sit, which she did so readily that I was concerned.

'Are you ill?'

'No – just shocked and upset.'

She was trembling. The tears had started to run down her cheeks, silently, as though she had no power to control them. I had never seen her cry before and it affected me powerfully.

'Mama? What did that man say to upset you so much?'

'He ... he was a reminder of something that happened long ago,' she said and wiped her tears with the tips of her fingers. 'I am being foolish, Jenny. He cannot hurt us now ... never again.'

'Why should Mr Allington wish to hurt us?'

'Oh no, not poor Philip,' she said, a faint smile lifting the corners of her mouth. 'He was merely the messenger, poor man. Bad news is never welcome.'

'Bad news? You have had bad news?'

'No...' She had recovered. She took out her lace kerchief and wiped her face. 'Good and bad – as they say of the curate's egg. It was really not Philip Allington's fault, Jenny. He brought me a message from someone – someone I do not wish to see. Perhaps I am a little unkind in view of ... but I cannot!' A deep shudder gripped her and I saw fear in her eyes. 'I cannot! What she asks is impossible. She should never have sent him here.'

'Who, Maman? Who should not have sent Mr Allington here?'

She blinked as I spoke and I knew her thoughts had been far away, buried deep in the past. Just what was she hiding from me? I felt a sense of unease, as though a dark shadow had fallen over me – but my mother grasped my hand, giving me a pleading look.

'Please do not ask, Jenny. One day I shall tell you. I promise I shall tell you – but not yet. Not today.'

The colour was returning to her cheeks, but I sensed she was still deeply distressed. Whatever could that awful man have said to upset her like this? I was angry with him and I thought that if I ever saw him again I would tell him he had no right to distress my poor mother in this way.

'As long as you are not ill?'

'No, my darling, I am not ill.' She stood up. She had conquered her emotions. 'I felt a little odd but I am better now.' She smiled and kissed me. 'My dearest girl. Everything I do is for you. Always remember that. If you feel hurt that I do not tell you everything, remember that I am thinking of you – protecting you from knowledge that would only distress or harm you.'

I have wished so often since that day that she had confided in me then, but at the time I was aware only of the warm flow of love from her, a love that wrapped around me, keeping me safe. From what little I had seen of the angry Mr Philip Allington I had no wish to know him. He had made my mother cry. I had only contempt for him and hoped that we should never meet again.

'Come along, darling,' my mother said, taking my arm. 'I have something for you ... a present.'

'But you have spent so much money on me already.'

'This is something special.'

She drew me into her elegant parlour. I saw the blue velvet box lying on her desk and looked at her as she picked it up, holding it out to me with a loving smile.

'I was given this by your father,' she said. 'As a proof of his love. I want you to have it, Jenny.'

She handed me the box. I opened it with a feeling of anticipation, giving a cry of pleasure as I saw what was inside. Nestled against a bed of blue satin was a fine gold chain with a small heart-shaped locket studded with pearls and diamonds.

'It's lovely,' I said in a hushed whisper, 'but I cannot take it, Mama. It must mean so much to you. If Papa gave it to you...'

'It is meant to be worn by a young girl,' she said. 'I have other trinkets. Besides, I want you to have it, my darling.'

'You are so good to me!'

We embraced affectionately. The unpleasant incident with Mr Allington was forgotten. I would have cause to remember it many times in the future, but it was not important to me then.

I had spent two wonderful weeks in Paris with my beloved mother and now I was about to begin a new life.

Three

The journey to my new school was uneventful. Mama introduced me to my teachers, kissed me fondly and took her farewell. If we felt like weeping neither of us gave any sign. We had grown used to partings over the years.

'Take care of yourself, my love,' my mother whispered as she kissed me on the cheek. 'We shall see each other very soon.'

I hugged her once, then let go and stood back, hiding my apprehension. 'I shall write to you,' I said. 'Mama...'

'Yes, dearest?'

She looked at me curiously but I shook my head. What I had almost said was unimportant at that moment. I had wondered if the man who had made her cry was the same one who had paid for our portraits from the street artist. At the time of Mr Allington's visit I had thought him familiar but been unable to place him, but afterwards it had struck me that he could have been the man I had glimpsed on the Left Bank that day. And I wondered why he had wanted the sketches – could it be that he wanted to show them to someone else?

Perhaps the woman who had asked him to come to Paris – the woman my mother had refused to discuss with me.

'It doesn't matter,' I said. 'You will write to me often?'

'Yes, of course.'

She smiled and went back to her carriage.

One of the nuns beckoned to me. I stood for a moment, watching as my mother's carriage was driven away, reluctant to follow Sister Anne. Then I realised that there was no choice. I was here now and I must make the best of things.

'Please do not run, Jeanette. I have told you before. It is not ladylike to run inside the school.'

'Yes, Sister Anne. I am sorry, truly I am.'

I slowed my pace until she had gone, then began to run again, because it was time for tea and I was hungry. I was always hungry in this place; the nuns did not believe in large meals – and I had been used to living on a farm and eating whenever I felt like it. Sometimes when I thought of Marthe's freshly baked pies and cakes I believed I could have died of longing, but in truth the life was not so very terrible.

I had thought I might feel lonely or that I did not quite belong at the school. Although

I had lived in France for most of my life I was English-born and not a Catholic, which meant I could not attend prayers with the other girls. Because of a special dispensation from the sisters, I was sometimes allowed to sit behind a pierced screen and listen to their singing, but this still made me different from the others – not quite one of them.

However, I was soon to have a friend: another English girl, whose father was a member of the British Diplomatic Service and attached to the embassy in Paris.

Kate had arrived at the convent two days after me. Sister Isobel had already told me that I would be sharing my room with someone called Catherine Blake and I was relieved when I first saw her. Smartly but plainly dressed, she had soft brown hair and bright eyes. I thought her pretty but not beautiful or proud, just a friendly girl to whom I took at once.

'I'm Kate. Please don't call me Catherine,' she begged as soon as we were alone. 'My father is the only one who does – and that's usually when he is angry with me, which is all too often.'

She pulled a face and I sensed that she was a little in awe of her father, who was, she told me, a secretary to the ambassador.

'That's why I'm here,' she explained with a wry twist of her lips. 'My mother died last year and since then Father simply doesn't know what to do with me. I am a nuisance, a piece of baggage he is obliged to cart around with him. He had almost decided to leave me in London with a paid companion but she left us suddenly to get married ... so here I am. Stuck in this awful place until I can be properly brought out.'

She pulled a face, which was meant to cover her grief but did not. I felt immediate concern for her. How awful to lose her mother and have no one to care for her! Even though my father had died before I'd ever known him, I'd had a real family to love me: Marthe and Pierre had been so good to me, and of course I had my own darling mother. I looked at Kate sympathetically.

'Don't you have any aunts you could stay with – no one at all?'

She shook her head. 'Both my parents were only children. My father has some distant cousins he dislikes and I have a brother – but Thomas is in the army. He will probably go into the diplomatic service in a few years, like Father, but for the moment...' She shrugged. 'It was either leave me with a stranger or bring me here.'

Poor Kate. I had hated being torn from all I knew and loved, but it must be so much worse for her, to be brought to a different country and to have to live amongst strangers, most of whom did not even speak her own language.

'I'm new here, too,' I confided. 'So we can comfort each other – if you'd like to be friends?'

'We can be best friends,' she said and took the pins from her long dark hair, which fell in soft waves about her face. Her eyes sparkled with mischief as she began to brush it with slow, deliberate strokes. 'Tell each other all our secrets.'

I smiled as I saw the look in her eyes. She was obviously going to be fun to know. I didn't have many secrets to confide, but perhaps I would tell her about André Bertrand and the kiss that had got me into so much trouble.

I discovered that Kate was nearly seventeen. There were almost twelve months between us, but the difference was not enough to matter. Perhaps it was natural that we should become friends, as most of the other girls were French-born and spoke very little English. I had learned to speak both languages from childhood, of course, my mother insisting that I spoke English with her most of the time, but poor Kate found it difficult to make herself understood. She had a terrible accent when speaking French and the others made fun of her behind her back.

In those first days I defended her fiercely and that made me unpopular with some of the other girls, but I didn't care. Kate was my special friend. We enjoyed being together and spent many happy hours lying on our beds talking late into the night. I told her about the farm and Tante Marthe, and she told me about life in the English country house where she had spent most of her childhood.

'It was a big, old house with tiny windows, and it was always cold. We used to spend the winter wrapped up in shawls to keep us from shivering. Father spent weekends and holidays with us so he didn't know how bad it was, and my mother never complained, though she was often unwell,' Kate said. 'Sometimes she went up to London to be with him ... then she started to have headaches and...' She stopped, a catch in her voice. 'It was terrible when she was ill, Jenny. I can't bear to tell you.'

'Then don't,' I said and hugged her. 'Unless you want to?'

She shook her head and I changed the subject, but some times, when I saw her sitting alone by her window, her eyes misted with sadness, I knew she was thinking of her mother and the terrible weeks when she had had to care for her almost alone, apart from a housekeeper and the doctor, who only occasionally visited.

As the weeks passed and I came to know Kate better, I learned that she had mercurial mood swings. At one moment she

57

could be teasing and full of fun, and then an odd quietness would come over her and she would withdraw, not speaking for perhaps an hour at a time. When that happened I knew she had been thinking of her mother and believed I understood.

'It was lucky for me that you were here when I arrived, Jenny,' she said once after we had been at the school for some weeks. 'I don't think I could have stood it otherwise. I should have had to run away.'

I smiled and hugged her arm, not truly believing her. It was a terrible thing to say, but Kate often made rash statements. Of course she wouldn't have run away. Where could she have gone?

'I'm glad you're still here, Kate,' I told her as we walked together in the ancient, walled gardens of the convent. It was autumn but the sun was still warm and roses scrambled over stone walls, giving off their heady perfume, the sweet sound of the nuns' singing mingling with the twittering of birds and the laughter of girls from inside the school building. 'What are you going to do at Christmas?'

'Thomas is coming to fetch me,' she said and her face lit up. She was really beautiful then. I saw a flicker of mischief in her eyes. 'We are going to stay with some friends of his. I think it will be fun. Sometimes I am so bored here ... I really could not stand it if it were not for you, Jenny.'

'Will your father be there, too?'

'No. He has to stay in Paris. It doesn't matter. We shall have more fun without him. He wasn't so bad before my mother was ill but now...' A shadow passed across her face but then she hugged my arm. 'We shall not talk about him. You will like Thomas, Jenny. He is the only one in the world I care for – except you, of course ... and someone else.'

There was an odd, secretive look in her eyes then, and I wondered why she didn't tell me who the other person was. I did not pry, however. Kate would tell me when she was ready.

'I am looking forward to meeting your brother,' I told her instead.

One day followed another as autumn moved slowly but surely into a mild winter. Our life at the school was calm, ordered and un-eventful. Kate often found it frustrating, but I liked the nuns with their quiet manners and gentle voices. It was a peaceful way of life and there was so much they could teach us if we were willing to learn.

'You are intelligent, Jeanette,' Sister Isobel had told me at the end of my first month with them. 'What's more, you want to learn, and that is good.'

It was true that I seemed to acquire know-ledge easily. It was because I found it all so interesting. My education had not been as full before this as it might have been; there was so much I wanted to know, so much I was ignorant of. I should probably have spent most of my time in the library with my head in a book if it were not for Kate.

'Not reading again!' she would cry, pouncing on me, dragging me from my refuge out into the crisp air of a winter's afternoon. 'Life is too short to waste. You must play as well as work, Jenny!'

Because of Kate I had my fair share of play. We laughed and teased each other all the time, especially on the rare occasions when we were allowed to go out together for tea in the village.

'It's so good to get away!' Kate exclaimed one particular afternoon two weeks before Christmas. 'I wish I was older so that I could make my come-out now. I can't bear being shut in with those dried-up old women. Sometimes I think I shall scream if Sister Isobel gives me another of her reproving looks!'

'Oh, Kate,' I said and giggled. She was in one of her rebellious moods, excited, almost nervous. 'I know what you mean, of course I do – but she is so kind. She doesn't disapprove of you, not really.'

'That's all you know.' Kate pulled a face and adjusted her hat so that it sat on her head at a jaunty angle, then slipped her hands inside her fashionable muff. She liked pretty clothes, though they were less fussy than mine and very English, and she seemed to have quite a lot of them. Her father might be strict with her, but he was certainly generous. 'Sister Isobel sees through to the real me. She knows I don't belong in a convent. She probably thinks I am a bad influence on you. Don't look like that; you know it's true!' Kate sighed deeply. 'How I long to be free, to be my own mistress ... if a woman can ever truly be free.'

'What do you mean?' I stared at her in surprise.

'We are ruled by men all our lives. You must know that, Jenny?'

'Surely not.' I thought of Tante Marthe's husband, who seemed to do whatever she asked of him, though in his own slow, un-hurried way – and of my mother. Her life had been hard at times, but she was her own mistress – wasn't she? ' Pierre always does what Marthe wants – and Mama lives her own life as she wishes.'

'Your mother is the exception, of course,' Kate said. 'I don't know how she has man-aged it all these years. Most widows live in poverty or are forced to marry again – unless they are lucky enough to inherit a fortune. Was your father very rich?' There was speculation in her eyes as she looked at me.

I shook my head, looking at her thoughtfully. She had put into words something that had been on my mind for a while now.

'Mama works in Paris as a seamstress to the quality; she is very busy and successful, that's why I had to live with Tante Marthe and Pierre at the farm. My father was an English gentleman but he had very little money. I think Mama must earn a great deal from her sewing, though she has recently inherited a little money.'

Kate wrinkled her brow. 'Your mother must be very clever, that's all I can say. Most seamstresses live very frugally. They couldn't afford the fees for this school.'

'She is clever – and beautiful. She's special, Kate. When you meet her you will understand.'

She hugged my arm. 'I am sure she is, Jenny. I can't wait to meet her.'

Kate's attention had wandered. I saw her glance across the wide expanse of the village green and smile. Her cheeks had gone quite pink and I sensed her excitement. Following the direction of her gaze I saw a young man staring at us. He could not have been much more than twenty-one or two, tall, of medium build and quite handsome with dark brown hair and eyes. He raised his smart beaver hat and started to cross the green towards us.

'Who is that?' I whispered.

'I've no idea,' she replied, 'but he is rather good-looking – isn't he?'

'Kate! We can't speak to a man we haven't been introduced to, you know we can't. Sister Isobel has warned us about it over and over again. It is against the rules and anyway ... it's not proper.'

Young ladies just did not do such things!

'Who cares about being proper – or Sister Isobel? I want to talk to him!' She was defiant, excited.

The young man seemed from his dress and manner to be a gentleman. He tipped his hat to us again, addressing himself to Kate.

'Excuse me, mademoiselle. I am a stranger to this area – could you please tell me if there is somewhere nearby where I might buy coffee or something to eat?'

'Oh, yes, of course.' Kate sparkled at him, her pretty face alive with mischief. Once again I sensed her intense excitement. 'We were just going to the café, weren't we, Jenny?'

'May I ask if you would be so kind as to direct me?'

Kate glanced at me uncertainly before replying. 'You could walk with us if you wish – couldn't he?' Her eyes met mine in a compelling look that seemed to beg for my agreement. 'You don't mind, do you, Jenny?'

I smothered a gasp of dismay. Such behaviour would bring a sharp reprimand from the sisters if it came to their ears – and there was always someone prepared to tell tales.

'Do you think we ought?' I whispered, but the man was introducing himself, offering his arm to Kate. He was an Englishman on business in France and his name was Richard Havers.

'I'm Kate Blake,' she said, her cheeks flushing and dimpling prettily. 'And this is my friend, Jenny Heron.'

'Mademoiselle Heron...' He glanced at me without interest. 'I am enchanted to have met you both.'

I had the oddest sensation – a feeling that this meeting was not by chance. They already knew each other. She was only pretending he was a stranger. It was a secret assignation! I could see it in Kate's face. She was excited – and guilty!

I dropped behind as they walked arm in arm. Kate had lowered her voice and I knew she did not want me to hear what she was saying to him, though every now and then they mentioned the weather or the village in voices loud enough to reach me.

Outside the small café Kate hesitated, looking back at me uncertainly.

'Mr Havers has offered to buy us coffee and cakes,' she said. 'I've told him I can't –

unless you will?'

'Kate...' I glanced uneasily over my shoulder. She must know what a risk we would be taking! Her eyes seemed to plead with me and I realised this was important to her. 'Well, if you really want to ... but be discreet. Please.'

It wasn't that I was afraid of breaking the sisters' rules, I had broken enough of them myself – but meeting a man was different to running in the house! Especially a man like Mr Havers – who seemed to me to be rather too forward in his manner towards Kate.

'Of course we shall be careful.' There was a flash of triumph in her eyes, as though she had been expecting me to refuse. 'Thank you, Jenny. Don't be cross. I'll explain later.'

I was nervous throughout the twenty minutes or so we spent drinking coffee and nibbling at tiny sweet cakes, because the girls from the convent were well known in the village and the other customers would be bound to gossip if they noticed us. But Kate was very careful to behave in a quiet, polite manner and, besides us, there were only two elderly ladies in the café. I kept my eyes cast down most of the time and tried not to show my feelings.

If we were lucky we might just get away with it.

I was relieved when at last Kate stood up,

thanked Mr Havers and said we must be going.

'I know I shouldn't have done it,' she said as we were walking back, hurrying through the gathering darkness so as not to be late for evening prep. 'I just couldn't believe my eyes when I saw him. He said he would surprise me one day – and he did!'

'You know him, don't you?'

'He is a friend of my brother,' she said. 'I knew he was in France, but I didn't think he would actually dare to come here this afternoon, even though he wrote—' She stopped and blushed, looking at me oddly.

'Have you been writing to him?'

She nodded, her cheeks pink. 'Oh, I know it is wrong of me. And not just because Sister Isobel says so! It will be another year before we could think of becoming engaged – and then my father may be against it. Even my brother would be shocked if he knew.'

'Why? Isn't Mr Havers suitable? He seemed to be a gentle man.'

'He comes from a good family,' she said and sighed. 'It's the same old story, Jenny – he is only a third son and has very little money. He will have to go into some sort of a profession – or the church.' She laughed at the thought. 'I cannot see Richard as a curate so he must find a profession, which won't be easy for him. I'm afraid he doesn't like the idea of being tied to a desk.' She seemed highly amused at the idea of his having to find employment.

'But everyone has to work.'

'Yes, of course. Unless they have enough money to live on without doing so. Richard will find something eventually – but my father would never agree to a marriage unless he was earning enough money to keep me.'

'But I thought you had some money of your own?'

'My mother left me a trust fund,' she replied, frowning. 'It's quite generous, really – but that only makes things worse. Father would think Richard was a fortune-hunter, which he isn't. It might seem that way, but really he isn't, Jenny.' Her face took on a stubborn expression. 'He loves me – and I love him. I shall marry him whatever anyone says.'

'Oh, Kate...'

I stared at her, not sure how to answer her rash statement. She was not quite seventeen, though she often looked older. She was surely too young to be thinking of marriage – and to a man her family would consider unsuitable!

Kate was silent for a moment, then said, 'Richard wants me to sneak out later this evening and meet him on my own.'

'You won't? You couldn't!' I looked at her in dismay. If she were caught she would be instantly expelled from the school. 'It's too risky, Kate. You'll be found out, you know you will.'

'Not if I stuff pillows in my bed.' She looked at me with pleading eyes. 'If Sister Isobel asks about me on her rounds you could tell her I went to bed early with a headache. Please, Jenny! If I miss this chance it may be ages before I can see him again.'

I recalled the innocent kiss André Bertrand had given me. Because of it I had been forced to leave Tante Marthe and the farm. Sneaking out to meet a man alone at night was a far worse crime than mine.

I still missed Marthe sometimes, missed my little room beneath the eaves and the smell of her cooking, but I was happy enough in my new life. Kate might not be so lucky. I knew from little things she had told me that her father was a stern disciplinarian: he would be furious with her if she was expelled from school.

'Supposing you get caught? Have you thought of what might happen – of what your father would say? What would you say if you were caught coming back in afterwards?'

'I'll think of something,' she said, giving me a hopeful look. 'Besides, I shan't get caught if you will help me. Please, Jenny? Please say you will?'

I hesitated, because I did not want to agree. I should find it difficult to lie to Sister Isobel ... but Kate was my friend. There was at that moment an odd defiance about her that frightened me: if I refused to help she would go anyway. I gave in reluctantly.

'Don't be too late back, then.'

'I knew you would help us,' she cried and kissed me. 'Thank you, dearest Jenny. Thank you!'

How I got through prep and supper that evening I shall never know. I was on edge, nervous, imagining that the sisters were watching us suspiciously, that they knew of our meeting with Richard Havers in the village and were waiting to punish us.

After supper, Kate slipped away to meet her friend, and I went up to our room alone to stuff pillows in her bed. It was quite effective and from the doorway might just convince someone she was lying there.

I read for two hours, my heart jerking each time footsteps passed our door, but fortunately we had no visitors that evening. Kate was not particularly friendly towards the other girls and they usually left us to ourselves in the evenings.

It was gone ten when I closed my book. Sister Isobel would soon come to tell us that we must put out our lamps and go to bed. I was beginning to feel anxious. Where was

Kate? She had promised to be back before this and I was starting to worry. If anyone suspected what she had done ... My heart caught with fright when I heard Sister Isobel's soft knock at our door.

'May I come in?' she asked as I opened the door slightly, standing so that she could only just see beyond me to Kate's bed. 'Is something wrong, Jeanette?'

'Kate had a headache,' I whispered, unable to meet her eyes because I hated lying to her. 'She is asleep now. I don't want to wake her.'

Sister Isobel nodded sympathetically. 'You should be in bed, Jeanette.'

'Yes, sister. I am just going.'

'Goodnight then. You know you can call me if Catherine needs me.' She glanced towards the bed once more. 'Poor Catherine.'

'Yes.' I could not look at her.

I closed the door as she walked away, breathing deeply as though I had been running very fast. Sister Isobel was a good woman and did not deserve to be deceived like this – and I would not lie for Kate again. I was suddenly angry with her for putting me in this position. It wasn't right or fair!

She burst into the room as I was undressing, laughing, her face flushed with excitement.

'That was a close one!' she cried. 'I had

70

to hide in the cupboard at the end of the hall or Sister Rosamunde would have seen me.'

'Sister Isobel was worried about you,' I said crossly. 'I don't like telling lies, Kate. Don't ask me to do it again, because I shan't.'

'Don't look at me like that,' Kate pleaded as she swiftly removed her clothes and folded them on the chair beside her bed. 'I'm sorry I was so long – but Richard didn't want me to go when I did.' She hugged her arms about herself, her face glowing. 'We had such a wonderful time. He wants me to run away with him.'

'Kate!' I cried in alarm and her glow faded. 'You won't. You mustn't. Think of your family ... of what it would do to them and your good name.'

'I told Richard I would think about it,' she said, looking a little sullen. 'It wouldn't be easy. Richard has so little money. My father controls my trust until I'm twenty-one – and I don't think he would let us have any money, even if we were married.'

'But you're so young, Kate.'

'Seventeen in January.'

'Don't you think you should wait – for a while at least?'

'Perhaps.' She made a dive for the bed as we heard someone in the corridor outside, pulling the covers over her at the same moment as Sister Isobel came into the room.

'I see you are awake, Catherine,' she said, putting her tray down on a table between the beds. I saw her glance at the neat pile of clothes on the chair beside Kate's bed, which had not been there earlier. 'Is your head still very bad, my dear?'

'It still aches,' Kate said. 'I was about to get up and come to see if you could give me something to help me rest.'

She lied so easily! How could she? My heart was beating very fast and I could not look at Sister Isobel. I felt troubled as the good nun laid a hand on Kate's forehead.

'You do feel a little heated,' she said, sounding concerned. 'Drink this hot milk and honey, Catherine. There is something in it that will help you to settle.'

'Thank you, sister.'

Kate took the cup and sipped obediently. Sister Isobel watched for a moment and then walked to the door. She paused there to smile rather oddly at us both.

'Good night, mademoiselles. Never forget that the good Lord is watching over you and sees all that you do.'

I looked at Kate as the door closed softly. 'She knows. I'm sure she guessed something.'

Kate pulled a face and put her cup down. 'Who cares? She can't prove anything. I'm going away with Richard as soon as he can arrange things. I've made up my mind. I don't want to stay here – and I don't want to wait for years to marry.'

'Kate ... you can't mean that!' I was horrified.

'What else can I do?' Tears welled up in her eyes. 'I'm so unhappy. You don't understand. You don't know what it was like living with my father after my mother died.'

I stared at her uncertainly. I knew she had been very unhappy, and a part of me understood how she felt, but I was more cautious, perhaps because of my French upbringing.

'I do understand, but I still think you should wait. Just for a short time – until you are eighteen, anyway. You ought to think it over more carefully, be sure that you love Mr Havers.'

'I do love him.' She pulled the covers up to her chin and closed her eyes. 'I'm tired. Goodnight, Jenny.'

'Goodnight.'

I lay awake long after Kate was asleep. Surely she wouldn't really run away with Mr Havers.

Mr Havers returned to England, and Kate did not see him again that term. We slipped back into our old routine of lessons, games and walks in the beautiful old gardens, and

I gradually forgot about the night my friend had gone to meet her beau.

Mama came to fetch me home for Christmas before Kate's brother arrived to collect her, so I didn't meet him after all. I introduced Kate to Mama, however, and they exchanged a few pleasant words, then, just as I was about to get into the carriage, my friend threw herself at me, giving me a fierce hug. I hugged her back and when I looked at her face I saw tears in her eyes.

'I'll see you after Christmas, Kate?'

'Yes. Of course.' She blinked hard, managing a watery smile. 'Have a lovely time, won't you? I shall miss you, Jenny.'

'I shall miss you too.' I kissed her cheek. 'Thank you for the lovely scarf. And I shall expect to hear all about your brother's friends next term.'

Kate nodded but didn't answer. I sensed she was trying to hide her emotions – that she was upset about our parting. Mama glanced at me curiously as I climbed into the carriage beside her.

'Your friend is rather an emotional young woman,' she remarked after a moment or two. 'Did you not tell me her mother is dead?'

'Her mother died a year ago last August – but she has a father and brother. She is staying with her brother and friends for Christmas.'

'Then why are you worried about her, Jenny?'

'I'm not worried ... exactly.'

'Would you like to tell me about it?' She raised her fine brows.

I shook my head. A part of me desperately wanted to tell her that I believed Kate was in danger of doing something very foolish, but I was afraid of what she might say or do. An innocent kiss had resulted in my being sent to the school: Mama would be horrified by Kate's reckless behaviour. She might forbid me to continue the friendship.

Afterwards, when it was much too late, I was to wish that I had confided in my mother then – but that was a long time in the future, when I was older and wiser.

'Very well.' Mama smiled at me. ' Marthe is so looking forward to seeing you, my darling. She will be surprised when she sees what a poised young lady you have become. I swear you've grown an inch.'

'Oh, Mama!' I cried. 'Surely not?'

'So very grown up,' she went on, her eyes dancing with amusement. 'Yes, my dear Marthe will be most surprised.'

Four

It was so good to be home again! I wanted to go everywhere, to see everything all at once. To my relief, nothing had changed. Marthe and Pierre were just the same, the farm as old and shabby and comfortable as it always had been. I had been so afraid it might have changed, and to find it the same was most reassuring: it made me feel that it would always be there, that I could run back to my dear friends if I had need of them.

We spent five days at the farm. Marthe cried into her kerchief when she first saw me, and even Pierre seemed affected. He blew his nose hard, patted my hand awkwardly and went outside to see to the cows.

'It's so good to see you, Jeanette,' Marthe said between snuffles. 'And such a young lady! How you've grown. I can't believe it.'

'There – what did I tell you?' Mama cried and clapped her hands. 'I felt just the same when I saw her – didn't I, Jenny?'

I nodded and kissed them both, my lingering fears for Kate receding to a corner of my mind. Kate would be with her brother.

Surely she would be safe enough?

I imagined her spending Christmas with Thomas and his friends. She had talked of parties and dances, and there was no reason for me to suppose that she would not be happy – and yet I could not forget that emotional farewell.

Those five days went by so swiftly I hardly had time to realise I was there before the visit was over and I was back in Mama's little house in Paris. This time she had arranged a small supper party for her friends to celebrate New Year.

'Of course you know Madame Leconte,' she said, greeting a woman I had met briefly on my last visit. 'And the Bruges – Madame Yvonne, Monsieur and their sons Marc and Jean.'

Jean was about my own age – sixteen, now – a skinny youth with spots and lank hair who looked at me shyly but smiled when he discovered I was not as sophisticated as he'd first thought. His brother was older, good-looking and a little too sure of himself. I did not like the way he stared at me with his knowing eyes, almost as if he were undress-ing me, seeing me naked.

After supper Mama suggested that we get up a little dance and the carpets were rolled back in her parlour. Madame Leconte played for us at the pianoforte and everyone took turns to dance. It was amusing and we all laughed and drank a great deal of wine. I was sorry when it was over.

Mama walked upstairs with me after our guests had gone. She smiled and touched my cheek.

'Did you enjoy yourself, my darling?'

'Oh yes,' I said enthusiastically. 'It was fun, Mama. I enjoyed the dancing very much.'

'And particularly with Marc Bruge, I think?'

I blushed and shook my head. The young man had flirted with me as the evening wore on but I had not found him attractive. I did not tell my mother that I thought he had held me a little too tightly and that I hadn't liked the musky smell of his body. André's kiss had been innocent and in fun. I thought that a kiss from Marc would be very different and decided to keep well away from him for the remainder of my visit with Mama.

'Well, I shan't tease you about it,' my mother said and smiled. 'You are growing up, my darling, but you are still too young to think of forming an attachment – and besides, Marc Bruge is not what I want for you. You are the daughter of a gentleman, Jenny. You must marry someone suitable. I am determined on it – when the time is right.'

'Why?' I gazed up at her. 'Why must I

marry? Could I not be like you and earn my living?'

'You would find it very hard,' she said and sighed, a strange, wistful look in her eyes. 'Life can be so unfair, my sweet Jenny. If things had been different, you would have lived in a fine house with a park and horses to ride around it all your life. You would have had pretty dresses and jewels and –'

'But I was happy with Marthe,' I reminded her. 'And I love being here with you. I can do plain sewing quite well – I thought perhaps when I left school I could divide my time between you and the farm?'

'Oh no,' she said with a determined shake of her head. 'That would not be suitable. No, not at all. It is not what I want for you. I have made plans, Jenny. We must both be patient but in time ... in time we shall have everything that is owed to us.'

'Owed us?'

Her eyes had a brilliant sheen as she looked beyond me into the future of her dreams. I wondered what she meant but I could see it would be useless to ask.

My mother had secrets she was not ready to share with me. She had promised she would one day, but until that day came I could only wonder and be patient.

Although I did not know why, I felt discomfited as I got out of the carriage and made my way back across the smooth lawns towards the school. My mother had been too busy to come with me this time, but I was not nervous and the coachman had looked after me well enough, so my unease was not for myself.

Where was Kate? I looked for her amongst the crowd of returning pupils but could not see her. It was then that I understood this feeling deep inside me, the feeling that something was terribly wrong.

'Jeanette ... may I speak with you, please?'

I jumped as Sister Isobel called me, beckoning to me to enter her small room. It was the room she used for dispensing medicines and for interviewing any girls who had misbehaved and needed discipline.

'Yes, sister, of course. Is something wrong?'

The look in her eyes made me tremble inwardly. That feeling of something unpleasant being about to happen was very strong. I sensed that she had something serious to say to me and I was afraid it was about Kate.

'I wanted to tell you before the whispers start,' she said as I entered the room and closed the door behind me. 'I'm afraid I have bad news for you, Jeanette. Your friend Catherine Blake will not be returning to the school.'

Kate not coming back! It was what I had

feared. She had been so emotional when we parted that I had suspected something was troubling her.

'Not ever?' I asked, my voice a mere croak. 'Why – what has happened?'

'Her father died suddenly and her brother has decided to take Catherine back to England with him.'

This was not what I had been expecting to hear. The shock made me feel faint and I moaned, swaying slightly. Sister Isobel caught my arm and helped me to a hard wooden chair. She looked at me in concern.

'I'm sorry, Jeanette. I know you will miss her.'

'Yes.' I nodded as tears stung my eyes. 'Poor Kate.' I glanced up at the nun. 'Are you sure that is the reason she isn't coming back to school?'

Sister Isobel looked at me in silence for a moment. 'Perhaps you would like to tell me what you are thinking, Jeanette? Is there something you know that I ought to know?'

'Oh, no.' I blushed. 'I thought...'

'You wondered if perhaps Catherine might have run away?' I gasped as I saw the knowledge in her eyes. She *had* known where Kate had been the night she had sneaked out to see Mr Havers. 'I believe there may have been some such intention but when the news of her father's death came...' Sister Isobel looked at me hard. 'I had suspected something for a while and intercepted a letter from Mr Havers a few days before the end of term. In the circumstances, I thought it my duty to hand the letter to Mr Thomas Blake when he came to collect his sister.'

'Oh.' I swallowed hard. 'I don't know what to say, Sister Isobel.' I hung my head in shame.

'You had best not say anything. You do not lie well, Jeanette. It does not become you.'

'No, sister.'

There was a hint of reproach in her eyes. 'I believe it was not your fault. I have been told that Catherine has always been a little ... reckless, shall we say?'

'She doesn't mean any harm.'

'Perhaps not – but her behaviour sometimes leads others into doing things that their own natures would not permit. If Catherine had returned to us it was my intention to separate you this term, for your own sakes.' She softened her words with a smile. 'I am sorry you have lost your friend, Jeanette. Mr Blake brought a letter for you when he came to tell me his sister would not be returning. I see no reason why you should not have it. I have not read it but I understand Mr Blake knows what is in it.'

'Thank you, sister.' I took the letter from her hand, my head down. 'I'm sorry ... for lying to you.'

Her face softened and I knew she had

forgiven me.

'You may go, Jeanette. I am putting a new girl in with you. I am trusting you to look after her – she is a year or so younger than you. You may regain my good opinion of you by showing me you know how to behave in future, and taking care of Elspeth.'

'Yes, sister. Thank you.' I went to the door and then looked back. 'I really am very sorry that I lied to you.'

'Please do not do it again,' she said. 'I was disappointed in you – I do not want to be disappointed again.'

I felt the shame wash over me as I saw the reproach in her eyes. 'No, sister. You won't be. I promise.'

I read Kate's letter swiftly and then more slowly a second and third time. She told me briefly that her father had died of a sudden heart attack, then launched into a description of her brother's friends.

They were all so kind to me because of Father. It was just like being one of the family. Edouard Duvalle and his wife are travelling to England for a short visit with some cousins and have offered to take me with them. Thomas says he will have found a companion for me by the time they return to France and promises that I need not go back to

83

school. I think he will let me become engaged to Richard very soon, but if he proves as stubborn as Father we shall go to Gretna Green in the spring ... Thomas thinks he has read my letter but I managed to substitute it when he wasn't looking. I shall send you my address when I can and I long to hear from you...

There was much more in the same vein, rebellious, defiant words that made me fear for my friend.

Oh, Kate! I sighed and refolded the letter, slipping it into my writing-case. I'd sensed that she did not particularly love her father but I was worried that she could still think of eloping when Mr Blake had so recently died. It was reckless and disrespectful. Was she so much in love that she could think of nothing else?

I wondered what it would be like to love a man so much that you were willing to risk everything for his sake, but could not imagine it. My one and only kiss had meant nothing serious to me.

The letter stayed at the back of my mind for several weeks but I had little time to dwell on thoughts of Kate. My new room-mate was a shy girl who had never been away from her home before. She cried into her pillow every night for days and I was too concerned about her health to worry about Kate too much. Poor Elspeth was a pale, sickly girl and suffered with chills and colds. I was forced to mother her and in doing so I allowed my concern for Kate to slip to the back of my mind – until the next letter came about six months later.

I recognised the writing at once and tore it open, but the shock of her news made me gasp with dismay. Surely it could not be true! I read it twice to be certain. Kate's brother had forbidden her to marry Richard and she had decided to run away with him. 'When you next see me I shall be Richard's wife,' she had written.

> I have time for no more now, dearest Jenny, but I wanted to tell you and I know that you will wish me luck. I shall keep in touch and hope we shall always be friends.

Oh, Kate, Kate, I sighed to myself. *I wish I could see you, talk to you.* If I could, I would have begged her not to do anything rash. I had not particularly liked Mr Havers – and I did not trust him.

I had hoped that she might have changed her mind once she had time to reflect, but it seemed that nothing would stop her. She was so reckless! She ought still to have been in mourning for her father, not behaving in

85

a manner that would cause her brother more pain and trouble. Although I had never met Thomas Blake, I felt sorry for him. How upset he must be that his sister had run away with her lover.

Her letter worried me. I read it several times, then destroyed it lest it fall into the wrong hands. I had the feeling that my friend was storing up trouble for herself, but there was nothing I could do to prevent her. One day I would come to understand, but at this time I was still too naïve, too much a product of my upbringing and education.

Oh, Kate, I said to myself. *Kate – why did you do it?*

If only I could have seen her, talked to her! But she had not sent me her address and I did not know how to reach her.

I heard nothing more from Kate, though I looked for a letter every day for the next six weeks or so. Then something happened that put everything else from my mind.

Elspeth took what we all thought was a nasty chill. She was really very unwell and I was excused classes for a couple of days to sit with her, because she begged the sisters not to leave her alone.

'You've been like a real sister to me, Jenny,' she said as I sat by her bed one day, holding her hand and stroking her forehead, which was hot and flushed with fever. 'Please don't leave me alone. I'm frightened of dying.' Her eyes filled with tears and she looked so young and vulnerable.

'You won't die, silly,' I scolded gently and bent to kiss her. I had become fond of her, seeing her as a younger sister, and I tried to comfort her. 'It's only a nasty chill.'

But it wasn't a chill, it was a virulent fever that turned in time to pneumonia – and I took it from her.

I remember very little of my own illness ... vague snatches of voices, pain and a terrible weakness that seemed to envelop my whole body. I believe that I was delirious for several days, but I knew nothing of it. It was as if I were caught in a mist, marooned on an island far from all my friends, and nothing was clear, nothing made sense.

Sometimes, I heard voices close to me. I heard people talking but I could not understand them.

'She must not die.' Was that anguished voice my mother's? 'She is all I have. How could you have allowed her to nurse that child? If she dies you will hear from my friend, and you will be sorry!'

'It was her own wish, madame. We none of us guessed how ill poor Elspeth was.'

'Elspeth,' I muttered through dry lips. 'Kate ... Kate, where are you? You must not ... you must not...'

A gentle hand stroked my forehead. 'Do not worry, dearest. Kate is well – and you must also be well again. Please, for my sake.'

I moaned and subsided back into that world of grey mists. But the voices came again. I heard them talking but from a great distance.

'This letter came for her.'

'Give it to me. I will keep it for her. My poor darling little girl ... If she dies I shall not know how to bear it!'

'Courage, madame. Jeanette is a strong girl.'

'But she is so ill ... I should never have taken her away from Marthe. She was safe there.'

'But it was her father's wish that she come here ... was it not?'

My father is dead. How could he have wanted me to be sent here?

The voices came and went and I forgot them in the agony of aching limbs and pain that seemed to go on and on endlessly, but then, at last, the day came when I woke to find my mother sitting at my side and there was no more pain, no more fever, just a blessed relief. She smiled and reached out to touch my forehead, stroking back the damp hair with her loving touch.

'You are better at last, my darling.' Her voice broke on a sob. 'We have been so worried about you, so very worried ... but you will be well now. I do not think I could have gone on if anything had happened to you, Jenny.'

'And Elspeth?' I whispered, looking across at the empty bed. 'What happened to Elspeth?'

My mother's face told me that my poor friend had not been as lucky as I and tears stung my eyes.

'Poor, poor Elspeth,' I said. 'Oh, Mama, she was so young and good. Why did it have to happen? It's so unfair.'

'Life is unfair, Jenny,' my mother said and bent to kiss my cheek. 'I am sorry you have lost your friend, but she was always a delicate girl.'

'Sister Isobel asked me to look after her...'

'And you did,' Mama said. 'You were devoted to her and that's why you took the fever from her.'

'Why did she die?'

I felt the sting of tears. It seemed that I was doomed to lose my friends. First Kate and now Elspeth.

'Jeanette – will you take the poetry class for me this morning?' Sister Isobel asked when she found me reading in the library one morning some months later. 'I have a very sick patient to look after – besides, the girls enjoy it so much better when you read to them.'

'Of course – if you wish it, sister.'

I was thoughtful as I made my way

89

towards the classroom. It was not the first time such a request had been made of me recently. Elspeth's death had shocked me more than anything that had happened to me before. I had grown up very quickly after that, and as my own health improved I had become quieter, even more studious than before. I had made it my duty to look after the new girls, taking them under my wing and protecting them as best I could, showing them how to adapt to life away from their families.

Because of this I went on to be nominated as Head Girl and my last year at the school was so busy that I hardly thought of Kate at all. She had not written to me again after the letter telling of her intention to elope and I thought that she might have changed her mind. I hoped she had. I hoped that she was well and happy, but I had too much on my mind to think about her often. I had made many friends now and found my life both rewarding and fulfilling.

On my last visit to her in Paris, Mama had promised that I should live with her once my schooling was finished. We had been shopping and were sitting in her pretty parlour when she looked at me, a rather odd expression in her eyes.

'We shall visit Marthe sometimes, of course,' she said. 'But I want to make you secure for the future, Jenny. It is my intention that you should marry well ... that you should have all the things that ought rightfully to have been yours.'

'What do you mean, Mama?'

'You will discover my meaning soon enough.' She shook her head and glanced away towards the windows. 'Do you ever think of Kate, Jenny?'

'Yes, sometimes.' I stared in surprise. 'Why do you ask? Have you heard anything of her?'

'You knew she ran away with Mr Havers, of course? She wrote to you about that?'

'Yes. She said she would write again – but she never did. How did you know? I never told you.'

My mother stood up and went over to her desk. She took a letter from her writing-box and handed it to me. It was addressed to me in Kate's hand, but had been opened.

'It came when you were ill,' she said. 'I think you had better read it, Jenny.'

I took out the letter and scanned the message swiftly. The writing was agitated and untidy, and as I read on, I understood why. It was an appeal for help. Kate had been abandoned by her lover; she was penniless and alone in France. She had written out of desperation, to beg me to do what I could for her.

I frowned as I looked up at my mother. 'Why have you never told me about this?'

'It was too late by the time you had re-covered,' she said. 'But do not worry, Jenny. I saw your friend. I gave her money.'

'You saw Kate?' I was stunned, and upset that she had kept it from me all this time. 'I wish you had told me this before.'

'She begged me not to,' Mama said. 'She was ashamed of what she had done, Jenny. She would not have written to you if she had not been desperate. After I gave her the money she went away. I do not know where.'

Something made me think she was not telling me everything.

'You know where she is, don't you?'

'No, Jenny, truly I do not.'

'Why have you given me the letter now?'

I was suspicious, angry with her. I was shocked because she had deceived me, and it made me vaguely uneasy. If she could lie about Kate's letter, what else had she kept from me?

'Because I wanted you to understand...' Mama's eyes were shadowed with memor-ies. 'I want you to know why it is so import-ant that you marry well, Jenny. Kate had many advantages which were denied you because of my circumstances, but she threw them away. I should not want you to do the same. You must have everything I could not give you.'

When my mother spoke in that way I was aware of a prickling at the nape of my neck.

I was looking forward to making my home with her, but uncertain of what lay further in the future. Mama seemed determined on marriage for me but I sometimes wished there was another way ... a way for me to be independent, as she had been.

I did not press her further, because I needed time to think. I was too stunned by the discovery that Kate had written to me – that she had asked for my help. And I was saddened to hear that my fears had been well founded. Mr Havers had treated her shamefully, just as I had suspected he might.

My poor, dear Kate. It hurt me that I had not been able to go to her when she needed me, and I was thoughtful as I left my mother to return to school. Where was Kate now? Was she well? Was she happy? If only she had left me some way of contacting her.

I wondered if my mother had been truthful when she told me that she did not know where Kate had gone – and for the first time in my life I began to doubt her.

What was it that she had always hidden from me?

As the end of my last year at school drew near, I began to think more and more of the future. If I must marry, I was determined that it would be to a man I could like and respect and not just for money and position.

Other girls sometimes talked of the husbands they would have one day. Many of them seemed to expect arranged marriages to men of their parents' choosing; some were already spoken for, though they would have their coming-out season first: parties and pretty dresses and a whirl of social engagements.

Surely my mother did not plan that for me? She had a little money besides what she earned from her work, but not enough for me to have a season. No, no, I must not expect anything of that kind. No doubt she would give a few dinner parties for me and hope that I met someone suitable amongst her friends – that was all she meant when she spoke of a good match.

What else could she mean?

I was looking forward to being with her when I left school; I wanted to help her in her business as much as I could – at least until I married. I often thought about how much we would enjoy being together, sometimes counting the days until the end of term – but then, a few weeks before I was due to leave, I had a letter from her.

'My dearest Jenny,' she wrote in a rather shaky hand.

I have been unwell this past month. Nothing for you to worry about, darling – but I may not be able to collect you from school myself. If I cannot, I shall ask a friend to do this for me. Do you remember Monsieur le Comte de Arnay? We met him with his cousin, Madame Rossi, the first time you stayed with me in Paris. He has often asked after you and I am sure you will like him...

I stared at the letter in dismay. My mother not well! How ill was she? I was consumed with anxiety. Mama was never ill. I had never known her to have more than a headache. It was so unlike her to write me such a letter.

I took the letter to Sister Isobel and showed it to her. 'I should like to go home at once, sister.'

She looked at me doubtfully. 'I'm not sure that would be a good idea, Jeanette. It might not be convenient for Madame Heron to have you home just yet.'

'Why?'

What was that odd expression in her eyes? I sensed she felt herself in a difficult position – that she knew something she did not wish to tell me. What was she hiding from me?

'Your mother may not feel well enough to have you there.'

'But don't you see? If she is ill, she may need me.' My voice held a quiet desperation. 'Please – I must see her. I must!'

'Very well.' Sister Isobel sighed resignedly. 'I shall write a letter today – but you must be patient. Promise me that you will do nothing foolish, Jeanette. Do you give me your word?'

'Yes, sister. I promise.'

'You will have an answer within a few days.'

It was useless to plead further. I had been foolish to suppose she would let me leave immediately. As I began to walk back to my own room a little voice in my head told me to disobey her and make my own way home.

Kate would not have given in so easily. Kate would have done whatever was necessary – but Kate had run away with a lover who had abandoned her.

For a few minutes I wished fervently that my friend was still at the school; then, as one of the younger girls came rushing up to me with a problem, Kate was pushed to the little corner of my mind she habitually occupied. She had not written to me since that last time, when I had been too ill to help her – and she had not wanted me to know where she was going when she left Paris. I doubted I would ever see her again.

Two days later I was helping some of the younger girls with their history studies when I was told Sister Isobel wanted to see me in her study immediately. The reply to her letter must have come sooner than we had expected! My heart raced wildly as I hurried to answer the summons. My packing was almost finished. I could be ready to leave within the hour. I was anxious to be on my way.

I knocked at the sister's door and waited for her invitation to enter. It was summer but the corridor was narrow and dark, chilly even on a warm day like this. I felt a shiver run down my spine and, as she opened the door, I was seized with apprehension.

Her expression was so serious!

'Come in, my dear.' Her voice was gentle and kind. 'You have a visitor.'

Why was she looking at me like that? Something terrible must have happened. Oh, no ... no! Not to my mother ... not that.

'Sister Isobel?' I hesitated and she took hold of my arm, leading me forward.

'Come along in, Jeanette. There is someone here who wishes to speak to you.'

A man was standing by the window, looking out at the gardens. I had only seen him once, in Paris, but I knew him instinctively. Sister Isobel glanced towards him as she spoke, an odd, slightly disturbed expression in her eyes as if she were not quite comfortable with the situation. 'I believe you have met Monsieur de Arnay?'

'Yes ... once.'

He turned at that moment, his face grave,

eyes intense. The look he gave me was so charged with emotion that my heart began to beat very fast and my apprehension deepened into fear. My mouth suddenly went dry and my legs felt weak. I reached for the side of Sister Isobel's desk and held on to it, fearing that I should faint. Because I knew; I knew what he was going to tell me even before he spoke.

'Mademoiselle Heron,' he said, his voice raw and husky, as if he were under a great strain. 'Forgive me – Jeanette ... I hardly know how to tell you...'

'Mama ... ?' One hand crept to my throat. I felt an awful sinking sensation inside and I understood what he was trying to say. 'She...' Tears built behind my eyes but I would not let them fall. I shook my head, vainly denying the truth I read in his face. 'She's dead, isn't she?'

'I'm so sorry,' Sister Isobel murmured from somewhere behind me. 'Poor Madame Heron ... it was very sudden.'

For one brief, terrible moment I was filled with a consuming hatred for her. If she had not denied me I might have seen my mother ... been with her at the last. The anger flared in me, but when I looked at her and saw her grief it died as swiftly as it had come. It was not her fault ... not her fault that I had spent so little time with my mother, that she had died just when my dream of living with her had seemed so near.

'Your maman died yesterday evening,' the comte said gently. 'She was peaceful at the end, though she had suffered some pain these past weeks. I believe it must have been a relief to her at the last.'

I heard Sister Isobel's hiss of disbelief that he should speak so openly of Mama's pain, but I was grateful for his honesty. It was better to know the truth than let my imagination take flight.

'What was wrong with her, sir?'

'The doctors cannot be certain. We think she may have picked up a fever. She had been visiting someone – some poor creature in desperate circumstances – and may have taken the sickness from her. Your mother had bouts of vomiting and chest pains ... but at the end she was peaceful. All she thought of was you. Your name was the last thing she said to me.'

'You were with her when she died?'

'Yes, I was.' He hesitated, then cleared his throat awkwardly. 'You may think that odd, perhaps?' I did not answer and my silence brought a frown to his face. 'We were friends for many years. I admired your mother very much, Mademoiselle Heron. She was an exceptional woman.'

'Yes.' There was a lump in my throat. I swallowed hard. It seemed so strange to be talking this way when my mother was dead.

I wanted to scream and throw myself down in a fit of grief, but of course I did not. These past years with the nuns, I had been taught to behave in a more seemly manner, to control my passions – but I was very near to giving way. 'I know ... she made the room light up whenever she came in.'

'Sit down, Jeanette.' Sister Isobel touched my arm. 'You look pale, my dear. This has been a dreadful shock for you.'

She sounded disapproving, as though she was angry with the comte for not breaking the news more gently.

'May I see her?' I asked, looking directly at him. His face was harsh as he struggled to contain what was obviously a powerful emotion at work within him. 'I want to see her. Please?'

Tears were beginning to trickle down my cheeks. I could not prevent them but I was not sobbing. I felt oddly calm, controlled ... removed from the scene, as if I had deliberately cut myself off from what was happening around me.

The comte handed me a large linen kerchief. I pressed it to my cheeks and tried to return it but he shook his head and I tucked it into my sleeve.

'Of course you may see her. I have come to take you to her.'

'My packing is almost done.'

'Leave everything as it is,' he commanded.

'Someone will see to it. Your mother entrusted your future to me, Jeanette. You have nothing to do but make your farewells. Say goodbye to your friends and meet me outside the front door in – shall we say fifteen minutes?'

He glanced at a gold watch that hung from his waistcoat on a fancy chain. I sensed that he wished to leave as quickly as possible and glanced uncertainly at Sister Isobel.

'We shall not say goodbye,' she said in soft, gentle tones. 'You will come to see me again one day, I hope?'

'Yes, of course.'

The moment of anger had passed. She was not to blame for Mama's death, and even if I had been there it could have made no difference to the outcome.

Sister Isobel smiled encouragingly and I went hastily from the room. As I hurried to collect a few personal things for the journey, I was stopped by a group of girls who were curious to know what was going on.

'I'm leaving today,' I said and walked on. 'Sister Isobel will explain if you ask her.'

There was no one I wanted to tell about my mother's sudden death, no one who was close enough to understand what I was feeling. If Kate had been there ... but she wasn't. If I wished, I could write to the other girls when I felt able.

The school had been an important part of

my life, but that was over. I felt no reluctance as I left. Indeed, I hardly gave it a thought. I was consumed by grief, my heart breaking as I realised that all my dreams of being with my mother in Paris had vanished in a moment like a summer mist.

Five

I joined the comte outside the school within the time he had allowed and received a nod of approval. News of my sudden departure had spread and several girls had gathered in the porch, watching curiously as I was helped into the elegant travelling carriage. I waved once from the window and then sat back, closing my eyes as the comte got in and took his seat opposite.

We drove in silence for some time, then he leant forward and touched my hands, which I had clasped tightly in front of me. I opened my eyes and looked at him, hoping desperately that he would say nothing to make me cry. I was fighting my deep sense of loss and grief by trying to pretend that none of this was real. Surely, any moment now, I would wake up and realise that it had all been a nightmare, that my mother was still alive and well, waiting for me to join her in Paris as we had planned.

'We must talk,' he said. 'Forgive me, but there are things you must be told.'

'Yes, of course.' I looked at him. 'It was

103

just the shock. I am ready to listen to you, monsieur.'

'I have made the necessary arrangements in Paris,' he said. 'Madame Leconte is at the house and will stay with you until after the funeral. I thought you would be more comfortable with someone you know?'

'Yes, thank you. You are very kind.'

His face was grave as he regarded me from thoughtful eyes. 'It is nothing. Your mother was my friend, mademoiselle. I am very happy to do what little I can for you.'

'You had known her a long time?'

'Since ... yes, for many years.' He gave me a rather sad smile. 'Recently, I had been advising her on a financial matter. She asked me to handle her business affairs and to take care of you if...' He paused and sighed deeply.

'To take care of me?' I stared at him, feeling a sudden, clutching panic. 'Did my mother expect to die? Did she know she was very ill? Why wasn't I told sooner?'

'Adele did not want to worry you.' He gave me a grave, sympathetic look. 'Towards the end I think she expected it, but Adele was always very aware that life could spring unpleasant surprises. She wanted to make sure that you would be protected in all eventualities. I think that must be why she appointed me as your guardian ... until you are twenty-one or married.'

'My guardian ... but...'

I had expected Tante Marthe and her husband to be my guardians until I was of an age to manage my own affairs. As yet I'd had no time or inclination to make plans, but I suppose at the back of my mind was the thought that I could always return to the farm and my friends.

The comte was studying me thoughtfully. 'You are surprised. It is natural that you should be since we have met only once previously – though I think you are better acquainted with Madame Rossi?'

'I have met her once or twice,' I admitted. 'She has called for fittings and to take tea with us when I've been staying with Mama.'

'And you like her?'

He seemed anxious that I should, so I smiled briefly and nodded.

'Yes, very much. She is good-natured and amusing company. I do not think that anyone could dislike Madame Rossi.'

'No.' He gave me an answering smile. 'Henriette usually manages to charm everyone – and to get her own way.'

'Sir?' I was not certain of his meaning. Was he criticising his wife's cousin?

He shook his head as he saw the question in my eyes. 'It was merely an observation. Of no importance. Henriette is herself. She has lived with us since her husband died. My wife is unfortunately something of an

105

invalid and cannot be parted from her dear Henriette.'

'I am sorry to hear that Madame de Arnay is unwell, sir.'

'Béatrix is not exactly ill – just delicate.' A flicker of what might have been annoyance passed across his face. I sensed that he was not close to his wife. 'She spends much of her time resting in her own apartments, but Henriette will be there to keep you company. You are not so much younger than she, after all.'

'Keep me company?' I stared in bewilderment. 'Forgive me, monsieur. I do not understand.'

His brow furrowed as he heard the surprise in my voice. 'I have decided that you shall live at my château until we can find a husband for you, Jeanette. Since I am your guardian it will be for the best that you reside at my home. I am not often in the country myself, though I visit from time to time. It would not be proper for you to stay with me in Paris – so you will go to the château, where my wife and Henriette can chaperone you.'

'Live at your château in the country?' I echoed foolishly. 'Until I marry? But...'

'You have some objection?'

He seemed annoyed and I quailed inwardly. Why was I questioning him? What real objection could I have? It was a very generous solution to an awkward situation. He could not have wished to be made guardian to a girl he hardly knew, even if my mother had been a friend of many years.

'No, sir. I have no objection.' I suppressed the odd feeling of panic inside me. This was nonsense!! He was making me a very generous offer and I was being foolish. 'I was surprised – but you are very kind. I fear I am causing you a great deal of trouble.'

'No, no, Jeanette,' he said, his frown easing. 'You have been well taught by the sisters, and will not disgrace me. You will be no trouble to my wife, and Henriette is looking forward to your company. When I am at home we entertain regularly, and I am sure it will not be too long before I have several gentlemen begging me for permission to speak to you. We shall have you suitably settled in an establishment of your own in no time. Just as Adele wished.'

I sat in silence, giving an appearance of acquiescence. To declare that I had no wish to marry would only make him angry. What could I say that would not seem churlish or disobliging? He had been kind to fetch me from the convent himself: he could easily have sent a servant. Besides, he was my legal guardian and for the moment I had no choice but to obey his wishes.

We are ruled by men all our lives.

Where had I heard that? I thought hard

and remembered that it was Kate who had said those words to me the afternoon we'd met Richard Havers. I'd laughed at her then in my innocence, but now I saw that she had been right. The comte was my guardian and would relinquish his rights over me only when I married a man of whom he approved.

Looking at his face now, I saw that I should be expected to obey his wishes in all things. It was a new experience for me, and for the first time I began to understand why Kate had run away with her lover.

The next few days were perhaps the saddest of my life. I spent some hours sitting quietly beside my mother's silk-lined coffin. She seemed to me to be even more beautiful in death than she had in life – so serene and happy. I could hardly believe that she would not open her eyes and smile at me – but when I kissed her cheek, she was as cold as marble.

I wept a little as I sat beside her, but still felt disorientated, as though gripped by some terrible nightmare. Surely none of this could really be happening? I imagined that at any moment I might wake up and find it was all just a dream. My grief was locked deep inside me. I dare not let it free, because I should not have been able to cope. Perhaps if I had been with Marthe and

Pierre it would have been easier to let go, but they were at the farm and I was in Paris with people I scarcely knew.

'Oh, Mama ... Mama...' I whispered. 'Why did you have to die and leave me ... why?'

Fate could be so cruel. I had dreamed of being with my mother, of all the wonderful things we would do together and now ... the world seemed an empty place without her.

I had really spent so little time with her, and yet she had filled my world. The future seemed bleak. What was there to look forward to now? I could not even begin to imagine my life without my dearest Mama. I knew nothing of the comte, his château or the life that awaited me there, and I clung to the past desperately.

'What will happen here ... afterwards?' I asked Madame Leconte as we sat together in the parlour the day before the funeral. 'The house ... Mama's things?'

'I believe Monsieur de Arnay proposes to let the house,' she told me gently. 'Your mother's personal things belong to you, Jeanette – perhaps you would like me to pack them for you when this is all over? I could have them sent on to you at the comte's château.'

'Is this the comte's house?' I asked, but she shook her head and said she was not sure.

'I have been told it will be let,' she said. 'That is all I know.'

I was silent for a moment, thoughtful. The idea of a stranger living in my mother's house was distressing, but what was the alternative? It could not be left empty and I knew my guardian would never allow me to live there alone.

Perhaps if Madame Leconte would stay on with me as a companion he might allow me to live here? But no, it was useless to ask. I was already aware of the comte's dislike of having his arrangements questioned. He was a generous man but used to having his orders instantly obeyed. I felt too much in awe of him, too vulnerable in my newly bereaved state, to speak my own mind plainly.

'If you would be so kind,' I said to Madame Leconte, 'I would like to have everything of Mama's, please – her clothes, letters, brushes. But I cannot face touching anything just yet.'

'Nor shall you,' she replied, patting my hand sympathetically. 'Leave it to me, my dear.' She hesitated as though she would have liked to say more, then sighed and shook her head. 'Now is not the time – but if ever you need to talk to someone who knew your mother well, I shall always be here. I was fond of her and you will always be welcome in my home.'

I smiled and thanked her for her kindness, the emotion welling up inside me so that the tears were very close.

'You are very thoughtful. If you don't mind, I think I shall go and help Marie. She is packing the things I had stored here, because Monsieur de Arnay wishes to leave tomorrow as soon as...' The words stuck in my throat and I could not continue.

Madame Leconte nodded understandingly but refrained from speaking further. She clearly thought that this was not the time for confidences and I could only be grateful for her forbearance. There were many things I wished to know about my mother's life, and perhaps Madame Leconte could tell me some of what I wished to know – but to speak of Mama now would be unbearable.

Why had she died so suddenly? No one had yet given me an explanation that made sense. If it was a fever, what kind of fever?

My heart was heavy as I walked upstairs. Mama had always seemed so young, so full of life. It hurt me just to walk past her room, to think of her lying there, sick and in pain.

When I entered my own room I saw that Marie had sorted out a pile of my old clothes, lying them on the counterpane side by side for me to inspect. I had outgrown most of the dresses and she was obviously wondering what to do about them. She turned as I entered, a bundle of old gowns in her arms.

'Will you want any of these, mademoiselle?'

'I don't think so.' I glanced through the pile just in case there was something I particularly liked. 'No, I don't want anything. Some of them are quite good, though – perhaps we could give them to someone?'

'Madame often gave her things to those who needed them.' Marie's voice caught on a sob. She had been walking around the house with red eyes ever since I'd arrived. 'There is a place ... a house for girls of a certain kind...'

'Of a certain kind?' I looked at her in surprise. She was flushed and embarrassed, and I suddenly realised what she could not bring herself to say. 'Do you mean women of the streets?'

'Your mother took things for them.' Marie was slightly disapproving, though not of her late mistress. She had been devoted to my mother. 'She felt sorry for them. I'm sure I don't know why.' She sniffed hard, screwing up her mouth. 'It is a scandal. Some of them are not much more than children – several years younger than you were when you first went to the convent.'

'Oh no!' I cried, shocked. 'Surely that cannot be true, Marie? You must be mistaken.'

She shook her head.

'That children of that age should be so

used ... it is wicked and disgusting!'

'You do not understand. You've been sheltered all your life,' she told me, a note of bitterness in her voice. 'And now you've fallen on your feet again. You don't know what life is like for the rest of us.'

I sensed anger and fear in her. What did she mean? Was she afraid of being turned off now that my mother was dead?

'I'm sure Monsieur le comte will retain your services for the sake of the tenants,' I said to reassure her.

'That's all you know. I am to have six months' wages and leave after you've gone tomorrow.'

'Oh, Marie!' I cried. She had been so devoted to Mama, and I was shocked that she could be dismissed so lightly. 'That cannot be right. It must be a mistake. The comte could not have thought properly...' I saw the stubborn set of her face and felt uncertain. 'If I were to speak to him, perhaps—'

'You would be wasting your time. Besides' – she raised her head proudly, an odd glint in her eyes – 'I do not need his charity. I can find a new place myself. I was asked many times to leave Madame Heron but I would not ... never, never would I have deserted her.'

'I know you were fond of her. I'm sorry, Marie.'

'It's not your fault,' she said and glanced at the clothes again. 'So I shall give these to those girls, then? Yes?'

'Yes.' I was curious. 'Did my mother often visit this particular house – was it there she caught the fever?'

Marie was silent for a moment. She turned away, her back towards me as she answered. 'Perhaps. Who knows? She visited lots of people. Women in trouble. She was always helping others, women who had been badly treated by men.'

'Was she?'

This was something new. I'd had no idea of Mama's good works amongst fallen women. It surprised me. Why had she never mentioned any of this to me?

'Your mother was a generous woman. Especially to other women who were less fortunate ... who were forced to earn their bread in *that* way. She always said that she might have been one of them if she hadn't been lucky.'

I was stunned, staring at her in disbelief and dismay. My mother ... a woman of the streets?

'What are you saying? How dare you! How dare you speak so disrespectfully of her?' I was outraged at such a suggestion. 'Take it back at once. I demand that you apologise!'

Marie's cheeks flushed red and she looked guilty, then upset.

'I wasn't being disrespectful, mademoiselle. I loved your mother. She was good to me.' A sob rose to her lips but she choked it back, her head going up proudly. 'She did say things to me. I was her confidante. She trusted me. I was always there when she needed to talk. She told me lots of things ... things I dare say you don't know.'

The look in her eyes made me angry. She seemed to be flaunting her closeness to my mother, shutting me out as if I could not possibly understand the relationship they had shared. How dare she! Without thinking, I stepped forward and slapped her face. She gasped and put a hand to her cheek, tears starting to her eyes.

'You shouldn't have done that.'

I was immediately contrite, shocked at my own violence.

'No,' I said. 'I shouldn't. I am sorry, Marie. Please forgive me.'

She stared at me for a moment, clearly trying to control her own temper. 'You'll be sorry for that one day,' she said. 'Madame spoiled you. She was always talking about you, planning your future – she wore herself out for your sake. I'll finish what I've started, then I'll leave. I don't have to stay here. I've been paid. I was only staying until it's all over for her sake.'

'No,' I said. 'Please don't leave in anger. I really am sorry. I don't know what came over me.'

She turned her back on me, beginning to fold the clothes. I apologised again and left her to her work. It had been very wrong of me to strike her the way I had, but her assertion that my mother had confided in her and not myself had upset me, perhaps because I suspected it might be true.

Again the sadness swept over me as I realised I had hardly known my own mother. To me she had always seemed a smiling, beautiful woman – but I had sensed the sorrow she kept locked inside her and I knew she had hidden her secrets from me.

Who was she really? Where had she come from?

I walked down the hall to my mother's bedroom. I knew she had always kept her personal papers in a large rosewood box on her dressing-table. For a moment I was tempted to go through them, but as I opened the door I was met by the smell of her perfume. It reached out to me, bringing back memories that were too painful to be borne at the moment, and I could not bring myself to go inside.

Madame Leconte would send Mama's things to me at the château. I had waited all these years to learn her secrets; I could wait a little longer.

I dreamed that night of my mother. She was

standing at the end of my bed and had been crying. She looked at me with reproachful eyes, holding out her hands to me as if in supplication.

'Everything I have done was for your sake, Jenny. Do not judge me so harshly. Do not think of me as a wicked woman. It was all for you ... for my dearest child.'

I woke with a start to find Marie opening the curtains, letting the bright sunshine flood into the room. It seemed that she had decided not to leave after all.

'It's time for you to get up,' she said and gave me a sheepish look. 'I'm sorry for what happened yesterday, Mademoiselle Heron. It is just that ... I cannot bear...'

'I understand. Of course I do!' There were tears in her eyes and something else ... another emotion I could not understand. Why should Marie feel guilt? Unless it was because of our quarrel? But that was as much my fault as hers. I jumped out of bed and went to her, my hands outstretched to take hers. 'Forgive me, Marie? Please say you will. I do not want to quarrel with you; I know you were fond of my mother. You looked after her when she was ill. I am grateful to you.'

Something flickered in her eyes. We clasped hands for a moment, then she released mine.

'I loved her. She was a good woman.

Never let anyone tell you different. There are some who did not always approve of things she did – but she was the loveliest, most generous lady that ever lived.'

'Yes, she was. Thank you, Marie.' I looked at her uncertainly. 'Will you forgive me – for her sake?'

'I'll forgive you for your own,' Marie said. Again there was that guilty, wary look. 'I've been upset since she was taken so ill. She would keep going to see those women despite my warnings. She wasn't well enough to nurse the sick but she would not listen...'

'The women you spoke of yesterday – did Mama take the fever from one of them? Is that what you think?'

'I'm not sure it was a fever.'

'Not a fever?' A cold chill ran down my spine. 'What do you mean, Marie? Didn't the doctor say it was a recurring fever she had picked up somewhere?'

'So he said ... but he was a fool.' Marie looked at me strangely. 'It was not like any fever I've ever seen before.'

'Then what was it?'

'I don't know.' She hesitated, then shook her head. 'Perhaps it was a fever. I do not know. She was ill for a long time before she saw the doctor – and he did nothing to help her. He gave her nothing for the pain.' Marie was angry, defensive. 'How should I know what made her ill? I am not a doctor

118

– but I know she wore herself out, visiting others when she was ill herself. And there was a visitor ... someone who upset her. It was after that that she took a turn for the worse.'

'A visitor?' I asked. 'A man or woman?'

'A woman, I think, but I'm not sure. Madame Heron usually told me things but she wouldn't talk about this. I think the visitor came from England, and I know something happened that worried her.'

'You have no idea what was on her mind?'

'No – but I think there was a letter...'

'A letter?'

She nodded. 'I saw her reading it and she was upset. She said that the past was reaching out for her.'

'What did she mean?'

'I don't know.' Marie looked uncomfortable, uncertain. 'It's just that I've not been able to forget the look in her eyes...' She turned away as the tears welled over. 'Take no notice. I'm foolish ... foolish!'

I watched as she ran from the room in tears. What was she really implying – that there was something strange about my mother's death? That the mysterious visitor might have contributed to it in some way? Surely not! It was a virulent fever. The comte had told me so and he had been with my mother at the end.

If there had been anything odd about

Mama's death he would have told me. He had been honest with me from the start. No, no, there could not be anything sinister behind Mama's sudden illness.

It was all in Marie's mind. It had to be!

'You are very quiet, Jeanette – is something troubling you?'

I looked at the comte as he sat opposite me in the carriage. He was dressed all in black, except for a snowy linen neck-cloth, which was fastened with a diamond pin, and I thought he looked even more aristocratic and distinguished than when he had fetched me from the convent school.

'I was thinking of Mama, sir.'

He nodded, his eyes thoughtful as they rested on my face.

'Yes, of course. It is natural that you should – but Adele would not want you to grieve excessively. You are young and have your life ahead of you. Adele wanted you to be happy.'

'Marie told me that she had had bouts of the sickness for more than two months ... that she had not been well for some time.'

'Yes, I believe that is so. These fevers come and go, it seems.'

'But she had always previously recovered within a few hours.'

'What are you asking?'

I met the comte's penetrating gaze. 'Is it

120

not strange that she should die of such an illness ... one that had previously been mild?'

His eyebrows rose. 'You are suggesting that her death was not natural?'

I was silent and he frowned. I thought he was annoyed.

'I see you have been talking to that foolish girl. You should have told me at once, Jeanette. Marie's tongue will get her into trouble one day. Adele was not poisoned, though I know that her maid had some suspicion of it. The doctors – and there were two of them – both confirmed it as a natural death.'

My cheeks felt warm. He had made me feel ridiculous.

'I see. Marie was very fond of Mama. I suppose she could not accept what hap-pened and became confused in her mind.'

'Or perhaps she is given to odd fancies? Some girls of her class are, I believe. She has not had the benefit of your education, Jeanette.' He smiled at me. 'Do you think I would not have suspected something if it had been so? Do you imagine I would have left any stone unturned if I thought that murder had been done?'

'No...' His slightly reproachful expression made me blush harder. 'No, of course not, sir.'

'Then please oblige me by putting all such

thoughts from your mind.'

'Yes, sir. It did worry me when Marie said – but I believe you are right. It could not have been poison. I shall not think of it again.'

'So I should hope.' He tapped his fingers impatiently against the silk hat he held on his knee. 'Believe me, it can do nothing but harm to allow such fancies into your mind. Once they have taken root one can never be free again.'

There was a look in his eyes then ... a haunted, strange expression that disturbed me. As if he were looking inwardly at something ... some memory he found almost too distressing to be borne. All at once, he seemed to recall himself, his gaze narrowing as he met mine and realised that I had been watching him.

'Henriette wanted to come up for the funeral but I instructed her to wait at the château. Perhaps I was wrong. You need cheerful company, Jeanette. You have a tendency to brood. It is a fault in someone of your age.'

I felt as if he had slapped me and was hurt. Mama's death had been very hard to bear. Why could he not see that I was merely grieving in my own way?

If only I had been allowed to go home to Marthe! Wrapped in her loving arms I could have sobbed out all the grief and pain

122

inside me.

My guardian had done his duty by me, but he seemed remote, withdrawn. At our first meeting in Paris, and even when he had fetched me from the convent, he had seemed much warmer – a man I could like – but this was someone different. I might have opened my heart to the man I had met in Paris, but now he was so stern, forbidding. Why had he withdrawn from me? What had brought that bleak look to his face?

I wished with all my heart that I need not go to the château. I had an odd feeling that I should not be welcome there and I wanted someone to comfort me. Someone warm and understanding.

Six

My poor, poor little one,' Henriette said the moment we were alone in the bedroom she had told me would be mine from now on. 'How pale and tired you look. And it is no wonder. Your sweet, lovely maman taken from you so cruelly!'

Tears rushed to my eyes. All at once I was weeping noisily, helplessly. As Henriette gathered me into her arms the grief I had held inside came pouring out.

'Yes, my little Jenny,' she whispered, her lips moving against my hair to comfort me. 'Cry, my dear one. Cry as much as you want. Laurent is a fool! He should have let me come to you at once.'

I think it was her use of the name 'Jenny' that made me cling to her the way I did then. Most people called me Jeanette, but Henriette had made my name sound more English, more the way Mama always said it, because she wanted me to remember that I had been born in England.

What a strange upbringing mine had been when you thought about it. Born of English

124

gentlefolk, I had been raised on the farm of a Frenchman only one step above his peasant ancestry. My mother had dressed me in clothes far above my situation, however, and I had been educated with the children of the best French families. Now I had been brought to live at the home of an aristocrat. It was not surprising then that I was feeling rather lost and confused. I hardly knew who or what I was any more.

But Henriette was talking again and I brought my wandering thoughts back to what she was saying, knowing that I must have missed some of it.

'Like a little Jenny Wren you were when you were born,' she murmured. 'So tiny and brown ... like a bird.'

Had she seen me as a new-born babe? How was that possible? I had been born in England as far as I knew. I wondered but did not question her – this was not the time for questions.

'Oh, Madame Rossi,' I wept. She smelled so good, and her arms were warm and tender. 'I miss her ... love her so much. I don't know how to bear it.'

'Shush, my sweet girl.' Henriette rocked me in her arms. 'I know it hurts to lose those you love but the pain gets better in time. I promise you it does.'

I lifted my gaze to look at her. 'Does it? Does it truly?'

'Yes. I promise you it will ease, my dear.' She stroked the hair back from my face, wiping tears from my cheeks with the tips of her fingers. 'You are so pretty, Jenny. Quite like Adele in some ways and not at all in others.'

She gave me a scrap of lace kerchief and I wiped my face. 'I should like to be as good as she was.'

'Would you?' An odd little smile tugged at the corners of her mouth. I thought she was amused about something. 'I'm sure she would be pleased to hear you say that, Jenny – but I think you need only be yourself. You are very loveable as you are, you know.'

'Am I?' I stared at her uncertainly. 'Sometimes I have such wicked thoughts, madame.'

'Henriette – call me by my name,' she reminded me and laughed. 'I am glad you have wicked thoughts sometimes, Jenny. I must confess that I do, too – very, very wicked.'

She looked so beautiful at that moment, her eyes alight with laughter, her hair curling about her face like threads of golden silk. She had masses of hair, which was piled up artlessly in curls and ringlets on top of her head. Her complexion was delicate but not pale, and her eyes were a greenish blue. Yet her true beauty came from within. I liked her because she was so warm, so

126

generous – and in a way she reminded me of my mother.

'I cannot believe that you have one wicked thought in your head.' My tears had dried and already I was feeling better, responding to her humour and charm. I smiled tremulously and she gave a small cry of triumph.

'That is good, my sweet girl. You hurt inside here' – she touched my breast lightly with her hand – 'but soon you will not hurt quite so much. You will learn to be happy again. I shall show you, Jenny. We shall be together as friends ... would you not like to be my friend?'

'Oh, yes, of course I would, ma – Henriette.'

Henriette's smile seemed to banish the dark clouds that had hung over me for the past few days. The ache was still there inside me, however; I could see that it might be possible to live here at the château, but I still felt cheated, angry at the cruel fate that had robbed me of my beloved mother. It was unfair that she should have died so young ... so suddenly.

'Yes, I should like to be your friend,' I repeated.

'Good.' She stood up, glancing at herself in the dressing mirror and smoothing her gown of creases that did not exist. There was a secret smile in her eyes, as if she were happy about something. 'So! Now I shall go and scold Laurent and you will have a little rest. When you are ready you will come downstairs – yes?'

'Yes. Where shall I find you?'

'Oh, in one of the salons or perhaps in the gardens,' she replied carelessly. 'One of the servants will tell you. You must not be frightened to ask. This is your home now, Jenny – and we all want you to be happy. Even that foolish Laurent who has so upset you.'

'Thank you.' There was one person she had not mentioned. I looked at her, feeling apprehensive. 'When shall I meet the comtesse, Henriette?'

'My cousin Béatrix?' Henriette glanced towards the mirror once more and smiled to herself. 'You need not fear her, Jenny. I have told her that you are my friend and it as such that she will welcome you to the château. Besides, you will not need to see her often. She seldom leaves her apartments, except when Laurent is here and we are entertaining his friends. And even then she cannot often be persuaded to join us for more than an hour or so.'

She nodded and smiled once more, then went out, closing the door carefully behind her.

After she had gone I splashed my face with water from a china jug standing on the mahogany corner wash-stand, patted my skin dry with a thick towel and smoothed wisps of my wayward hair into a confining knot at the nape of my neck. I then began to look around, to take stock of my surroundings.

Set in the lush, fertile regions of the Loire Valley, the château was no more than a hundred years old, having been built on the site of a much older house that had been destroyed by fire during the revolution. It was a pretty, family home, not a medieval fortress as so many of the great houses of France had been; the long windows were flanked by green wooden shutters, which looked well against its honey-coloured walls and there was a dovecote over the arched gateway.

As I glanced out of my window I could see smooth lawns, rose gardens and, on a sloping hill, the vineyards beyond. For a moment a wave of nostalgia swept over me as I thought of the farm and the vineyards of Monsieur Bertrand, but I made up my mind not to cry. I must look to the future now.

As Henriette was bringing me upstairs, I had noticed that the house was furnished in an elaborate style with intricate marquetry cabinets, huge gilt-framed mirrors over matching pier tables, and fragile chairs which looked as if the legs might snap if one actually sat on them. Everything was lavish, the rooms filled with priceless treasures.

The room I had been given was less formal than those I had seen downstairs, however, and was not, I suspected, one of the best guest chambers. It was still large enough to hold a double bed, wardrobe, dressing-chest, desk and chair, and a comfortable window seat. I would be able to curl up near the window with a book if I felt the need to hide away – but why should I?

I had been told that this was my home, and that I was welcome here, but I was still apprehensive, still nervous. I felt as if I were an intruder in this place despite all that had been said to the contrary.

Henriette had welcomed me with open arms, but she was not the mistress here. I had been assured that the comtesse hardly ever left her own apartments, yet I had sensed her presence the moment I entered the house. It was probably very foolish of me but I was anxious about meeting her. I had an uncomfortable feeling that she would not welcome me to her house.

What a silly girl I was! It was unlikely that she would even notice me. I glanced at my reflection once more as I prepared to leave. My hair was under control; I was neat and tidy, presentable. There was no reason for the comtesse to dislike me. Why should she?

I walked unhurriedly along the landing, pausing now and then to study one of the many pictures which hung on the walls.

They seemed to be mostly family portraits in this part of the building, and I stood for several minutes looking at the likeness of a young man. He had a sweet, gentle face, pale blond hair and bright blue, rather naughty eyes. Surely the artist had flattered him? No one had eyes that colour!

I wondered who the young man was and made a mental note to ask Henriette. At the foot of the stairs I hesitated, wondering where I would find her – would she be in the house or the gardens? It was lovely out, a warm still evening, the air heavy with the scent of jasmine and stocks. As I lingered uncertainly in the hall, I heard the sound of laughter and turned instinctively towards it.

To my right was a small parlour furnished in shades of green and gold, but beyond that was a much larger reception room with impressive, carved double doors. The doors were opened wide, allowing me a clear view of the two persons standing by the window at the far end. Henriette was gazing up at the comte with a teasing smile on her face. There was something very intimate in her manner, something that made me feel awkward, as if I were intruding on a private moment.

I hesitated for a few seconds, not sure whether it would be better to withdraw or make some noise to warn them of my approach. My dilemma was solved when the comte suddenly moved away from her, and in doing so, turned and saw me.

He frowned, looking annoyed and guilty. 'Jeanette,' he said in a harsh, abrupt tone. 'Don't hover, girl. Come along! Henriette is waiting to show you over the house. It is larger than you might imagine and we don't want you getting lost.' He glanced at his embossed gold pocket watch. 'You must both excuse me. I have business to attend.'

He strode past me without glancing Henriette's way. I felt he was escaping from something, some situation that he found either awkward or embarrassing. When I looked at Henriette there was both regret and amusement in her eyes.

'So...' she said in a soft tone that was meant more for herself than me. 'The time is not yet but it will come ... it will come.'

'I beg your pardon?'

She shook her head. I thought she seemed well satisfied, as though whatever had been said just before I arrived had pleased her.

'So – you are ready?' she said and smiled at me. ' Laurent insists that you meet Béatrix at once. And since he is master here...' She shrugged her shoulders expressively, and held her hand out to me. 'Come, Jenny. I shall take you to her now.'

I hung back reluctantly. 'Are you sure we shall not disturb her? You told me that she likes to rest during the heat of the afternoon, didn't you?'

'Laurent says she is impatient to meet you – so we must not keep her waiting.'

There was something in Henriette's voice then that made me look at her – a note of resentment, perhaps. Did she dislike being reminded that the comte's wife was the mistress here? If so, why did she stay in this house?

My mother had told me that Monsieur Rossi had left his wife a more than adequate fortune. She could have been mistress of her own establishment had she wished – so why stay here as a companion to her cousin? It was not a position many women would choose for themselves and was usually the lot of a poor relation, who had no chance of making a good match.

Henriette was both beautiful and wealthy. She must live in this house because it suited her to do so. It was surprising that she had not remarried before now.

The comtesse's apartments were in the west wing of the château, a little detached from the main reception rooms as befitted her need as an invalid for peace and quiet. I was immediately aware of the atmosphere, which was somehow sombre and depressing.

Henriette led me down the rather dark, wood-panelled hallway then paused outside a door, giving me an encouraging smile.

'Do not be nervous, Jenny. Béatrix has a sharp tongue, but she will not play a large part in your life here. Except for those times when Laurent is visiting, she almost always stays in her rooms.' She knocked softly, calling through the door, 'It is Henriette. I have brought Mademoiselle Heron to see you, Béatrix.'

For a moment there was no response, then we heard sounds of movement and the door was opened by a sour-faced woman dressed in severe black. She did not speak but indicated with a slight nod of her head that we might enter.

'Thank you, Flore.' Henriette glanced at me. 'Jenny – this is the Comtesse de Arnay's personal maid.'

I looked at the woman nervously but her expression was so forbidding that I did not dare speak.

Henriette led the way through what was obviously the comtesse's parlour into a smaller boudoir, which led in turn to a bedroom beyond. It was in the middle room that the mistress of the house had chosen to receive us. She was lying on a day bed, her legs covered by a light cotton quilt; the windows closed and curtained against the sun. It seemed stuffy and airless in the little room, which smelt of a strong perfume and sickness.

The comtesse had been working on a

piece of tapestry, which she laid down as she saw us, so that all I could see was the ugly criss-cross of multi-coloured threads on the back. They looked rather like a spider's web, tangled and jarring to the eye.

'Good afternoon, Béatrix,' Henriette said and bent to kiss her cheek. 'How are you now?'

'As always,' the comtesse replied in a querulous tone. 'Well, where is she? Laurent insists it is my duty to greet her – let me see her. Bring her forward.'

Henriette beckoned. I had lingered at the doorway feeling awkward, and the comtesse's words did nothing to dispel my unease. Her attitude showed quite plainly that she did not want me here: I was unwelcome in her house. At Henriette's bidding, however, I moved forward so that I could both see and be seen.

Close to, the comtesse looked old! I was shocked by her appearance. Her face was grey and etched with lines of suffering from her illness, her hair heavily streaked with grey. She looked almost old enough to be the comte's mother rather than his wife.

'So...' Her eyes focused on my face and I saw that she still had a strong spirit despite her obvious ill health: those eyes were angry, resentful. 'You are Mademoiselle Heron. Your mother was once my dressmaker. But not for a long time. I have no need of new gowns. I spend my life here in these rooms. I want only peace ... only peace.' She sighed heavily.

'Yes, madame.'

'Speak up, girl. I shan't bite you. What is your name?'

'I am Jenny Heron, madame.'

She nodded, her heavy lids hooding her eyes and hiding her thoughts. 'My husband tells me you are to live with us for a while. You have been well educated. I trust the sisters taught you how to behave?'

'Yes, madame.'

'I shall expect good manners and obedience while you reside under my roof, mademoiselle.'

'Yes, madame.'

She moved her hand agitatedly and the tapestry frame fell to the floor at my feet. I picked it up and gave it to her, glancing at the subject briefly. It looked very odd, rather as if it depicted a dark cavern lit by flames. Not at all what I had expected.

'It is rude to stare. Did I invite you to look at my work?'

'No, madame. Forgive me. I did not mean to—'

'It is one of a set,' she said. 'This is of Persephone being carried down into the underworld.'

'It looks interesting.'

She gave a harsh crack of laughter. 'I

doubt you would think so if you found yourself carried off by demons. But what can you know of the torments suffered by others? You are too innocent ... too child-like.'

'Yes, madame. I'm sorry.'

'You're sorry? Always sorry ... everyone is always sorry ... but what do they know of suffering?' She looked at me with contempt. 'Is that all you have to say for yourself? You are sorry. You irritate me, girl. I do not want you near me. Never come here unless I send for you – do you understand? I cannot be bothered with foolish, naïve girls. I am too ill to have young people near me.'

'Yes, madame – I mean no...'

She snorted in disgust and waved her hand in a gesture of dismissal. Obviously she had seen enough of me.

'At least her mother had some spirit. Take her away, Henriette, and come back in an hour. I want you to read to me. You must not neglect me now that you have a new companion to amuse you.'

'As if I would,' Henriette replied in a chiding tone. 'You are out of sorts. I suspect you have one of your headaches, Béatrix. Shall I tell Flore to make you a tisane?'

'Make one yourself when you come,' the comtesse said. 'You are so much better at it. I don't know how I should manage without you. No one else cares whether I live or die.'

'You are feeling unwell,' Henriette said, her expression one of tolerance mixed with concern. 'Try to rest for a while. I shall return to you soon, Béatrix.'

'Laurent unsettled me,' the comtesse complained, her voice rising bitterly. 'His visits always leave me feeling exhausted. He is demanding and unkind. I know he hates me. Sometimes I wish he would stay in Paris and never come here again. He comes only to torment me ... to make me suffer. And I suffer enough ... no one knows how I suffer...'

Henriette gave me a meaning look and a little push towards the door. I was only too glad to leave them together.

Flore glared at me as I entered the parlour. She was such a surly, plain woman, as unlike the flower she had been named after as it was possible for a woman to be. I sensed her dislike of me and did not linger, preferring to wait outside in the hallway until Henriette came.

As I sat there on a hard, wooden chair, I heard a low, moaning cry that was quickly hushed. I wondered what ailed the comtesse, what had made her look so much older than her years ... put that haunted, weary expression in her eyes.

Why should she think her husband hated her?

I did not have to wait long. Henriette

joined me moments later.

'There,' she said, pulling a wry face. 'That was not so very bad, was it?'

'The comtesse resents my being here – doesn't she?'

'Take no notice, Jenny. She was in one of her black moods, that's all. They come and go – and she can be charming when she chooses. Besides...' Henriette paused, an odd, slightly triumphant expression on her face. ' Laurent is master in his own home. Béatrix has everything she wants, but Laurent will not give into her all the time. He thinks she enjoys being an invalid. For many years he tried to force her to be a part of his life, to leave her rooms and walk in the fresh air daily – now, since I came to live here, he does not bother so much.'

'What do you mean?'

'Laurent is a very sociable man and likes to entertain his friends; he wants the house to be full of people, laughter and music. If Béatrix is too ill to join his guests I often take her place as his hostess.'

'Oh, I see.'

Henriette's expression gave her away. It was obvious that she enjoyed being the comte's hostess when he entertained. I suspected that she liked to think of herself as the mistress here ... that she would like to be mistress of the château ... and its master.

Such a wicked thought! I blushed for

shame as it entered my head and squashed it at once. What an ungrateful wretch I was! After all the comte's trouble and Henriette's kindness ... to suspect that they might be lovers, that the reason she stayed here as a kind of superior companion to her cousin was because she wanted to be near him...

Henriette's gaze narrowed as she looked at me. 'What are you thinking, Jenny?'

'Nothing,' I answered in a choked whisper, knowing that my face had given me away. 'I am just being foolish, that's all.'

There was knowledge in her eyes as she nodded, obviously having interpreted my thoughts. 'Do not read more into anything you may have seen than is there, Jenny,' she said, and I felt chastened at the note of warning in her voice. 'We are neither of us fools and you will guess soon enough that I have certain feelings for Laurent – feelings that are perhaps stronger than I have any right to – but neither of us have done anything that could harm my cousin.'

'Oh no, of course not!' I cried, anxious to reassure her. 'I did not think ... I mean—'

'But of course you did,' she said, a teasing smile on her lips now. 'And you are not the only one – but it is not so. Laurent has had a mistress he dearly loves for years. She lives in Paris. Béatrix knows that he has ... an arrangement. It would be impossible for such a man as he to live like a monk and my

140

cousin has not been a proper wife to him for years. She accepts his need for that kind of comfort. Indeed, she is grateful that he no longer expects anything of an intimate nature from her. She did not mean what she said just now, of course – but their marriage has for many years been in name only. It might have ended years ago if they had not both been good Catholics.'

'Oh.' I stared at Henriette, my cheeks pink. 'I – I see.'

Her laughter rang out. 'What an innocent child you are, dearest Jenny. Have I quite shattered your illusions? Do not be upset. It is not unusual in marriages such as this – my cousin comes from a good family, an old family, and was a considerable heiress. She is older than Laurent by several years and knew what to expect when she married him.'

'Did she love him when they married?'

'Love has very little to do with it in such cases. He married her for her money, and she for ... reasons of her own,' Henriette replied, an odd expression in her eyes. 'I was fortunate in being able to love my husband, even though he was many years my senior – and of course my marriage made me independent for the rest of my life.'

'Is that why you have chosen not to marry again?'

Again that little secret smile flickered

about her full, sensuous lips. 'Perhaps I shall tell you my reasons one day,' she said, 'but not now. Come, Jenny – I want you to meet my son. Charles is almost five years old now and becoming a handful for his nurse. Soon I shall have to engage a governess for him, because I cannot be with him all the time.' She frowned slightly. 'I want a young woman for him, but she mustn't be too pretty. I need someone who isn't likely to leave at a moment's notice to get married.' She glanced at me. 'Was there anyone like that at the school? Should I write to Sister Isobel for her advice?'

I was about to reply when we both heard scuffling and then a child's cry of triumph. Turning, we saw a small boy running full pelt towards us, his harassed-looking nurse in pursuit.

'Maman ... Maman,' he cried. 'Tell Rose-anne she is bad. She wouldn't let me come to you. Naughty, naughty Roseanne.'

Henriette glanced at the middle-aged woman who had come puffing up to join us. She was stout, obviously out of breath, and in some distress.

'What a naughty child you are, Charles,' she said, trying to grasp him. He retreated behind his mother, looking at her defiantly. 'Come here. You know you are not allowed in this part of the house.'

'Leave him to me now, Roseanne,' Henriette said. She bent down to sweep her son up in her arms. He promptly covered her cheeks in kisses, his face a picture of angelic innocence belied by the triumph in his eyes. 'Jenny – this is my terrible son.' She caught his hand, nipping his thumb with her teeth in mock reproach. 'Bad, wicked boy to tease poor Roseanne so.'

Her expression and her tone were so indulgent that the child chortled with glee. It was obvious that he was spoiled and petted so much that he believed he could do no wrong in her eyes.

'Here is Jenny come to visit with us as I promised,' Henriette said, turning him so that he looked at me. I saw speculation in his eyes. 'Isn't she pretty?'

'Maman pretty,' he responded, patting her cheek with his hands, which I noticed were none too clean.

'Hello, Charles,' I said. 'Do you want to play ball in the gardens?'

'Roseanne doesn't let me play,' he said, and I saw something leap in his eyes. 'Will you play with me, Maman?'

'For a little while,' she replied, 'and if you are good, perhaps Jenny will play with you longer.' She set him down and I held my hand out to him. ' Maman has to read to Cousin Béatrix. Jenny might play with you if you ask her nicely.'

'Will you?'

He had the face of an angel combined with devilish eyes and was very much Henriette's child. He had her smile, her charm – yet beneath it I sensed a vulnerability that touched my heart.

'Yes, of course,' I replied. 'And afterwards, if you are as good as you can be, I might tell you a story. But only if you are good and no trouble to your maman.'

His hand slid into mine and he gave me a winning look. 'I'm always good ... except sometimes with Roseanne. She is so silly and she can't run as fast as me because she's too big.'

'That is not nice,' I reproved gently. 'You must try to be nice to Roseanne if you want to be my friend.'

'If I'm nice to everyone will you always tell me stories?'

'I will – for as long as I stay here.'

'She must stay, mustn't she, Maman?' Charles turned to his mother immediately. 'I want her to stay so she must.'

I sensed that his demands were usually granted, if only for the sake of peace.

Henriette's eyes met mine over his head. 'I suspect Jenny has a mind of her own,' she said. 'We shall just have to persuade her to stay here – shan't we?'

An unspoken message passed between us in that moment. Henriette was asking for help with her son in return for all that I was being offered at the château.

'Of course I shall stay for as long as I can,' I replied. 'Now – let us go into the gardens, Charles. I want you to show me your home.'

A little smile tugged at the corners of my mouth as I sat before a dressing-mirror brushing my hair that evening. I had enjoyed spending an hour or two in the company of Henriette's son, and I believed I could teach him to respect me. If I could establish myself as Charles' unofficial governess I should feel that I was earning my place here in this house ... that I was not just a dependent of the comte, to be tolerated and despised by his comtesse.

Laurent had already done so much for me, fetching me from the school, taking care of all the necessary arrangements after my mother died and bringing me to his home.

I was wearing one of the new black gowns he had provided for my period of mourning: it had a large white collar, lace cuffs and a sashed waist, which made it more stylish and becoming than my school clothes. I glanced at my reflection in a large oval mirror on the wall, then fastened a cameo brooch at the neck of my gown, tied my hair back with a ribbon and got up to wander over to the window.

It was a warm, pleasant night and my window was open. I heard a woman's laughter and knew that she must be standing directly beneath, though I could not see her without stretching out as she was hidden by an overhanging trough of flowering plants.

'How wicked you are to tease me, Laurent,' the woman said, and I realised it was Henriette. 'I am almost jealous. Jenny is so pretty ... so like Adele.'

'You have no need to be jealous,' he replied gruffly. 'If I do not respond to you as you would like ... it is for your own good.'

'You remind me of my duty to Béatrix.'

'I think you would find it impossible to remain here if we became lovers. You know how suspicious she can be ... rather than expose you to that I would prefer that you should leave.'

'Why?' There was passion in her voice now. 'You do care for me, Laurent. I can see it in your eyes ... I know you want me. I feel it when you are close.'

'I care too much to insult you by asking you to become my mistress, dear Henriette. And there is my wife to consider.'

'I should not think it an insult.' She paused, then continued, on a note of mild accusation: 'You have not always been so considerate of Béatrix's feelings.'

'She understood my feelings for—' He broke off as if in some distress. 'What I choose to do in Paris is one thing but I will not have her embarrassed in this house. She has suffered enough. I have not always been kind to her, but I will do nothing to hurt her more. If you cannot accept this, Henriette...'

I moved back from the window, feeling uncomfortable. I must not listen to any more of their private conversation.

My suspicions concerning Henriette's reasons for staying at the château had been confirmed ... and yet I sensed there was more. Somehow I did not believe that she would be content merely to be the comte's mistress.

Did she think the comtesse might die soon? Was she hoping that the comte would turn to her if that happened – that he would ask her to be his wife?

Monsieur de Arnay had a mistress in Paris. Henriette knew that and yet she believed he cared for her ... if I had not misunderstood what I had just overheard, she wished to take that woman's place in his life, to become his mistress.

She must be in love with him! There was no other explanation for her behaviour. She must surely have had plenty of opportunities to marry men of equal birth and fortune, though I knew the comte to be a wealthy, generous man. If Henriette chose to live at the château despite the awkward circumstances, she must be deeply in love with its master.

The Comte de Arnay was an attractive man. Although he was often stern, he could be charming when he chose. I could understand Henriette's feelings, why she chose to stay in this house, though I believed in her place I should have gone away and tried to make a fresh start somewhere else.

How complacent and foolish I was! How young and naïve.

What did I know then of love or the overwhelming passion that can flare unexpectedly between a man and a woman? I was almost nineteen but an innocent girl, still untouched by the darker emotions that sometimes drove human beings to unwise behaviour. Little did I know as I prepared to go downstairs that evening that Fate was already laughing at me, preparing to ensnare me in its coils...

Seven

I decided it was time to go downstairs. I knew where the dining room was and also that it was the custom of the household to gather in the adjoining drawing room before dinner, but I was anxious not to intrude on another intimate scene between the comte and Henriette. I made my way instead to one of the smaller reception rooms at the front of the house.

I halted on the threshold, surprised to see that someone else was already there. A young man I judged to be perhaps twenty or so turned as he heard the startled gasp which escaped me at the sight of him, and I realised almost at once that he was the young man from the portrait I had admired earlier. I had meant to ask Henriette who he was but finding her with the comte had put it from my mind until now.

'And who have we here?' he asked, a twinkle in his eyes. My heart missed a beat. The artist had not lied. This stranger had the bluest eyes I had ever seen, and they were regarding me in a very wicked way.

'Why was I not told that we had a beauty staying with us? Have they been hiding you from me?'

My cheeks flushed scarlet and I gave a nervous laugh. I felt suddenly tongue-tied and shy. He was young but very self-assured, a man of fashion – and so handsome!

'Has the cat eaten your tongue?' he asked teasingly. 'Or have I scared the life out of you? Pray tell me, mademoiselle – why will you not speak to me? Am I such a rogue?'

'No, of course not.' I felt my confidence flow back as he smiled: a smile so full of approval that it made me blush. 'I am Jenny Heron. My – my mother made gowns for Henriette and the comtesse. She died recently and Monsieur de Arnay told me I was to live here ... until other arrangements could be made for me.'

There was amusement in the young man's eyes as he studied me in silence for a moment, then he nodded. 'So they're planning on giving you to the most suitable applicant, are they?'

'What do you mean?'

'Marriage, of course. You must know it's the only choice open to you – unless you've been left a fortune?' His brows went up, then he shook his head. 'You haven't, of course. So – there's nothing else for it. You'll be married off before you've had time to

150

draw breath. It's always the way with girls as lovely as you.'

Something in his manner put me on the defensive. I raised my head, looking at him proudly. 'Perhaps I shan't ... perhaps I'll find work instead. As a governess.'

'As a governess?' He was definitely laughing at me now. 'No, I don't think so, Jenny Heron. You are far too pretty. No woman of sense would have you in her house – they would be afraid their husband would fall in love with you. Or that you might seduce their sons into marrying you. I'm not sure which would be the worst sin.'

'Please don't mock me. I have been well educated. I can play the pianoforte, embroider and sketch tolerably well – and I speak two languages fluently. I also read Latin.' He *was* mocking me. I felt the colour staining my cheeks, but my head went up again as I looked into those blue, blue eyes. 'I could be a governess – I have been taking care of Henriette's son this afternoon.'

'That young rascal! He has been thoroughly spoilt. You will be a fool if you let Henriette push him on to you too often.'

'I like Charles. I enjoyed playing with him.'

'Playing is different from teaching him lessons. He likes to play games in the garden, because it's pleasure. You would not find him so amenable if you tried to confine him to a schoolroom, believe me.'

'I don't see why lessons should not also be enjoyable.'

'Don't you?' His fine brows arched mockingly. 'You will if you continue with him. I love him dearly but he is a brat. You will come to realise it if you stay here long enough.'

I sensed a slight annoyance behind the bantering tone, as though he resented the fact that Charles was spoiled.

'And who are you, sir?'

He laughed again as he realised I was indignant on behalf of Henriette's son, seeming much amused at something. Why must he mock everything? His smile was charming, and I might have liked him very much had he been more serious.

'Haven't they told you? How remiss of me not to have introduced myself at once. Vain as I am, I did not imagine it to be necessary.' He made a little, arrogant bow. 'I am Gérard de Arnay. My father is the comte.'

I was so shocked that my mouth fell open. No one had ever mentioned his name to me. I'd had no idea that he existed – except for the portrait, of course.

'I see you are surprised.' His face reflected wicked enjoyment at my discomfort. 'I know I am not exactly the apple of my father's eye – especially at the moment – but I would have thought he might warn you.'

'Warn me?' I was suspicious of him now, because I had guessed that he liked to tease and provoke where he could. Why did he find it necessary to put on this show of bravado? Was it possible that behind his arrogant manner there was a different man – a man who was not quite as sure of himself as he liked to pretend? And yet there was no doubt that he was enjoying himself as he teased me!

Those blue eyes glinted with malicious pleasure. 'I have a terrible reputation with the ladies, Jenny Heron. I should probably have been in Cambridge for some months yet – my father insisted on my being educated in England for some obscure reason of his own, I suspect because it kept me out of his sight – but I've been sent down for seducing the wife of one of the dons.'

Again that slight resentment was there, and I could not but wonder what had made him feel that way. Did he think of himself as an outsider in this house, perhaps? Yet surely that could not be so? He was the comte's son!

'Seducing?' I gasped. 'That was very wicked of you, sir.' And even more naughty of him to tell a young lady he had only just met!

'She did not seem to mind, though her husband was a trifle upset.' He was obviously unrepentant, his tone light, careless as he shrugged his shoulders. 'Please don't call me sir, Jenny. I'm not going to call you mademoiselle – or even Mademoiselle Heron. My name is Gérard and I have decided we shall be friends.'

'Oh – have you?' For some reason his assumption that I would be grateful for his friendship annoyed me. Perhaps we would become close, for I could see he would make a pleasant companion if he were not being so arrogant. But he ought not to take me for granted. I lifted my head defiantly as I said, 'I am not sure I want to be your friend ... Monsieur de Arnay.'

'Perhaps you would rather we were lovers?'

Outrageous! How could he say such a thing to me when we had only just met? My heart leaped with fright and I gave him a frosty stare, which served only to make him laugh.

'Now I really have ruffled your feathers, haven't I, my pretty bird?' He reached out to touch my face but I stepped back hastily. 'You are cross with me, Jenny, but I think perhaps we *shall* be friends once you get to know me. I am not really so very—'

He broke off as we both heard the tap of heels on marble tiles and then Henriette came into the room bringing a cloud of delicious perfume with her. She looked both beautiful and elegant in a gown that seemed to swathe her body in folds of peach silk.

'Gérard – darling!' she cried. ' Laurent has just told me you were home – and how naughty you've been!' She arched her brows at him but her eyes sparkled with amusement.

He gave her a look of warm affection. 'Hello, Hettie my love. How beautiful you look. I hope you are not going to scold me? I've had enough of that from my father for one day. Anyone would think I had committed an unforgivable sin.' At that moment he resembled nothing more than a sulky child, reminding me forcibly of Charles.

Henriette went to him with hands outstretched and they embraced warmly. There was an obvious affinity between them, the closeness of good friends.

'No, I shan't scold you – even though you are a very bad boy,' she said and tilted her head to one side as she gazed up at him. ' Laurent should not either. You have done nothing so very terrible after all – nothing he has not done before you. All young men must have their amusements, no? That is all it was – an amusement.'

'You should know that I can never please the comte.'

There was a shadow in his eyes. Once again I sensed his resentment, and this time I could tell there was deep, smouldering anger simmering inside him – against his father, I thought, but I was unsure what was behind it. I only had my earlier guess that he felt hurt ... excluded in some way, perhaps ... to go on.

Something brought a cold sensation to the nape of my neck and I had a presentiment of some impending disaster, but then in another moment, Henriette tucked her arm through Gérard's. She turned to smile at me and the odd chill passed.

'How pretty you look this evening, Jenny. Doesn't she look lovely, Gérard? Do you not agree with me? Most girls of her age would look dreadful in black, but she can wear it, yes? I think it is because of that glorious hair.'

I put up a defensive hand to my hair, which had already begun to escape from its ribbon and curl in wisps about my face and neck. No matter what I did, it would never stay tidy for long.

'Mademoiselle Heron *is* beautiful,' Gérard replied with a wicked glance at me. 'But I fear I have offended her. She is determined to keep me at a distance – as perhaps I deserve. She knows that I am a wicked seducer and not to be trusted.'

Henriette's eyes narrowed as I blushed. 'Stop teasing my poor Jenny,' she commanded. 'I won't have it, Gérard. Do you hear me? You must be nice to her. She is going to live with us and help me take care of dear Charles – aren't you, Jenny?'

'Yes. I hope to be of help – if I can.'

'But of course you will. Charles adores you already – and he is not the only one.' Her eyes were very bright as she gazed up at her captive. ' Laurent is like a bear with a sore head this evening. It is all your fault, Gérard. Come and have a drink with us before dinner – and try not to upset him any more. Do not quarrel with him. For my sake.'

'For your sake?' His expression was mocking once more, but the resentment had gone for the moment. 'Very well, Hettie. For you I shall listen to Father's lectures with a good grace – but you must give me something in return. Perhaps a kiss? Or something more...' He whispered mischievously in her ear.

'You wicked boy!'

She shook her finger at him, then laughed huskily, drawing him from the small parlour, across the hall towards the elegant drawing room. I followed behind, trying to reconcile my thoughts with the odd behaviour of my heart.

Gérard was by his own admission a rogue – charming but selfish and careless of proper manners or the harm he did to other people's feelings. To seduce the wife of one of his teachers! It was scandalous! I ought to be wary of him, to keep a barrier between

us, but I had been attracted to him instantly
– perhaps from the moment I had first seen
his portrait. He had so much warmth and
was undeniably the most handsome man I
had ever met – and I had felt the hurt he
tried so hard to hide from the world.

*Foolish, foolish Jenny! Why should the comte's
heir need to hide anything?*

I chided myself for my ridiculous thoughts,
making a resolution to avoid him as much as
possible. I should indeed be foolish if I were
to allow myself to fall for him. Gérard de
Arnay was a sophisticated flirt. He might
tease and flatter me for amusement's sake,
but he would never seriously consider
asking me to marry him.

Nor did I want him to! All this talk of
marriage had taken over my mind. I did not
particularly want to marry, and if I should
change my mind – well, I was sensible
enough to know that neither the comte nor
the comtesse would approve of such a
match. The daughter of a seamstress would
not be good enough for their son, even if my
father had been an English gentleman.

Early the next morning a thick haze of mist
hung over the land, which gave the gardens
a rather eerie atmosphere. Unable to sleep
and feeling restless, I had risen before
anyone else was about and was walking in a
small walled garden at the rear of the

château when I saw the comtesse coming towards me. She appeared suddenly out of the mist like a wraith, wearing a thin satin robe belted loosely around her waist and looking untidy, her grey hair hanging about her shoulders as if she had just risen from her bed.

Perhaps this was her part of the garden! I shrank back behind a flowering shrub, not wanting to intrude on her, hoping that she would pass by and not see me.

'Who is it?' she called. 'Is it you, Maurice? Where are you – why are you hiding from me?'

'It is Jenny Heron,' I said and stood forward so that she could see me. 'Forgive me. I did not know I was not allowed to come here.'

'Who are you?' she demanded. Her eyes looked strange, half drugged with sleep. 'Are you spying on me? Why have you come here? Did he send you to spy on me?'

'Who, madame? I do not know what you mean. No one sent me. I like to walk in the mornings before the sun is too hot … it is a quiet time, for reflection.'

'I know you.' Her eyes had narrowed to suspicious slits. 'You are *her* daughter. He brought you here to punish me. He hates me … he will never forgive me.'

'Are you ill, madame? Should I fetch someone – Henriette?'

'You are his spy,' she muttered and moved closer to me, a menacing look in her eyes. 'Go away ... go away, little spy. Leave this place before it is too late. Don't be like me ... don't be like me...'

For a moment her eyes seemed to glitter with hatred, then she walked on past me, disappearing between the bushes.

I turned to watch her until she was out of sight, then hurried back to the more formal gardens at the front of the house. I should not come here to this place again unless invited.

Gérard was coming down the main staircase as I entered the house. He stopped at the bottom, barring my way as I tried to pass him.

'Where have you been so early?'

'Just for a walk.'

'So you like to walk alone at dawn,' he said, a wicked smile about his mouth. 'I shall remember that, Jenny.'

'It was just that I could not sleep.' I blushed as he looked at me, a speculative gleam in his eyes. 'Please let me pass. I should like to tidy myself before anyone sees me.'

'Have you been meeting a lover?' He was mocking me again, challenging me. 'No one rises at this hour unless it is to meet a lover.'

I was tempted to tell him I had met his mother walking in the walled garden, but something stopped me. Her manner had been so strange that I should be embarrassed to speak of it.

Gérard laid a hand on my arm.

'Will you meet me at dawn tomorrow, sweet little Jenny?'

'No – no, I shall not,' I said. 'Now let me pass.'

'Go, then,' he said, laughing as I fled past him and up the stairs. 'If you were meeting a lover I shall find out. You had much better meet me, Jenny.'

His laughter followed me up the stairs, making me feel hot and uncomfortable. I should take care not to walk early in the morning again – and his mockery had made me determined to stay as far away from my tormentor as possible.

'We have guests for lunch,' Henriette told me that morning. 'Friends of Gérard's. Madame Testud, her daughter Catriona, Mademoiselle Lasalles and Monsieur Bertrand. I believe you may find them on the lawn – if you care to join them. Gérard has set up a target. Mademoiselle Testud is a toxophilite and I understand her aim is excellent.'

'Surely they will not expect me to join them?' I said. 'I have never used a bow and arrow, and I am sure I should not be any good at the sport.'

161

'Gérard particularly requested you should meet his guests,' Henriette said. 'You need not join in if you prefer not to – but it should be amusing to watch.'

I reluctantly left the house in search of the archers. The target had been set up on the lawns in the formal gardens. I could hear laughter and voices as I made my way slowly towards them.

The ladies were dressed in the height of fashion. The most outstanding of them was wearing a skirt made of some heavy, silky material in an off-white, the jacket falling well below her hips, bunched and frilled at the back and edged with a thick cream lace. She had a sash of pale lilac tied in a huge knot at the back and a hat trimmed with the same colour ribbon sat jauntily on the back of her head.

She was a very beautiful woman of a similar age to myself, but far more stylish and confident. As I watched from a distance, she took aim with her bow, pulling the string back with her gloved hand, a look of concentration on her face. As the arrow flew towards the target, I knew that she would hit the very heart of the coloured rings – and I realised that this must be Mademoiselle Testud.

A round of applause greeted her efforts, and I watched as another, smaller lady took her place before the target. She seemed to hesitate, as though she were uncertain of how to hold her bow. She threw a look of appeal at Gérard and he came up to stand behind her. He put his arms about her, showing her how to hold the bow steady, how to fix her arrow, and then helped her to draw back the string so that her arrow flew straight and accurately, entering the target a few centimetres from Mademoiselle Testud's.

'That is unfair,' a young man of about Gérard's age protested. 'You should have let Jeanne shoot for herself.'

'I do not mind,' replied Mademoiselle Testud. 'It is only a game, after all. Come, Monsieur Bertrand – I shall challenge you to a contest. You will be a fairer test of my skill.'

The young man laughed, obviously more than willing to take up her challenge. I saw that Jeanne Lasalles did not particularly mind her place being taken by Monsieur Bertrand. She was smiling up at Gérard, obviously more interested in him than in the game of archery.

I was about to turn away when he glanced my way. He beckoned to me, but I shook my head, unwilling to intrude.

'Jenny,' he said and, murmuring something to his companion, brought her towards me. 'Mademoiselle Lasalles, I would like you to meet my father's ward, Jenny

Heron. Jenny, this is Jeanne – a cousin of my friend Paul Bertrand, who you see making a fool of himself at the target. He hasn't a hope of beating Catriona. None of us has ... unless you are a toxophilite?'

I shook my head, smiling as Mademoiselle Lasalles offered her hand. 'I am pleased to meet you, mademoiselle.'

'Then I shall teach you,' Gérard told me, his eyes gleaming with mischief.

I pictured his arms about me as they had been about Mademoiselle Lasalles and I was determined to resist.

'You are very kind,' I said. 'But I beg you will excuse me. I came only to greet your friends, Gérard. I am needed in the house.'

He knew why I had refused. I saw the laughter in his eyes, but he did not try to stop me.

'Another day then,' he said. 'Fly away, little bird. I shall not cage you, but remember ... there is always another day.'

I gave him a nervous glance, then turned and walked back towards the house, my heart fluttering as if it were indeed a bird in a cage.

Before lunch, I was formally introduced to the other guests. The food was a rather lavish buffet, which had been set out on tables in the gardens, and we all helped ourselves to the various dishes, sitting in little

164

groups as we pleased.

I chose a seat on a bench a little apart from the others, but after a while Mademoiselle Testud came and sat next to me.

'I was sorry you did not stay to shoot with us,' she said. 'I should have been glad to show you how to arm your bow.'

'That is kind of you, mademoiselle,' I replied. 'But I fear I should have disappointed you. I was never good at any sport at school.'

'But you must learn,' she said, her eyebrows arching. 'Surely you ride, mademoiselle?'

'No, I do not ride – not properly. I have ridden on the farm as a child – but not side-saddle.'

Gérard had wandered over to join us. I could see the mischief in his eyes as he said, 'Not ride, Jenny? Shame on you. You must learn.'

I shook my head, but I could see that the idea had taken root in his mind.

'This afternoon we are all to take a walk to the stream,' he said. 'You will not say that you do not like to walk, Jenny?'

'No, of course not.' I blushed. 'Of course I should like to walk with you and your friends – but I must bring Charles. He loves to sail his boat and he will be disappointed if he is left at home.'

'Of course you may bring Charles, if it

makes you feel safer,' Gérard said, giving me a wicked look as he walked back to where Jeanne Lasalles and Madame Testud were sitting.

Seeing my blush, Catriona laughed. 'Do not allow Gérard to tease you,' she advised. 'The more you resist him, the more he will pursue you. Jeanne would snare him more easily in her net if she did not show her feelings so plainly. He is a flirt, Jenny – not to be taken seriously. One day he will marry, but I do not think he is ready just yet.'

'Jenny – you have a visitor.' I had just come in from the garden with Charles that afternoon when Henriette greeted me with the news that someone was waiting to see me. 'He arrived a few minutes ago. I asked him to wait in the front parlour until you could be found.'

'Who is it?' I looked at her curiously. 'I am not expecting anyone.'

'He said his name was Captain Blake.' Her eyes rolled expressively, her smile teasing. 'He is rather handsome, Jenny – is he your lover?'

I blushed and shook my head vigorously, wondering if my visitor could possibly be who I thought it must be. 'Oh, no! I think ... I think he may be the brother of a friend of mine.'

'Well, I shall not tease you about him,'

Henriette said. 'He is waiting for you, my love.'

I blushed again and turned in the direction of the parlour, feeling apprehensive. What could Captain Blake want with me? Had he news of Kate? How strange that he should come to see me, after all this time!

My heart was beating faster than usual when I entered the parlour to find a man standing looking out at the gardens. He was tall and well built, with broad shoulders, and his hair was dark brown. When he turned to look at me, I saw that he was very like Kate in his features and his smile was pleasant, though hesitant.

'Forgive me for coming here without warning,' he apologised at once, looking awkward. 'I would have written first, but I discovered your whereabouts only yesterday from Sister Isobel – and I have to return to England tomorrow before sailing to Italy to take up a post as secretary to the ambassador.'

'There is no need to apologise, Captain Blake. Have you brought me a message from Kate? You are her brother, aren't you?'

'Yes, I am.' His gaze narrowed as he looked at me. 'I was hoping ... I am trying to trace my sister, Miss Heron. I came to see you in the hope you might know where she is living.'

'I have not heard from Kate in years,

Captain Blake.'

'Do you have any idea where she is?'

'No, I'm afraid not. She wrote to me after...' I stopped abruptly. 'I was ill and only received that letter quite recently. She was in trouble at the time and my mother helped her.'

'Your mother helped Kate? Would she know where to find her?'

'My mother died recently, sir.'

'Oh ... forgive me. I did not know.' A flush swept up his neck as he realised I was in mourning. 'I should not have come at such a time. It was not well done of me.'

Again I begged him not to apologise. I saw that he was a very precise gentleman, and not at all like his sister.

'I asked my mother if she knew where Kate was when she gave me the letter, but she said she didn't.'

'And you have not heard from my sister since then?'

I shook my head. 'No, though I have thought of her often.'

'She ran off with that rogue Havers, you know. He deserted her. They were never married.' There was anger in his eyes, but also regret. I sensed that he was very fond of his sister, and thought that perhaps he did not always find it easy to show his feelings.

'I was afraid something like that might happen. I only met Mr Havers once – but I

168

did not like him.'

'All he wanted was her money. When he discovered that I held the purse strings ... he left her alone in a cheap hotel in Portsmouth. She had no money and was forced to leave under cover of darkness owing for her board. I paid the debt later, but they could not tell me where she went when she left Portsmouth.'

'I am so very sorry.'

'I saw him recently,' Captain Blake said, his face tight with anger. 'He was in court for debt. I demanded news of Kate ... but he knew no more than I. He suggested that she had friends in France, and I remembered her speaking of you.' A low moaning noise escaped him before he could control it. 'You were my last hope, Miss Heron. I know she was always fond of you. I thought you might know where I could reach her.'

'I'm sorry. I have no idea where she went after my mother gave her money.'

'I want to help her, Miss Heron. My sole reason for seeking her is to give her some security, to restore her inheritance to her. She has no need to hide from me; I would not harm her. I give you my word. I want only to help Kate.'

'If I see her I will tell her that,' I said, 'but I really do not know where she is.'

'Then I shall not take up any more of your time.' He hesitated, then took a card from his waistcoat pocket. 'This is the name of my solicitor in London. Should you discover anything, I would be obliged if you would contact me through him.'

I took the card, placing it in the pocket of my gown. 'Of course, Captain Blake. But Kate is my friend. My first loyalty is to her. I could only do so with her permission.'

'Yes, I see that – but just to know she is safe would relieve my mind so much.'

'If I hear from her I will let you know, sir – that is all I can promise.'

'Very well. Thank you for seeing me, Miss Heron.'

He bowed and walked from the room. I stood by the window and watched him walk to where a groom stood holding his horse. He mounted and rode away without looking round.

Where was Kate? The grief of my mother's death had overshadowed everything else, pushing my friend's fate to the back of my mind, but now it returned to haunt me.

I wondered if she was in France. And if she was – what steps could I take to trace her?

Perhaps when my mother's things were sent on to me I might find something amongst them that would give me a clue to Kate's whereabouts, but for the moment there was nothing I could do.

I had other things on my mind – and not

least of them was the behaviour of the comte's son! He seemed to like nothing more than to tease and torment me, and I had made up my mind to avoid him whenever I could.

It was easier to take the decision to avoid Gérard as much as possible than to carry it out. Over the next week or so he sought my company wherever I was, seeming determined to make me yield to him, to force me to admit that I wanted to be his friend. Perhaps my show of defiance at the start had intrigued him – I thought Gérard would always need to have his own way in all things – and he was a self-confessed flirt. Or it might just have been that he was bored.

'Poor Gérard,' Henriette said to me as we were walking together in the gardens some three weeks later. 'He is so restless here. Laurent should either send him on a grand tour or make him a generous allowance so that he can set up his own establishment in Paris. Laurent thinks of his son as a high-spirited youth – but he is a man. He should be allowed to have his fling before he settles down; it is only natural – no?'

'How old is Gérard?'

'He will be twenty-one next month.'

'And there is no chance of his returning to England to continue his studies?'

'They would not have him back at Cambridge. Besides, he would not consent to go. Gérard never had a great desire for an academic life. Laurent was wrong to try and force it on him.'

'Then what will he do with himself? Can he not find some kind of employment?'

Henriette smiled and shrugged her shoulders. 'He might settle in the army, but Laurent is against it. He thinks Gérard should learn to manage the estates. Laurent has others besides this – in the Languedoc and Provence. They *are* Gérard's inheritance, after all.'

'Is the comte very wealthy?' I looked at her curiously. 'I had not realised there were other estates besides this one.'

'This house was a part of Béatrix's dowry,' Henriette replied with an odd smile. 'That is why she chooses to live here – and it is not so very far from Paris, which makes it convenient for Laurent to visit. Of course Laurent has people to look after his property – some of which is in England – though he spends most of his time in Paris.'

'With his mistress?'

Henriette hesitated, looking at some point just beyond my shoulder. 'That is over,' she said. 'I misled you the other day. There was someone ... but no longer.'

I absorbed this new information in silence. Henriette had known that the comte's long-standing affair was over – that was why she had hoped to become his mistress, of course. Did she believe that she would one day be his wife? I suspected she hoped for it, but naturally I could not ask her, so we resumed the fascinating subject of the comte's son.

'But you think Gérard has no interest in managing his father's property?'

'He is still very young, for all his sophistication,' she said. 'He must have some time to be a little wild, after all. Laurent expects too much of him. He is too strict. It is as if ... he can show no affection to his son. I know I spoil Charles but Laurent ... Laurent can be a tyrant with his son. If he is not careful Gérard will rebel and there will be trouble between them.'

'What do you mean? What kind of trouble?'

Henriette shook her head. 'How can anyone know what may happen?' She glanced at a small gold watch pinned to her waistband with a pretty bow. 'My cousin will be waiting for me – and I think Charles will be looking for you shortly, Jenny. He has become so fond of you – and you are so good with him.'

'I enjoy being with him,' I assured her. 'I shall take him for a walk down to the stream. He likes to sail the boat Gérard made for him.'

'You will be careful he doesn't fall in?'

173

'Of course.' I met her eyes frankly. ' Charles is an adventurous child, Henriette – but I watch him all the time.'

'Very well. I trust you to take care of him.' She pressed my arm. 'Now I must go or Béatrix will be in a sullen mood all day.'

We parted company in the main hallway, she hurrying to the west wing and the comtesse's apartments, while I made a more leisurely journey up to the nursery to collect my charge for the afternoon.

It was as we were walking back after a pleasant hour or so by the stream that we met Gérard coming towards us. Charles was fond of his honorary uncle and rushed to greet him with a cry of delight. Gérard swept him up and they engaged in a few minutes of rough and tumble before the lad was hoisted on to his 'uncle's' shoulders.

'We've been sailing boats,' Charles cried, pointing to the splendid model yacht I was carrying for him. 'You should have come with us. You could have helped me sail my boat.'

'And I would if anyone had told me where you were.' Gérard's eyes met mine in amusement. 'I think Jenny has been avoiding me. She thinks I am a wicked ogre.'

'No, of course I do not – and I have not been avoiding you.' I blushed, because I was lying and he knew it. He seemed to find it all too easy to read my mind. 'Besides, I'm quite sure you have more important things to do with your time.'

'More important than sailing boats in the stream?' His brows went up. 'What could be more vital than that?'

'You are making fun of me.'

'Jenny ... Jenny,' he chided me. 'Haven't you learned that I am never serious – unless confronted with dire need?'

'You should be studying,' I said. 'Just because you have left college it does not mean that you must spend your whole day in idle pursuits.'

'How virtuous she is,' he said, and lowered the child to the ground as we saw his nurse come out of the house. 'It is time for your supper, Charles. Run to Roseanne like a good boy – and take your boat with you.'

'Will Jenni come and tell me a story later?' He looked at me as I handed him the boat. 'Will you?'

'Yes – if you do what Gérard tells you now.'

He hesitated, clearly reluctant to return to the confines of the nursery, but, as Gérard frowned, he turned and ran across the lawn to the impatient Roseanne.

'Must you go in just yet?' Gérard held my arm as I made to follow them into the house. 'It is such a lovely afternoon. Could we not walk together for a while?'

'Yes, I suppose so – if you wish.'

175

I sounded reluctant, but my heart was racing wildly as I saw the expression in his eyes. He looked so intense at that moment ... so passionate ... that I caught my breath, my gaze dropping in confusion. Common sense told me that I must not become involved with this man, but there was something about him that I found greatly attractive, and my heart was urging me to forget caution.

We turned and strolled towards an avenue of climbing roses, which clustered over a long wooden pergola in heavy clumps of highly scented white flowers. There was a slight breeze and the petals showered down on us, like confetti at a wedding. Neither of us said anything until we emerged at the other end of the tunnel, then Gérard touched my arm, and as I turned towards him, he caught me up in a sudden passionate embrace, looking down at me for one brief moment before crushing his mouth to mine.

I am not sure why I did not immediately repulse him. Perhaps his impulsive action was surprising – or perhaps my foolish heart had been willing him to do just this. For a few wonderful, dizzying seconds I allowed myself to respond to his kiss; then, as he released me, I saw the light of triumph in his eyes and gasped, my cheeks beginning to flame. If he was only mocking me, playing with my affections, I should be hurt. I spoke next out of a need to protect myself.

'You should not have done that, Gérard!'

'Why – was it distasteful to you?' His wicked look made me turn away in distress. I would have run from him then but he reached out and took my arm, preventing me. 'No, do not run away, Jenny. It was wicked of me to use you so – and to tease you afterwards.'

I glanced back, tears burning behind my eyes. 'You should not have kissed me like that, Gérard. It was not fair of you.'

He touched my cheek gently with the tips of his fingers. 'Poor Jenny,' he murmured. 'Have I confused you, my little one? Was that your first kiss?' He seemed contrite for a moment, but the spark was back in his eyes as I defied him.

'No.' My head went up, pride making me speak out. He should see that I was not so easily to be conquered. 'I've been kissed once before.'

'So – sweet, innocent Jenny did have a lover!' he teased. I saw that my defiance had brought out the hunting instinct in him. 'Tell me, did he make your heart beat fast ... as fast as it is beating now?' He placed his hand against my breast and the heat of his flesh seemed to burn through the flimsy material of my summer gown, making me jerk away in fright. 'No, not a lover, then – a clumsy boy, perhaps?'

'It was because of that kiss that my mother sent me to the convent school,' I confessed. 'I was not quite sixteen and I had lived with Tante Marthe all my life until then – but Mama took me away after that kiss. I have never known why ... why they were all so upset. It was after the wine-treading and we were all excited. It meant nothing – but Mama sent me to the sisters because of it.'

'And who shall blame her?' Gérard's eyes danced with mischief. 'Could she see what I see in you, Jenny?' His voice dropped to a husky whisper. 'I believe there is passion in you, my sweet little bird. You look so meek and mild, and I should not tarnish your innocence ... but I know there is a fire inside you. Do you want me to show you the real Jenny?'

Something in his eyes at that moment made me feel weak at the knees. I longed for him to take me in his arms again and kiss me, but a little voice in my head was telling me not to listen to his teasing. If I were not careful I should fall in love with this charmer – and he would break my heart.

'No, I do not,' I said. 'I am not the wife of your teacher, Gérard. I shall not be so easily seduced.'

'What a fool I was to tell you about that,' he said, a half-serious expression on his face. 'You cannot imagine I think of you in the same way, Jenny?'

'Don't you?' I asked uncertainly.

'No, of course not. I told you at the start: I want us to be friends – at least for the time being, though perhaps one day we may be something more.'

'Then you should not have kissed me like that,' I said. 'If we are to be friends I must be able to trust you. I do not know you, Gérard – your wild talk and your kisses frighten me.'

'Forgive me,' he said and smiled in a way that melted my resistance. 'Will you trust me – if I promise it won't happen again?'

'Yes...' I felt a surge of joy. How handsome he was – and how charming when he looked at me that way! I liked him so very much. 'Yes, of course I will, Gérard.'

'Then we shall be friends,' he said. 'Now – let us -finish our walk. I want you to tell me all about yourself, sweet Jenny.'

'There isn't much to tell.' I looked at him doubtfully, but he took my hand and placed it on his arm. 'I'm afraid I haven't done anything very exciting.'

'Poor Jenny,' he murmured, the mocking note back in his voice. 'We shall have to find some way of changing that – shan't we?'

My heart leaped as I saw the look in his eyes. He was flirting with me again – but somehow as time went on I minded less. It was exciting just to be with him, to listen to his voice and see him smile.

'Why don't you tell me what you did at Cambridge?' I asked. 'Apart from seducing that woman.'

'Shall I tell you about the balls?' he asked, his eyes full of wickedness. 'About dancing with beautiful ladies and drifting down the river in punts afterwards ... breakfasting on the banks without ever having been to bed...'

'That sounds wonderful,' I said and sighed. 'I've never been to a dance ... not a proper one.'

'Poor Jenny,' he said and pulled me against him, whirling me round in a madcap waltz. I was intoxicated by the smell of him, by the way his touch seemed to melt my insides, and I could have swooned from pleasure.

'How well you dance, Mademoiselle Heron.'

'My friend taught me,' I confessed with a laugh. 'Kate was always bemoaning the fact that the sisters wouldn't let us dance properly. You would like Kate, Gérard.'

'It is unfair that you have never been to a dance,' Gérard said. 'I shall ask Henriette to persuade my father to give one for you.'

'Oh, no,' I gasped and pulled away from him. 'She mustn't. Your father has already done so much for me. Bringing me here – introducing me to people as his ward—'

'Inviting a few of his own friends to

180

dinner?' Gérard's brows rose in disbelief. 'They are all far too old for you, and so boring. I could not allow you to be condemned to such a fate. How are we ever to find you a suitable husband that way, Jenny? No, no, I shall take charge of the business and find you someone suitable. We must have a dance. I shall speak to my father myself.'

He was teasing me, deliberately needling me. Surely he must know that I did not want a husband ... or at least none that he might find for me. Foolishly, I was already beginning to let myself dream.

'He will never agree.'

'Oh, I think he might,' Gérard said. 'Once upon a time he often entertained his neighbours with a grand ball – but I think a small dance will suffice this time, don't you? You would like to dance with me – wouldn't you, Jenny?'

'Oh, yes,' I breathed, my heart leaping suddenly. 'If you think it would be no trouble for your father.'

Gérard's head went back as he laughed. 'My father never allows anything to trouble him, Jenny. It may cause a great deal of work for the servants, but who cares for that? We shall have our dance, my little bird – and see what comes of it.' He looked down at me with mock severity. 'But you must promise to be guided by me in this matter of a

181

husband. I will not have you accepting some old fool just because he has money and can provide you with a home of your own. No, you must let me find someone who will make my little Jenny happy.'

'I am in no hurry to be married,' I replied, avoiding his provoking gaze. 'I'm quite happy here with Henriette and Charles.'

'Oh Jenny, Jenny,' he murmured. 'Why no mention of me? Are you not happy with me?'

'I'm not sure that I should be wise to rest my happiness on you,' I replied, gazing up at him seriously.

'No, perhaps not,' he said and the laughter had gone from his face. 'Believe me, Jenny, I shall never intentionally hurt you – but I am not sure that I could make you happy, or anyone else either.'

'What do you mean?'

My heart caught as I glanced up and saw his expression. There was such a bleak ... almost haunted ... expression in his eyes. Why did he feel he was incapable of making me happy? What secret grief haunted him?

He shook his head. 'Take no notice, my little bird. It is too nice an afternoon to be serious.'

He slipped his arm about my waist and smiled once more in the way that always made my heart beat faster. I had told him he must not kiss me again, but the sadness in his eyes had touched me and I wanted to comfort him.

Impulsively, I kissed his cheek. 'I think any woman would be happy to love you, Gérard.'

He smiled but surprisingly did not make the mocking response I might have expected.

Eight

I was already halfway to being in love with Gérard by the time we walked back to the house that afternoon. He might at times be the most infuriating man, but I sensed so much more in him – and it was that inner self that made me so attracted to him.

We stood for a moment on the lawns overlooked by the west wing, gazing at each other in perfect harmony.

'So...' He reached out to touch my cheek with his fingertips as I looked up at him. 'Such big eyes ... so clear and grey, like the English sky in winter. What is going on in your head, my Jenny? Have you forgiven me? Are we friends now?'

'Yes, of course.' His teasing expression brought a flush to my cheeks and I turned my head. As I did so, I caught sight of a woman standing at one of the windows. We were not close enough for me to be certain but I thought it might be the comtesse herself. 'Oh ... someone is watching us.'

Gérard followed the direction of my gaze and frowned as the woman withdrew into the room. 'Do you suppose that was my mother – or the dragon who guards her?'

'I'm not sure.' I pulled a laughing face at him. ' Flore is a bit of a dragon, isn't she?'

'Her looks don't pity her,' he said, smiling oddly, 'but she isn't really so very terrible. I tease her – but she is devoted to Maman, and sometimes she gets upset because...' His smile faded and I saw the smoulder of resentment in his eyes. He was silent for a moment, lost in thought. 'If it was Flore she will tell Maman that she saw us together ... so I must pay my mother a little visit.'

'Your mother does not approve of me, Gérard.' I looked at him uncertainly.

'Only because she doesn't know you,' he said and touched the tip of my nose with his forefinger. 'We shall have to try and change that, Jenny. I should like you to think kindly of Maman. She has not had an easy life.'

My instinct was to reply that his mother would never like me, nor I her, but something in his expression held me silent. It was clear to me in that moment that Gérard was fond of his mother. I began to understand his resentment against his father and to suspect that he knew about the comte's long-standing affair with the woman in Paris.

'I do not want to be any bother to the comtesse.'

'She would not allow it,' he said and

185

laughed. His eyes danced with mischief. 'Believe me, Jenny. I am under no illusions where Maman is concerned. She is difficult and demanding – but I understand her, I care for her.'

His concern for his mother made me like him even more. 'Of course you care for her. She is your mother. I should think it unkind of you if you did not.'

'I care for her ... but I also care for you, Jenny.'

I caught my breath, unsure how to reply. What did he mean exactly? That he cared for me as a friend or ... what ? He could not mean that he loved me? My heart raced with anticipation as I gazed up at him.

Before either of us could speak again we heard Henriette's voice calling to us from the house.

'Ah, there you are,' she cried. ' Laurent wants to speak to you, Jenny. You will find him in the small front parlour.'

'Have I done something wrong?'

She laughed as she heard the note of alarm in my voice. 'Not to my knowledge,' she said. 'I think some things have arrived from Paris for you.

'Mama's things? Madame Leconte promised to send them.'

I read the answer in her eyes and hurried into the house.

★ ★ ★

The comte was waiting for me. I paused as I saw him standing at the window, his back towards me. He turned as I entered, looking at me gravely.

'Henriette told you some things have arrived from Paris? There is this box – and a trunk full of clothes, which I thought you would want stored.' I nodded silently and he indicated my mother's writing-box. 'Shall I have this stored with the rest – or taken up to your room?'

'Where would you store it?'

'I'm not sure. Does it matter? No one will touch it.' His forehead furrowed. 'Would you rather I kept the key safely for you?'

'I will have the key – and her writing-box.' My throat felt tight as a wave of grief threatened to bring tears. 'But I would be grateful if you could store the trunk with her clothes and personal possessions ... just for a while, please?'

'Whatever you wish. When you are ready you have only to ask for it to be brought to you.'

'Thank you. You are very kind.' I took the key and was about to leave but he began to speak again and I realised there was more. I waited, blinking hard to cover my emotions.

'Were you aware that your mother has relatives in Cornwall, Jenny?'

When had he started to use that name? It

187

was odd to hear it on his lips, though not really surprising as both Henriette and Gérard used it all the time.

'I knew she had a family in England once. I'm not sure where Cornwall is exactly...'

'At the southern tip of the country,' he said, his expression thoughtful. 'Adele cut the connection years ago. She wanted nothing to do with her family. Do you know why?'

I shook my head: my heart had begun to thump and my hands felt moist, sticky as I waited for him to continue. I had always sensed some mystery in Mama's past.

'There was a quarrel many years ago. Adele left her home and vowed never to return. I am telling you this so you will be aware of her feelings, Jenny.'

I was silent, watchful, waiting for him to continue.

'I have received a letter from a Mr Philip Allington.' His gaze narrowed, becoming more intent, even angry, as I gasped. 'I see the name is familiar to you. Has he dared to write to you himself?'

'No. I saw him only once – at the house in Paris. My mother was upset by his visit. She cried afterwards. I don't know why.'

The comte nodded, his eyes studying me thoughtfully. 'He has written asking for permission to speak to you, Jenny. It appears that he has something of importance to tell you concerning your mother's family.'

'I do not wish to see him!' My answer was so emphatic that his brows rose, and I blushed beneath his intense gaze. 'At least, I would rather not – just yet.'

He nodded. 'Then that is what I shall convey to Mr Allington in my letter of reply. You wish me to say that you do not feel ready to see him yet – is that right?'

'Yes, please, sir.'

'Jenny...' He took a few steps towards me then stood gazing down at me, an odd expression on his face. 'You are happy here, aren't you? You have settled into your life with us?'

For a moment I thought I saw tenderness in his face and a strange wistfulness ... as if he wanted to reach out to me, to tell me something important.

'Yes, sir. Of course. It was kind of you to bring me to your home.'

'Jenny—'

His hand lifted as if to reach out to me. I thought he meant to touch my face but then we heard footsteps and he drew back as someone knocked at the door.

'Come in,' he said, the old harshness in his voice once more. 'You may go, Jenny.'

I passed one of the servants as I went out. There was a small army of them in the house and I was not yet sure of all their names.

'Madame la comtesse would like to see you, monsieur.'

I heard the comte answering as I went up the stairs to my own room. I thought his voice sounded angry – and I wondered why.

Once alone in my room, I set the writing-case on a chest of drawers and put the key in my dressing-case, then I went to perch on the window seat and look out at the gardens, though I was at that moment only vaguely aware of the beautiful vista set out before me. I was glad my mother's things had been sent on to me, but I wasn't quite ready to go through them, even though the sharp edges of my grief had begun to dull these past weeks.

I wondered why Philip Allington had written to my guardian. I supposed it must have something to do with the visit he had paid Mama in Paris and remembered her stricken face after he'd left. It was the first and only time I had ever seen her cry and I'd been angry with him for upsetting her. I'd asked her what was wrong but she had begged me not to press for an answer, promising that I would know the truth one day.

Would I find the answer to the mystery amongst her things? Had she left a diary, perhaps, or letters for me? A part of me wanted to find out, and yet I was nervous ... afraid of what I might discover.

I felt cold all over, as if someone had walked on my grave. Mama had kept her secrets to protect me from something she thought might harm me ... something that Philip Allington might be a part of.

If I had allowed him to visit me ... No! No, I did not want to see him. I did not want to pry into the secrets my mother had carried with her to the grave. I felt that there was some danger ... something evil hidden in the past ... and it made me afraid. If Mama had told me herself ... but it was too late.

She was dead and I would never see her again, never feel the loving touch of her hand or see her smile light up the room. As a terrible sense of despair swept over me, I bent my head and wept.

'What did my father want?' Gérard asked when he saw me later that day. He looked at me suspiciously, tipping up my chin to gaze into my eyes. 'He upset you – you have been crying.'

'Yes, for a while,' I admitted, 'but it was not your father's fault. He merely wanted to tell me about some things that had come from Paris for me – and to discuss whether or not I wanted to see someone.'

'Who?'

'A man called Philip Allington,' I said, frowning. 'I think he must be some kind of distant relation or a friend of my mother's family. Your father asked me if I wanted to see him ... he told me that there had been a quarrel, that my mother cut the connection years ago.'

Gérard too was frowning. 'You realise that he was trying to influence your decision, don't you? He probably has reasons of his own for not wanting you to see this man.'

'Gérard!' I was shocked. 'How can you say that? I am sure he had no such intention.'

'Are you, Jenny? Have you not yet realised that my father is still a royalist at heart?' His mouth twisted wryly. 'He may pay lip service to the Republic, but he still believes in the *droit du seigneur*.'

'That is a terrible thing to say,' I cried, looking at him in disbelief. 'I cannot believe you really mean that!'

'Not literally,' he admitted. 'I do not imply that he would actually take an unwilling virgin to his bed on the eve of her wedding – he has too much pride for that – but he believes he has the right to dictate to us all. Just as if he still had all his feudal powers.'

'You are too hard on him,' I said.

The Comte de Arnay was a stern man, who was used to being obeyed, but he could not really be as autocratic as his son imagined. It was obvious that Gérard's resentment against his father ran deep. Something more lay beneath the surface, but it was not for me to pry into family secrets. I was here at the château as a guest.

'Now *I*, of course, am a good Republican,' Gérard said, and the mockery was back in his eyes as he whistled a few bars of the Marseillaise, the song the revolutionaries had sung as they stormed the Tuileries. 'I have no need to drag unwilling maidens into my bed.'

I dropped my gaze, my cheeks flushing.

'Oh, Jenny, Jenny,' Gérard laughed huskily. 'What a wretch I am to tease you so. Say you will forgive me?'

'You do not deserve that I should.' I looked at him, but there was no anger in me. I was only too relieved to see that his black mood had passed.

That night, for the first time in weeks, I dreamed of my mother. It seemed to me that she came to me as I lay in bed. I felt the touch of her hand as she bent over me, and I could smell her perfume.

'Remember your heritage,' she said. 'Remember that I gave it to you, Jenny.'

'Mama,' I cried out to her as I woke, and for a moment I thought I could still feel her there. But it was only the breeze from my open window which stirred the curtains. *Why did you come to me? What were you trying to tell me?*

It had seemed to me as I slept that she was trying to warn me of something, but now I realised it was just a dream.

'Oh, Mama,' I sighed as I drifted back to sleep. 'Why were you taken from me so cruelly? Why did you have to die?'

In the morning I remembered the dream, and I took the key to her writing-box from my own dressing-case, thinking that perhaps it was time I tried to discover something of her past. When I opened the box, however, the smell of her perfume brought tears to my eyes and I sat for several minutes just staring blindly at the contents.

I caught sight of an envelope marked 'personal documents', a pile of letters and various bits and pieces that looked like bills tied up with blue ribbon. I was reaching for the first envelope when Henriette knocked and came into the room.

'Are you busy?' she asked. 'Only Béatrix has a headache and I promised Charles I would play with him this morning ... but if you have something important to do...?'

'No, of course not,' I said. I closed the box, locked it and returned the key to my own dressing-case. 'I shall go to Charles at once.'

It was cowardly of me to feel relieved by Henriette's interruption, but although I knew I ought to make myself go through Mama's things, in case there was something important I ought to know, I still did not feel ready.

I would look soon, I told myself. The comte was taking care of her business affairs; if there was anything I should know, no doubt he would tell me.

I was in the parlour when Gérard came in that afternoon. I had been reading a book of poems, and he walked across to where I was sitting and took it from me, glancing at what I had been reading.

'You *are* a romantic!' he cried, looking at me accusingly. 'All this time you have pretended to be so sensible – and now I find you reading this.'

'That does not make me a romantic,' I said and blushed. 'I just happen to enjoy poetry.'

'What were you reading when I came in? Which is your favourite?' He handed me the book, as imperious at that moment as he accused his father of being. 'Read it aloud to me.'

I hesitated, then began: "Ah, what can ail thee, wretched wight, Alone and palely loitering—"

'*La Belle Dame Sans Merci*!' Gérard cried triumphantly. He snatched the book back and flipped through the opening pages. 'I researched the life and work of John Keats at Cambridge for my thesis. Did you know that the first version of this poem was written in a journal-letter to George Keats and his wife? This book you have is the second volume of Keats' works published by Lord Houghton in 1848 – how did you come by it?'

'My mother gave it to me, because she wanted me to read an English poet. I have always treasured it.'

He nodded, looking at me thoughtfully as he stroked the soft leather cover, then glanced at the inscription inside. 'It is a handsome copy, with a good thick binding – not the original, I think, but added later. Your mother must have had it done specially for you. And this is your favourite poem. Oh, Jenny, Jenny ... shall you lead me astray like that faery's child? Would you leave me alone and palely loitering?'

'You will always mock me, Gérard.'

'No, I think not,' he said, and there was something in his eyes then that made me believe he might be in earnest. 'I believe you have me in thrall, Jenny. And if I were to awake and find you gone—'

'Jenni! Jenni!' Charles came rushing into the parlour at that moment. 'Will you take me to sail my boat?'

'We shall both take you,' Gérard said. 'You are a rogue, young sir, but I suppose you must have your way or we shall have no peace in the house.'

The strange, haunted look had gone from Gérard's eyes, and I was glad. He looked at me and laughed. He was his usual confident self once more, and I could not be perfectly sure that he had not been mocking me after all.

Gérard had decided he would teach me to ride. Henriette gave her approval and lent me a habit which had been hers at about my age. It was black, with a long full skirt and a short, fitted jacket: there was also a snowy stock and a smart hat with ribbons at the back. Her boots were too large and we had to send for some from town, so it was more than a week before I could begin my lessons – something which did not suit Gérard.

He was always so impatient, and could be sulky when his plans were thwarted. But at last the boots arrived and I was ready. His eyes went over me with approval when he first saw me.

'You look very proper,' he said, his smile mocking me. 'Like an English miss. I think Henriette must have had this habit made in London.'

I was surprised. 'Does she often have things made in London?'

'She spent some time there as a young girl,' Gérard replied. 'And I think she went there with her husband when she was first married. Why – does it matter?'

'No, of course not.'

It did not matter in the least where the

habit had been made, but I was remembering something Henriette had once said to me. She had mentioned seeing me as a new-born baby, and I had wondered at it – for I understood I had been born in England. But if Henriette had visited England many times ... and yet had she known my mother before she became a seamstress in Paris?

It was a mystery, but I had no time to ponder it now. Gérard was impatient to begin my lessons.

His hands were strong about my waist as he helped me to mount. He looked up at me, smiling in the way that always affected my heart in that funny way.

'I shall lead you round the paddock for a start,' he told me. 'You will be quite safe, so there is no need to be nervous.'

'I am not nervous.' I gave him a proud look and he laughed.

If I was nervous it was not of the horse; Pierre had put me up bareback on the farm horses as a child. But I had never learned to ride properly – not as a lady should – and it was this that Gérard meant to teach me.

'No, you're not,' he said, approving the way I held myself. 'You are a natural, Jenny. We shall be able to go riding together in no time. But you have to learn poise – keep your head up and your back straight. Remember you are a lady! When people look at you, they should be able to tell your quality from the way you sit your horse. That's better ... much better.'

After a while, he let go the leading rein and allowed me to take the horse myself, sending me round and round the field until he was satisfied. He was a hard taskmaster, and I was quite tired when he lifted me down.

'You've done well,' he said, his hands lingering about my waist for a moment. My heart raced as he smiled at me. 'Another lesson or two and we shall be able to ride in the park together.'

'Gérard...' My breath caught as I saw the look in his eyes. 'I...'

'What now, little one?' He saw I was flustered and touched my cheek. 'You are wondering about the dance, I suppose? Impatient Jenny. I shall arrange it, do not fret.'

I blushed and looked down. We both knew it was not the dance that had brought the fire to my cheeks.

'Henriette...' I spoke to her when we were alone in the parlour that same afternoon. 'Gérard said he thought you bought the riding habit you lent me in London?'

'Yes.' She looked at me in surprise. 'I went there with my parents when I was ten – and then again when I married at nineteen. Why do you ask?'

'You spoke of seeing me as a tiny baby. I wondered how you knew my mother – before she became a seamstress in Paris?'

'Did I say that?' There was an odd, guarded expression in her eyes. 'I meant when you were still only a few months old. If I said new-born I was mistaken. Of course I did not meet Adele until she came to Paris.'

I had the oddest feeling that she was lying – but why should she? If she had known my mother in London, why did she not just say so?

'Leo says there's an English fair come to the village,' Charles said as he came flying into the parlour where Henriette and I were sitting the following afternoon. 'May I go, Maman? Will you take me? Please take me!'

'I have told you not to listen to stable gossip,' Henriette said with a slight frown. She fanned herself languidly. 'It's too warm for such things, unless ... I suppose, as it is an English fair ... you might like to go, Jenny?'

'An English fair?' I looked at her curiously. 'I have never been to anything like that.'

'Then it's time you did.' We both turned at the sound of Gérard's voice. He was standing in the doorway, a teasing smile on his lips. 'It is a travelling fair, Jenny. They have performers from many countries, and they take their show all over Europe, but because the owner is English, we call it the English fair.' His eyes gleamed with mischief. 'If Henriette will permit, I shall take both you and Charles.'

Charles immediately demanded his mother give her permission, which of course Gérard had known he would. Henriette looked at me, arching her eyebrows.

'I shall go and put my hat on,' I said, and saw the satisfaction in Gérard's face.

I was amused as I ran upstairs to get ready. It seemed to me then that Gérard would always get his way somehow or other.

'Now – are you not glad you came?' Gérard's eyes mocked me as I gasped with delight at the scene that met my astonished gaze. The normally quiet village green had been transformed into a hive of activity. 'I knew you would like it, Jenny.'

Gaily painted swings and roundabouts were set up between stalls selling everything from sticky sweets to gingerbread men and hot pies. Charles was already running everywhere, demanding to go on all the rides in turn.

Gérard paid for him to ride on one of the smaller painted horses, and we watched as he shrilled his delight and tried to snatch the 'gold' ring without success.

After Charles had had enough of the

painted horses, we all went on the swings, then wandered round the side-shows, enjoying the excited atmosphere and the sunshine. There was so much to see: the fire-eater from Hungary, a troupe of tumblers and dancers from Russia, fierce-looking men who shouted wildly and did the most amazing things while a fiddler played faster and faster. There were clowns with sad faces, and a man on stilts, who walked through the crowd throwing little bags of sweets to the children.

Charles caught one, but after looking at the lurid-coloured sweets, Gérard said he thought they might not be suitable and bought the boy a bag of wholesome-looking fudge instead. Such arbitrary action would have brought cries of protest had either I or Henriette attempted it, but Charles seemed in awe of his uncle and accepted the change equitably.

'It amazes me how good he is with you,' I whispered and Gérard laughed.

'The little devil knows he can twist you and Henriette around his finger,' he said, 'but I am up to all his tricks.'

'Yes, I am sure you are.' I pulled a face at him and he grinned wickedly.

It was then that we saw the gypsy woman sitting outside her tent. She was wearing a full-skirted scarlet dress, a scarf around her long, black hair, and large gold earrings.

'Tell your fortune?' she offered, her dark eyes intent on me. 'It will bring good luck, lady. Show me your hand and I shall reveal mysteries to you.'

I shook my head and would have passed on, but Gérard gave me a push forward. 'Go on, Jenny,' he urged with a look of mischief. 'Let her tell your fortune. What harm can it do?'

I hesitated, then held my hand out reluctantly. She took hold of it, her skin dark beside mine, her long nails like yellow claws. She ran her finger over the lines in my hand, tracing them over and over. I felt strange, as if a cold chill had blown over my skin, and I would have withdrawn my hand had she not held on to it. She glanced up at me, an odd glow in her eyes.

'You do not belong where you are,' she said. 'Your destiny lies over the water, but before you reach the calm you must first pass through the storm. You will know grief and despair, but at the end of your journey is peace.'

I pulled my hand free, feeling a start of fear, and she gave a cackle of laughter. 'You'll fight your fate, my beauty, but you cannot avoid it.'

'That's because it lies with me, and she has no choice,' Gérard said, and dropped a gold coin into her hand. 'What does the future hold for me, old woman?' He was obviously amused and threw out the challenge as the knights of old might have thrown down their gauntlet.

Her eyes seemed to flame for a moment as she looked at him, then she shook her head. 'Your fate is in your own hands, sir. You will forge your own way. I cannot tell it.'

Gérard laughed, and pulled me away to a stall selling trinkets. He glanced at my face, grinning as he saw I was still looking uneasy.

'Take no notice of her,' he said. 'She says the same things to everyone. We all make our own lives, Jenny.'

'Yes, yes, of course we do.' I laughed at myself, shaking off my feeling of unease, and beckoned to Charles, who had run on ahead of us. 'Why don't we all go on the swings again?'

'In a moment,' Gérard said. 'I want to buy you something first – a keepsake.' He scanned the items the peddler was selling, then picked up a tiny pendant made of green stone. 'What about this? I think it must be jade.'

'It's very pretty,' I said, 'but I don't need anything, Gérard.'

'I'm going to buy it anyway,' he said, and turned to the stall-holder. I walked off to join Charles, who was watching one of the jugglers throw clubs into the air.

Gérard followed us a moment later. He pressed the jade pendant into my hand and when I looked at it properly, I saw it was fashioned in the shape of a heart.

'One day I'll have it set in gold so that you can hang it on a chain,' he said. 'But for the moment you can keep it to remind you of me.'

'Thank you,' I said. 'It is very pretty.'

There was no point in protesting further. I had come to realise that when Gérard made up his mind to something, he would not be swayed.

Nine

'I told you I would arrange it, didn't I?' Gérard's eyes sparked with mischief as looked at me in the garden one morning some days later. 'Father has written to give permission for the dance to be held next month, and he will come down himself a day or so earlier.'

The comte had returned to Paris the day after my mother's trunk had arrived. I had not seen him again after the brief interview during which he had given me her key, for he had been dining out that evening and had left early the next day. Nor had I yet found the courage to open Mama's writing-box again.

I had not attempted it since the morning Henriette had interrupted me. It was too painful, and I did not suppose, when I thought about it rationally, that I would find anything of real urgency there.

For the moment I had put aside my hopes of tracing Kate. If she had wanted to reach me, she could have done so long ago – and I had other things to occupy my mind for the moment.

Since the comte's departure, life at the château had become very quiet. Unless Gérard brought his friends we seldom had visitors, though Madame Testud and her daughter called to take tea with us occasionally.

Gérard was out almost every evening. Henriette said that his nights were spent with young men in drinking and gambling, and from her expression I gathered that she thought his companions wild and an unwelcome influence on him.

'He is young and must have his fun,' she said, 'but I think he drinks too much. He will burn himself out.'

It was unlike her to criticise him, and I thought it unjust. If Gérard drank to excess, he never did so when he was at home. I knew that he was often restless, and sometimes moody, but when he was with me he seemed to throw off his moods.

Most of my time these days was divided between Charles, Henriette and studying. Increasingly, though, Gérard would seek me out as I walked alone in the garden and I found myself living more and more for those precious, stolen moments, though I knew it was foolish to allow myself to dream.

When he told me about the dance, I was excited. I had never before attended a real dance, and I had suspected Gérard was only teasing me when he said he would arrange one for my sake.

'I am so looking forward to it,' I cried. 'But what shall I wear?'

'Father will send something from Paris,' he said, looking amused. 'You must be properly dressed for your first dance.'

'Oh, Gérard,' I said and slipped my arm through his. 'You are so good to do this for me. I can hardly wait!'

'A dance?' Henriette stared at me in dismay as I told her the news later that afternoon. 'Whatever was Gérard thinking of to suggest it – or Laurent to agree? Adele has not been dead more than three months. You cannot possibly attend, Jenny. You will be in mourning for at least another three months and should not be thinking of a dance for at least a month or two past that.'

'But...' My heart sank as I looked at her. 'You can't mean it? I've been in mourning ever since I came here, but I've still been meeting people. What difference could it make if I attended a dance? It would not mean that my grief for my dear mama was any the less – and she would not have wanted me to weep for her endlessly. All she ever wanted was for me to be happy.'

'A few of Laurent's oldest friends at a quiet dinner? That is different, my dear.' She shook her head, giving me a look of regret.

'I am so sorry to disappoint you, Jenny. Of course we shan't hold the dance at all – not until you can attend. I shall write to Laurent myself. I cannot imagine why he even considered it – he thought me wrong to go out in company even after nine months of seclusion following my husband's death.'

It had not occurred to me that it would be improper for me to attend a small country dance such as Gérard had planned before six months of mourning had passed. I was bitterly disappointed but once Henriette had made me aware of the impropriety, I accepted it.

Not so Gérard.

'That's so ridiculous!' he cried, annoyance flashing in his eyes. ' Henriette interferes too much. Father has given his permission. I shall insist on holding the dance.'

'You may do so if you wish – but I shall not attend. It would look as if I were uncaring, be an insult to my mother's memory. I know she would not mind, but others would misunderstand. It is too soon, Gérard. Henriette is right.'

'So you are to be miserable for months simply because of an outmoded convention?' He was angry and frustrated at being thwarted. 'Don't let them dictate to you, Jenny. Surely your mother would not have wanted you to be miserable? She would not have minded you having a little pleasure?'

'No, I am sure she would not,' I admitted. Laurent himself had told me that. 'But both Henriette and your mother—'

'I shall speak to Maman. She is the mistress here, not Henriette.'

'No! Please, Gérard. It doesn't matter. I don't want to cause trouble.'

He refused to listen. I watched unhappily as he strode off towards the west wing of the house. Gérard was so headstrong. He believed he could always have his own way, but this time it just was not possible.

It was not until that evening that I discovered what had happened. Henriette was waiting for me alone in the drawing room.

'Where is Gérard? I thought he was dining at home this evening?'

'He has gone off to stay with some friends.' She sighed and looked disapproving. 'I'm afraid he left in a temper. He demanded that his mother give her blessing to your presence at his dance and of course she would not.'

'Of course not. I tried to warn him but he refused to listen.'

'Gérard never listens to anyone.' Henriette frowned. 'I am surprised that Laurent gave his permission. He must surely have known it was impossible for you to attend.'

I agreed but believed I knew the answer. The comte had been prepared to forget the conventions in the hope of finding me a husband all the sooner. I was, after all, merely the daughter of a seamstress. He had clearly thought it would not matter if I flouted the rules of society by attending his son's dance.

Since he was in Paris and likely to remain there for some weeks neither Henriette nor anyone else could be certain of his opinion, but the comtesse made me very aware of hers.

She sent Flore to fetch me the morning after Gérard left the house in a temper. It was the first time I had been summoned to her apartments since Henriette had taken me there and I was nervous.

'You're to come at once,' Flore announced, a flicker of malice in her eyes as she saw my discomfort. 'Madame is angry with you. Very angry.'

My heart thumped with fright as I followed her along the dark, narrow passages, our shoes echoing on the marble floors. What had I done? Was I going to be sent away in disgrace?

The comtesse was seated in an upright chair by the window, dressed very formally in a dark green silk gown, her hair rolled into a coronet around her head. Despite the signs of illness in her face she looked regal and forbidding. An opened book lay on the table beside her, a piece of fine needlework

211

on her lap. As I entered she looked up, an expression of dislike in those penetrating eyes.

She was very much awake, not dulled and confused as she had been the morning I saw her walking in the walled garden.

'You are a wicked, ungrateful girl,' she said as soon as she saw me. She was clearly very angry. 'It is your fault that my son has gone off in one of his tempers. If anything happens ... if he quarrels with his father ... you will be to blame.'

I thought I saw a flash of something like fear in her eyes then, and wondered at it. She seemed more concerned for her son than angry with him – but what was she afraid of?

'I'm sorry if Gérard quarrelled with you, madame. I begged him not to – but he wouldn't listen.'

'Do you suppose he would listen to you? Gérard is like his father: he listens to no one. He is sorry for you.' Her eyes held both scorn and contempt. 'Do not imagine that he is in love with you. He will never marry a girl of your lowly order – scheme as you will, you will never marry Gérard. Do you hear me? It is out of the question. He is the son of the Comte de Arnay, and far above such as you!'

'I have not schemed, madame.'

'Do not answer me back!' She glared at

me. 'I should send you away at once. Laurent was a fool to bring you here.'

My head went up, pride bristling. 'I shall leave if I am not welcome here, madame.'

'Little fool!' She leaned towards me and I caught the sour odour of her body: she smelt of sickness and stale perfume. 'You cannot leave any more than I can send you away. My husband is your guardian – and the master of us all.' Her sharp, mirthless laugh made me jump back in fright. Her lined face was contorted with grief and hatred, yet somehow pitiful. 'Women babble of emancipation and the freedom to vote. What good will that do them, answer me that?'

'I – I'm not sure, madame.'

'Go to that *secretaire*,' she commanded, pointing at a tall piece of furniture with a glass cabinet and several drawers beneath, one of which could be pulled out to make a writing desk. 'In the bottom drawer you will find my tapestries. Bring them to me.'

I opened the drawer and saw a bundle of canvases; they were rolled over and over so that all I could see was the tangled web of colours on the backs. I took them back to her.

'Unroll them – lay them out on the table and then look and tell me what you think of my work.'

'Madame...' I looked at her uncertainly.

213

'Do as I say, girl!'

'Yes, madame.'

The tapestries were all worked in vivid shades of red, orange, gold and black and it soon became apparent that each one was of a woman being tortured or tormented in some way. Three of them depicted either saints or witches being burnt at the stake, another was of a woman being torn to pieces by wolves, another of a young girl being tormented by demons.

I felt an icy trickle down my spine. What had caused the comtesse to make such terrifying pictures? Why had she portrayed women as victims time and time again?

'They – they seem to all be part of a theme,' I said. 'I think they are a little frightening. Such terrible things are happening.'

'See how they treat us?' she demanded, her voice rising querulously. 'Women have always been the slaves of men ... throughout the ages. Violated, tortured ... tormented for their beauty and their sins. Sins that are forced upon them by the nature of men. Do you see it, girl?'

'Yes, madame. I see what you have done – but I don't understand.'

She gave a harsh laugh, her face twisting with scorn.

'You are young, naïve. You believe in love. You think that women have rights. I tell you they have none. All this talk of emancipation will not help them.' Something flickered in her eyes, though whether it was anger or fear I could not tell. 'Not until they have equality in all things. And that will never be. Not in my lifetime or yours. Perhaps never. Laws cannot control the beast that is man. They like to control, to manipulate us. If I had been free...' Her eyes glittered like ice for a moment and I sensed a deep resentment in her, even hatred; then she sat back and the intensity faded. She looked tired and old. Her hand clenched on the arm of her chair, thin fingers beringed with jewels. 'It's too late ... too late for me. Even if he were dead I should not be free. Only my death can release me from these chains.'

'Madame?' Her words had chilled me. Sitting there in her finery, chained to her rooms by ill health, she was like a magnificent bird of prey – caged and dying, wearied of life by her confinement. I sensed pain and bitterness festering inside her.

'Too late for me but not for my son ... He must not suffer because of ... Nothing else matters now.'

What did she mean? Why should Gérard suffer?

She seemed to me to be rambling in her mind. She was mistress of the château and obeyed in most things: she could have gone out into society had she wished and it was by her own choice that she stayed incarcerated in these stuffy rooms. Only when the comte was visiting did she have to defer to his wishes – so why did she stay here when she so obviously hated her life?

She had closed her eyes for a few moments; now she opened them and looked at me. Clearly too weary to continue her lecture, she waved her hand in dismissal.

'Remember what I have told you.'

'Yes, madame.'

I was thoughtful as I left her apartments. What *had* she been trying to tell me? Was she afraid of her husband? What had happened to her to make her the way she was?

She had a sharp, spiteful tongue, but somehow I was no longer as afraid of her as I had been. I pitied her for the waste of her life. Once she must have been young and full of hope – what had turned her into the bitter, twisted invalid she had become?

Had her illness affected her mind? No, I did not think so. It seemed to me that she was not mad but confused: she had been shut up alone in her rooms for far too long.

As I walked up to the nursery to find Charles, I had already dismissed her warning. Gérard was thoughtless and selfish, but I believed that he did care for me. All those pictures of martyred saints and witches being put to the torch meant nothing to me. What had such legends to do with my life?

Gérard had stormed out of the house after

his argument with his mother. I did not know where he had gone or for how long, but I was eager for his return.

It was a warm, sultry night. I lay sleepless, tossing and turning in my bed, thinking of what the comtesse had said to me. I had thought she would deny a marriage between her son and the daughter of a seamstress, because I was not of the right social standing ... but it was more than that. She had seemed to be warning me of something. What? What lay behind her cryptic words? Why did she weave those tapestries that told such vivid stories of the damned?

Remembering the morning I had seen her wandering about the garden in a state of distress, I wondered what had caused her such pain. Gérard had spoken of her unhappy life – and I knew that the comte had had a mistress in Paris for many years. Yet Henriette had said that the comtesse welcomed her husband's absence from her bed.

Unable to sleep, I rose from the bed and walked over to the window. Had her husband treated her cruelly? I knew that Laurent could be harsh and even Henriette, who loved him, had spoken of him as being a tyrant where Gérard was concerned.

It was a mystery.

★ ★ ★

I dreamed of my mother again that night. She came to me as I lay sleeping and I saw her standing at the foot of my bed, her eyes reproachful and sad.

'Mama,' I whimpered, reaching out to her. 'Mama ... I need you.'

I felt her lips touch my forehead, but she said nothing and when I woke there was no sense of her in the room. It was just a dream, nothing more.

The next morning I spoke to Henriette. I asked her why the comtesse should dislike me so much – and why she was so unhappy.

'You must not mind her ways, Jenny. It is not you she dislikes particularly. She is tired and ill – and sometimes says things she does not mean.'

Her eyes did not meet mine and I knew she was embarrassed, that she did not want to discuss this subject.

'She showed me her tapestries.'

'Did she? You thought them odd, I expect?'

'Yes ... a little. She seems so unhappy ... so bitter.'

'Do not ask me to tell you my cousin's secrets, Jenny, for I cannot. I know that she has been unhappy for a long time, and that her illness was brought on by an accident that happened long ago – but even I do not understand what has made her the way she

218

is in her mind.' Henriette looked at her sewing. 'Please try to forget what she said to you, Jenny. I am sure she did not really mean to upset you.'

I understood that Henriette was not prepared to tell me more. Whatever had happened to the comtesse was her secret and only she had the right to tell me, which of course she never would.

Why should she? I was only the daughter of a seamstress and she had never wanted me in her house.

What kind of hold had her husband over her that he could force her to accept me? Gérard had spoken of his father as being a tyrant, who rode roughshod over us all, regardless of our feelings. I had not really believed him, but the comtesse had made me wonder just what kind of a man my guardian was.

Gérard returned before the week was out. He apologised to everyone in his most charming manner, admitted he had been wrong, then told us he was going to Italy for a few months.

'Must you go?' I asked when we were alone in our favourite place in the rose gardens. 'It will seem so ... quiet ... here without you.'

I meant that I would miss him unbearably, but of course I could not say it so openly.

'It is for your sake as much as my own.'

'Why – what do you mean?' I gazed up at him in dismay. How could he think it was for my sake?

It was warm and the air was heavy with the perfume of flowers. A slight breeze had scattered petals everywhere and they lay like a carpet on the lawn. I gazed up at him, tears hovering on my lashes, my heart aching with the knowledge that he was so soon to leave us.

'Silly Jenny,' he said softly and bent to kiss my lips. 'You know why I must go – surely you know?'

I shook my head, feeling the sadness begin inside me. Did he not know that I would miss him? Did he not he know that my life would seem empty without him?

'Because I love you too much to stay.'

'Gérard,' I breathed shakily and a tingling sensation started deep down inside me. 'Please don't go. I love you.'

'Sweet Jenny.' He bent to kiss my lips. 'I must go, if only to protect your innocence. I shall come back in a few months; by the spring, anyway. You will be out of mourning by then and there will be none of this nonsense. I'll ask Father to give a dance for you on my return and we'll announce our engagement then.'

Announce our engagement? But he had said nothing of this to me! We had spoken of love and feelings, but this was a huge step. I was confused by conflicting emotions – pleasure and great happiness because he wanted to marry me, but also apprehension, because I knew that his parents would be against the marriage.

'But you know he will never agree. Nor will your mother. It is hopeless even to think of it, Gérard.'

I thought of my strange interview with the comtesse, and remembered her warnings. Had she been trying to tell me that I would suffer the torments of the damned if I allowed myself to love her son?

'I usually get my own way in the end – haven't you noticed?'

'Gérard!' I smiled through my tears. 'You won't find it easy to win them over this time – your mother or your father.'

'I shall have money of my own when I'm twenty-two – a legacy from my maternal grandfather. Neither of them will have the power to order my life then. If necessary I shall take you away.' He gazed down at me, his eyes dark with passion, more intensely blue than I had ever seen them. 'You do love me, Jenny? You do want to be my wife?'

'Of course I do, but—'

He hushed my protests with a kiss that left me breathless, my head spinning.

'You won't say anything yet, will you? Please, Gérard. Everyone will be against us.

I couldn't bear it if you were not here with me – they would all be so angry.'

'It would not be wise to say anything just yet,' he agreed, his eyes serious now as he looked into mine. 'But I wanted to tell you how I felt – because they may try to push you into marriage with someone else while I'm away. Promise you won't let them, Jenny. Promise me now!'

His look was so compelling, so thrilling. He was young and had so much energy and confidence. I felt that anything might be possible. No one could deny Gérard when he was set on a particular course. If he was determined we would marry then I believed it would happen, despite all opposition.

I gave my promise eagerly, willingly. I had thought I did not wish to marry, but that was before I had fallen hopelessly, helplessly into Gérard's trap. He had been determined that I should from the beginning, and he had had his way – how could I doubt that he would do so in the future?

'Oh, yes, yes,' I cried. 'I love you. Of course I want to be your wife. You won't stay away too long? Please, Gérard! Please say you will come back to me soon!'

'A few months,' he said, but his eyes were looking beyond me and I sensed that he was eager to be gone, restless. 'I can't stay. Not the way things are ... not even for you, Jenny.'

I clung to him as he kissed me, but I knew that he would go. Gérard had a wayward spirit, a little demon inside him that would not let him rest long in one place. He spoke of love and fidelity, but even when he held me close and kissed me passionately, there were vague shadows hovering near by.

Gérard loved me – but did he love me enough to come back and claim me despite all the opposition we would have to face?

Ten

'I am going to take you to Paris, my love. You have been sad recently, and I think it is time you had a little pleasure.'

I stared at Henriette in surprise when she made her announcement two weeks after Gérard's departure for Italy.

'But I am in mourning.'

'Yes, I know,' she said, 'but that is no reason for us to stay here all the time. I want to buy some new gowns, and I think you should have some too, Jenny. Black is so dreary. I think you could wear grey or even lilac occasionally.'

Only two weeks earlier she had been insisting that it was too soon for me to be seen at a dance, now she was suggesting that we should go to Paris. It seemed a little odd – unless she had had another reason for wanting the postponement of our dance?

I looked at her doubtfully. 'Will the comte permit it?' I asked. 'He will not be angry with us?'

Henriette shrugged her shoulders. 'If Laurent is cross I shall deal with him,' she said. 'Besides, you cannot stay here all the time. You should meet other people.'

Her eyes avoided mine and I wondered if this was a little ruse she had come up with of her own accord. I knew neither Henriette or the comtesse would approve of my marrying Gérard, and I suspected that they hoped to find me a husband before he returned from Italy.

I had no wish for any other husband, but despite all Gérard's promises, my common sense told me it was unlikely we would ever marry. Since I believed I would have to leave the château one day, I thought it might be wise to make some enquiries about finding a position for myself. I was not as clever with my needle as my mother had been, but I still thought it might be possible to find work as a governess.

In Paris I could contact my mother's friends. Perhaps Madame Leconte could help me? It might be that one of my mother's clients would be prepared to offer a place in their household to Madame Heron's daughter.

Our days at the château were so quiet, that it was almost as if time stood still, but in Paris I was suddenly alive again. In the busy streets with the flower-sellers, the press of carriages, delivery vans and an occasional sight of the new horseless carriages, which sometimes made strange bangs with their engines and sent out little clouds of unpleasant-smelling smoke, I felt as if I had woken after a long sleep.

I had wondered if it would be unbearably painful to be in Paris again, but with Henriette I was to see a different, more sophisticated city. My mother had taken me to sites of historical interest, to museums and art galleries – but my friend had no interest in such places.

With Henriette, I visited all the more fashionable shops in the Avenue Montaigne and the Rue Faubourg St-Honore, and the best restaurants. We went to the theatre and the opera, and I asked her if perhaps we might one day visit the Moulin Rouge.

'Maman promised we would go one day, when I came to live here with her.'

Henriette raised her brows, a twinkle in her eye. 'Did she indeed? I have not been there since before the trouble with the students.'

'The trouble with the students?' I frowned at her: there was often trouble with the students of Paris.

'Surely you remember? It was three years ago. The Bal de Quat'z Arts got a little out of hand. Some of the artists' models participated in a striptease contest.'

'Oh, yes, of course!' I laughed. 'I do remember, now. The matter was investigated and one of the girls imprisoned, wasn't she? That's why the students were so angry.' They had set up barriers and protested against the government for three days. The windows of St Germain church had been broken and two students had been killed.

Henriette nodded and shrugged her shoulders. 'It is always so with the people of Paris, Jenny – they will make their feelings known no matter what the cost.'

We were approaching the establishment of Monsieur Worth, and the subject of a possible visit to the Moulin Rouge was dropped as we entered the premises.

'Jean-Philippe has taken over the business with his brother Gaston,' Henriette informed me in a low voice. 'Some say he is an even better designer than his father – who you must know died some four years ago – but I am not so sure. I have one particular gown that Monsieur Charles designed for me himself when I married. It is heavily beaded on the bodice and the work is exquisite; it is still my favourite gown despite being so old now.'

'I am sure I shall find something I like,' I replied. 'I do not think I could afford to have a gown created just for me. But I shall be more than happy with something from the rails.'

'It is a pity,' Henriette said with a sigh, 'but I dare say you are right, my love. See, here is

227

a pretty tea-gown that would suit you very well...'

We spent several happy hours looking at the gowns, finally buying two tea-gowns and a morning dress, which were to be delivered to the comte's house later that day.

After leaving the shop, I stopped to buy a newspaper from a stand. I was reading the headlines, amongst which was the second trial of Dreyfus, who was still considered guilty of treason but had been pardoned because of new evidence, when something made me turn and glance at a woman approaching the stand. For a moment we stared at each other, then she turned and walked away very quickly.

'Wait!' I called out to her, but was obliged to pay for my paper and unable to follow immediately. 'Kate – please wait!'

As soon as I had given my money to the newsagent, I rushed after her without waiting for change. He shouted to alert me, but I could not have cared less about the coins owing to me. I could see Kate a few yards ahead of me, disappearing into a side street, and I started to run – but as I did so, a man came out of a shop and bumped straight into me.

I almost fell but he caught my arm, steadying me. I glanced up to thank him, trying to detach myself in my haste to follow my friend, but he held on to me determinedly.

'Please allow me to pass,' I said, without really looking at him. 'I am sorry for knocking into you, monsieur, but I was trying to catch up with a friend.'

'Jenni,' he said, staring at me intently. His grip tightened on my arm. 'It is Jenni Heron, isn't it?'

'Yes, but who—' The question died on my lips as I looked at him properly. 'Marc?'

'Marc Bruge,' he confirmed, his smile widening. 'This is wonderful, Jenni ... to meet so unexpectedly. How are you? I was sorry to hear your mother had died. I would have written to you, but I was away at the time and no one seemed to know where you were.'

Henriette had arrived by this time. She looked a little annoyed at having to chase after me. 'What on earth was wrong with you?' she said. 'Why did you run off like that?'

'I saw a friend – a school friend.'

'Where is she?' Henriette frowned. 'And who is this young man?'

Marc tipped his hat to her, giving her an engaging smile. 'Forgive me, madame. I bumped into Jenni and stopped her following her friend, then I discovered that we knew each other. I am Marc Bruge – Madame Heron and my mother were friends.'

'Oh, I see.' Henriette was regarding him in

a different light now. I could see the interest in her face. She shook hands with him and smiled, at her most charming. 'Monsieur Bruge. How pleasant to meet one of Adele's friends. You must take tea with us one afternoon; we are here for another two days. We should both like that – shouldn't we, Jenny?'

I was forced to smile and agree. 'Yes, of course.'

'Tomorrow is my afternoon off,' he said. 'I am working now, as a journalist for *Le Morceau.*'

He had named a magazine which I had heard of and knew specialised in writing about famous – or rather infamous – people, and was known for its scandal-mongering.

Henriette frowned over that, but did not rescind her invitation. Instead, she gave him our address and made a firm arrangement for the following afternoon.

After we had left him, she looked at me curiously. 'Who was the friend you thought you saw, Jenny?'

'Her name is Kate – Kate Blake. Her brother called at the château to see me some weeks ago; do you remember?'

'Yes, of course. Why did she not stop when you called to her?'

'She couldn't have seen me,' I said, not meeting Henriette's enquiring gaze. 'We lost touch with each other when she left the school and I have not heard from her since then. I wanted to ask her to come and see me one day.'

'It was unfortunate that she did not hear you,' Henriette said. 'But, never mind, my love – you have found another friend.'

She was so obviously pleased to have arranged another meeting for me with Marc that I could not tell her I did not particularly like the young man. I suspected she thought it was an opportunity for me to become acquainted with a man of my own station. Marc was well educated, attractive and, although she might not approve of the magazine he worked for, she thought it a good sign that he had found such a position.

He was clearly enterprising and personable – and in Henriette's mind a candidate for marriage.

The comte's house was set in a quiet, exclusive area on the outskirts of the city. It was furnished in the Empire style, which had been so fashionable some years earlier, and was rather lavish, with lots of gilt, velvet drapes and paintings by Fragonard, Daubigny, Jean-Marc Nattier and others of the same rather romantic school.

I was sitting the next morning by the window of a parlour overlooking pleasant gardens at the rear, when the comte entered. He saw me with an open book on my lap and came over to sit next to me on the little sofa.

'What are you reading, Jenny?'

'Cyrano de Bergerac.'

'Where did you get this?' He picked it up and flicked through the pages with a frown.

'Gérard lent it to me before he left.'

'Ah, I see.' He nodded and returned the book to me. His eyes were thoughtful, but he seemed in a good humour, not in the least like the tyrant Gérard had named him. 'Henriette tells me you have invited a friend for tea this afternoon?'

'Yes ... at least, Henriette invited him.'

'And how do you know this young man?'

'We met at my mother's house.'

'And do you particularly like Monsieur Bruge?' His smile was pleasant, the enquiry indulgent.

'I hardly know him, sir.'

'But you would like to get to know him better?' His eyes were intent on my face. He seemed anxious to hear my answer – as if he were truly concerned for my happiness.

'I don't know – perhaps.'

'Well, we shall see,' he said. 'There is no hurry for you to marry after all. In a few months you will no longer be in mourning. I shall give a dance for you, introduce you to my friends – many of them have sons of near your age, Jenny. Do not be in a hurry to form an attachment before then.'

What had Henriette been telling him? I could not say I was uninterested in Marc Bruge without making her appear foolish, so I remained silent. The comte gave me another penetrating look, then nodded as if to confirm his own thoughts, got to his feet and left the room without another word.

The book no longer held any interest for me. I could not concentrate after such an odd conversation, and I decided I would go for a walk. Henriette was having fittings for a special evening gown that morning and I could please myself: this was my chance to visit Madame Leconte and ask her if she could put me in touch with any of my mother's clients.

'It is lovely to see you,' said Madame Leconte, embracing me warmly as I was shown into her front parlour. 'Come in, come in, Jeanette.' She indicated that I should sit, then asked the maid to bring coffee and cakes.

'I do hope it is not inconvenient,' I said. 'I ought to have written, but I wasn't sure when I could come.'

'If it had been this afternoon, I should have been out,' she said, 'but this morning is quite free.' Her eyes moved over me, taking in the pale grey, rather smart gown I was wearing. 'How are you now?'

'A little better, thank you. I still miss her

terribly, but...'

She nodded in sympathy. 'Of course, of course – but you are a little more able to cope now, I think?'

I agreed that I was, then told her why I had come to see her.

'The comte and Madame Rossi are very kind,' I said, 'but there may come a time when I shall have to leave the château.'

'You can always come here,' she assured me at once. 'My home is always open to you. And should you need to find work, I may be able to help you. I do not know the names and addresses of your mother's clients – but you may find them amongst her things. However, I have worked in many of the good houses of Paris, Jenny. Before I married, I was a hairdresser and I used to go to the homes of my clients to dress their hair for a party. I could make a few enquiries, discover if there is likely to be a position you could fill.'

'I thought I might be a governess,' I said. 'Or perhaps a lady's maid?'

'If you were willing to consider something like that, I am sure I could help you.' She looked at me a little doubtfully. 'But Adele wanted much more than that for you, Jenny. She often spoke of her hopes for you – that you would make a good marriage. Do you not think you should stay at the château?'

I could not meet her kind gaze, nor could

I explain why I might find it necessary to look for work.

'It was just in case I needed to find a position,' I said, blushing slightly. She nodded, but her eyes were thoughtful as they dwelled on me.

'You are very pretty,' she said. 'Not in the way your mother was – but you are still a very attractive young girl. I can understand that you might want to make your own life, and I am always here if you need me.'

I thanked her and asked if she had seen Marie recently. She said that they met occasionally in the market, and then she surprised me by asking if I had heard from a young Englishwoman who had come to her house asking for Madame Heron.

'I told her why the house had been let to strangers,' she explained, 'and I offered to give her your direction, Jeanette – but she seemed very distressed to learn of Adele's death and went away without it.'

'An Englishwoman?' I looked at her eagerly. 'Did she tell you her name?'

'No, she merely said she knew Adele – why?' Madame Leconte looked at me curiously. 'Do you think you might know her?'

'I was hoping it might be Kate,' I said. 'She was my friend – but my mother helped her once when she was in trouble.'

Madame Leconte nodded. 'Adele helped a lot of young women in trouble. She was very generous with her money, and her time.'

Her words brought tears to my eyes. She saw it and changed the subject, talking instead of a cabaret at one of the café concerts in Montmartre, to which her nephew and his wife had taken her recently. It had been a little risqué, and rowdy, with some noisy youths in the cheap seats throwing cherry pips and orange peel at the rest of the audience.

'It was amusing, but some of the young men were rather drunk,' she said with a frown. 'I saw Marc Bruge with them. I do not imagine his mother would approve.'

'No, I do not suppose she would.'

I did not tell her that Marc was coming to tea that afternoon, but I was thoughtful after I left her and walked home a little later. Somehow I was not surprised at what she had told me, and it confirmed my own opinion of him.

Marc was on his best behaviour that afternoon, however. He was dressed very elegantly in what looked like an expensive suit of pale grey, his waistcoat a slightly darker silk and striped, a gold watch hanging importantly on a chain across his chest. He could have been a young gentleman of fortune, and I thought his work as a journalist must pay well, for I did not imagine he had very much in the way of private means.

We had been talking for some minutes

when the comte entered. Marc stood up at once, and I saw Laurent's eyes assessing him, but it was impossible to read his thoughts. He was very polite, very correct in his manner.

'I am glad you could come,' he said. 'It is good that Jenny has friends to visit her.' His gaze narrowed. 'So – tell me what you do for a living, Monsieur Bruge.'

For the next ten minutes, he subjected Marc to a searching questionnaire, probing into his life and his prospects with a thoroughness which made me squirm. Marc turned pink and looked most uncomfortable, as if he wished to escape.

'So,' Laurent said, seeming satisfied at last. 'You have an interesting career ahead of you, monsieur. I wish you well.' He stood up, shook hands with Marc, then smiled at me and left the room.

Henriette got up at once and followed him.

'Is he always like that with your friends?' Marc raised his brows at me. 'I feel as if I have been grilled by the secret police.'

I was embarrassed. 'I am sorry. I do not know why he did that – it was not necessary.'

'Perhaps he wanted to make sure I was suitable for you to know?'

'Perhaps – but it was wrong of him. I wish he hadn't done it.'

'You have no need to be embarrassed; I'm not.' Marc grinned at me. 'I don't suppose I fit in with what your family thinks is right for you. I probably shouldn't be here – but it was so good to run into you like that, Jenni.' He realised what he had said and laughed. 'No, I didn't mean it quite that way. I hope I didn't hurt you yesterday?'

'It was my fault. I was in a hurry. I wasn't looking where I was going, I'm afraid.'

'No, you weren't.' He looked at me thoughtfully. 'Did you find your friend?'

'No. She had disappeared by the time we left you. Besides, I'm not sure she wanted me to catch up with her.'

'That sounds intriguing. Tell me more,' he invited. 'I have lots of contacts in Paris. If you're looking for a missing person, I might be able to help. Have you thought of placing an advertisement?'

'No, I hadn't thought of that,' I said, wondering about the possibility. 'The thing is ... Kate might not read French papers.'

'Kate – is she English?'

'Yes.' I hesitated, reluctant to tell him more. If Kate was avoiding me, she might have good reason – and this man worked for a magazine whose journalists liked to write about people's private lives. 'We were friends at school, but I don't think I should advertise. I don't think Kate would like that.'

He looked as if he were going to try to persuade me, but Henriette came back into the room at that moment and the subject was changed. A few minutes later, Marc took his leave.

'I should like to see you again one day,' he said. 'Perhaps when you are next in Paris.'

'I am not sure when that will be.'

'If you have time off from your work you could come down to the château and visit with Jenny for the afternoon,' Henriette offered. 'I am sure you would be most welcome, wouldn't he, my love?'

I murmured something that might have been agreement, and Marc bowed over her hand and kissed mine.

Henriette smiled at me as he went out, a sparkle in her eyes.

'So, my love, you have made a conquest – no?'

'No, of course I haven't. He is just a friend of my mother's. I hardly know him.'

'But he likes you.' She nodded, looking pleased with herself. 'If he is willing to come again – after what Laurent put him through – then he likes you very much, Jenny.'

I thought it best not to argue. It was unlikely that Marc would bother to come down to the Loire Valley. He had friends in Paris, and from what Madame Leconte had told me, liked to enjoy himself at the more risqué cafés. He had come to tea because he was curious, but he would not bother to visit me at the château.

However, when I thought about his idea to advertise for Kate it occurred to me that it might just work. I had seen her near a newspaper stand which sold papers from England; they were usually a few days old by the time they reached the stands, but it would be one way for Kate to keep in touch with her home, to know what was going on in her own country. I could place an advertisement in a shop near the newspaper seller in the hope that Kate might see it.

But why was she still living in Paris? I would have expected her to return home long ago.

Eleven

I was wrong to suppose that Marc would forget me. His first visit to the château was three weeks later, and to my surprise he told me that he had begun to make a few enquiries concerning Kate's whereabouts.

'But how do you know her name?' I asked, looking at him suspiciously.

'I asked Madame Rossi and she told me. Besides, I saw the advertisement you placed in the window of that shop. I often buy a paper there in the mornings and I noticed it at once.'

I was annoyed with Henriette for telling him Kate's name without first consulting me, and with myself for having placed the advertisement, which had so far brought no response.

'I did not ask you to make enquiries on my behalf.'

Marc stared at me oddly, his eyes narrowed. 'You are afraid I shall discover some scandal about her and write a report for the magazine, aren't you?'

My cheeks flushed. 'Kate would hate that.

You must promise me you won't, Marc – whatever you discover!'

He laughed, seeming amused. 'She isn't famous enough, Jenni. The magazine wouldn't be interested – unless she's done something very wicked?'

'Of course she hasn't!' I glared at him. 'If you do anything to harm her, I shall never forgive you.'

'Do not be angry with me, Jenni,' he said. 'I only wanted to help you find your friend.'

'I'm sorry.' I realised I was being unfair. 'Perhaps I misjudged you ... but I am so fond of Kate.'

'Then I shall try to find her.' He smiled ruefully. 'Besides, it will give me an excuse for visiting you, Jenni.'

I did not answer. I would have liked to stop him coming to the château, but if he could help me to find Kate ... Besides, if Henriette imagined I had a follower, she might forget about trying to find me a husband.

I had promised Gérard that I would not be persuaded into marriage while he was away, but it would not hurt if Henriette and the comtesse thought otherwise for the moment.

Over the next few months, Marc visited the château on at least four occasions. Since it would have been rude of me to send him away without offering him refreshment, I

242

was obliged to entertain him to tea in the small front parlour.

He came ostensibly to bring me reports of Kate. He had actually traced her once to a small pension, a lodging house in a rather dilapidated area of the city, but when he returned to see her, she had paid her bill and left in a hurry.

'She must have been frightened to hear there was someone looking for her,' I said. 'You must not do so any more, Marc. If Kate does not wish to be found, we should respect that and not look for her.'

He agreed, but the gleam in his eyes warned me that he was not prepared to let it go. He was curious because Kate had run away, and now he wanted to discover the truth for himself.

The long months of Gérard's absence were hard to bear, and yet they were also a time of healing, as my grief for my mother became softer and I was able to remember the warm affection between us, the blessings of being her daughter. Sometimes, I was tempted to open her writing-box, to read the letters and documents I had glimpsed inside, but somehow I never did. It was easier just to leave things as they were and wait.

I missed Gérard and I longed for a letter from him, which never came, but I was growing accustomed to my situation, accepting that the past was gone and I must look to the future.

Sometimes I took out the tiny jade heart he had bought for me at the fair, holding it in my hand as I remembered the gypsy's warning that my destiny did not lie here in France. Gérard had laughed and dismissed it as nonsense, but I had never quite forgotten the look in her eyes ... as if she were warning me of something.

Gérard's mother had warned me, too.

I had not seen the comtesse since the day she'd sent for me to show me her tapestries. Henriette told me she was getting weaker and I sensed that she was worried for her cousin. I felt sorry for the comtesse, but it was her own choice to remain cloistered in her apartments.

Occasionally, I wondered why she had chosen to retire from normal life, why she had become so bitter and twisted in her view of life. It was not my business to pry, however, and though I sensed there was some mystery – some tragedy – here, I dismissed the comtesse from my mind as my own life resumed its pleasant routine.

Usually, I spent my days playing with Charles, teaching him a few words of English, telling him historical stories, careful always to disguise the lessons as a game.

Henriette was pleased with his progress.

'He is much calmer now. You are so good with him, Jenny,' she said. 'You will make a fine mother one day.'

We had become close companions, spending as much time together as we could, though she was often with her cousin. The comtesse refused to venture from her apartments even when her husband gave Christmas parties for his friends.

For the four days Laurent stayed with us the château was filled with guests. Lots of greenery was brought in from the gardens, as well as expensive garlands tied with gold ribbons and flowers sent from an exclusive florist in Paris. There were presents and festive meals, and the comte had engaged the services of musicians who played for us in the evenings after dinner. All at once, the big house seemed to come alive with laughter and voices.

And yet the comtesse stayed in her rooms the whole time.

When I asked Henriette why she did not join us, she frowned and said that her cousin was not well enough to leave her apartments.

Once or twice, I saw the comte coming from her part of the house, so I knew he visited her, but he had not forced her to join his guests, so he must have accepted her illness as genuine this time.

I had noticed something different in the

comte's manner towards me. He smiled more often, his voice soft, almost caressing, when he spoke to me, and he made a point of drawing me forward when we had company, keeping me at his side as his friends arrived.

'This is my ward, Jenny,' he would say. 'Such a sweet, charming girl. Henriette adores her. I scarcely know how we shall bring ourselves to part with her when she marries.'

Yet I had noticed that whenever I was in conversation with one of the gentlemen, he watched me with an intent air that made me vaguely uneasy. What was behind those looks he sometimes gave me? What was he thinking?

Sometimes I felt that he struggled against strong emotions in my presence. There was a look of despair about him at times, a wistfulness that disturbed me. Almost as if ... he saw me as a desirable woman ... a woman he desired but could never have.

No, no, that was foolish! I was ashamed of such thoughts, which surely sprang from vanity. The comte was not attracted to me in that way. Of course he wasn't! If he seemed to watch me, it must be because he hoped I would show an interest in one of his friends. He wanted to find me a husband and relinquish the burden of his guardianship into the hands of another.

I was foolish to feel uncomfortable in his presence. Foolish to feel threatened ... afraid of this intensity about him. And yet I could not help remembering those tapestries, the comtesse's bitterness. Something terrible must surely have happened to her at some time in the past to make her the way she was ... something her husband had done, perhaps?

When he chose, Laurent could be charming, generous and good company – but charm sometimes hid a violent nature. Was there something in his nature that had caused his wife to fear him?

I could not help my thoughts, but I often berated myself for them. I was wrong to imagine such things. I had no real reason to believe him unkind to his wife, nor should I fear him myself. He meant me no harm. He wanted only to find me a suitable husband.

I had met no one I would have wished to marry even if my heart had not belonged to Gérard. The men who visited the château were mostly of a similar age to my guardian, though some brought their sons occasionally. Sometimes I caught admiring glances from the younger men, but I kept myself deliberately aloof and, perhaps because I was still in mourning, none of them had so far pressed their attentions on me.

The comte returned to Paris before the new year. On the morning of his departure he sought me out in the small front parlour, which was where I usually sat when alone.

'Jenny.' He smiled at me. 'I thought I might find you here. Reading again, I see. You study too much. You are too young ... too pretty to waste your life. It is a pleasant day. You should be out walking, taking the air. It is not good to sit indoors too long.'

'I shall walk for an hour or so this afternoon. I always take Charles into the gardens in the afternoons.'

He knew that, of course. It had become a habit that never wavered.

'I came to say goodbye – and to give you this.'

His eyes were brooding and thoughtful as he held out a small black velvet box. I hesitated uncertainly.

'You gave me a Christmas gift, sir.'

'Writing paper and money.' He dismissed my protest with a careless shrug. What did that odd expression in his eyes mean? I found it disturbing. 'You have a birthday soon, and I shall not be here. I wanted you to have this now. Please take it, Jenny.'

I took the box. Our fingers touched and he flinched as though he had been stung. Opening the box, I gasped as I saw the thick gold bangle with a heart-shaped clasp studded with pearls and rose diamonds. It was so like the pendant my mother had given me when I first went to the convent school that they might have been part of a matching set.

'It is beautiful.'

'I had it made to match your pendant.'

'Thank you. I shall always treasure it.'

He nodded, looking pleased. As our eyes met and held I felt something pass between us and sensed that he was struggling with some emotion deep inside him.

'Jenny...' He cleared his throat. I thought he would speak but instead he reached out to stroke my cheek with his fingertips. 'So like her and yet so different.'

I was silent. There was an underlying tension beneath the surface. I felt a strong, dark force in him, then he moved away to stare out of the window.

'I leave for Paris almost at once,' he said, his back towards me. 'I shall not return until the spring. Gérard will be home then. We shall have a splendid ball. You will meet a man who stirs your heart. You will marry.' Slowly, he turned to face me. 'You will be married this summer, Jenny. It will all be as Adele wished.' Then he walked past me and out of the room.

I was trembling. I could no longer doubt that my guardian felt some deep emotion for me and it frightened me. He had barely controlled his desire, if desire it was. Yet what else could it be? Surely not love? There were too many years between us.

Gérard loved me. He intended that we should marry when he returned in the spring. I longed for him to come home, and yet I feared that moment when we must confess our love. From the beginning I had sensed a bitter resentment between father and son – and I was afraid of what might happen if Gérard saw his father look at me with such a desperate hunger in his eyes.

It was almost spring. I could feel the change in the air; there was a new warmth, and with it a feeling of anticipation in my heart. Surely Gérard would return soon?

Henriette looked at me as I came down the stairs that morning. She smiled and held a letter out to me, an expectant, triumphant expression in her eyes.

'This has just arrived for you, Jenny.'

'For me?' My heart raced with excitement. 'Is it from Italy?'

'You mean from Gérard?' Henriette's forehead wrinkled. 'No, it is not from him, Jenny. I should be very surprised if it was. Gérard never writes to anyone. This has come from Paris by special delivery. I would imagine it is from Marc.'

'Oh.' I took it from her hand and slipped it into my pocket. It was almost two months since Marc's last visit and I had hoped he might have grown tired of what even he must see was a futile pursuit.

'Do you not wish to read it?' She looked disappointed when I shrugged my shoulders. 'Well, no doubt you will do so later.'

She obviously thought it was a love-letter. I said nothing to make her think differently.

'I thought I would go for a walk – unless you need me?'

'Charles is with his nurse,' she said, 'and I must go to Béatrix. She is not well today.'

'Then I shall see you later.'

We parted and I went into the gardens, seeking solitude in my favourite rose arbour. The roses were in bud, but would not bloom for a while yet.

I sat for several minutes, enjoying the warmth of the sun and thinking. Soon Gérard would come home – and what would happen then? Would he still want to marry me? It seemed so long ago that he had kissed me and told me he loved me. For months I had looked for a letter, but he had never once written.

All at once, I remembered Marc's letter and took it out. Reading it swiftly, I discovered that my fears had been well founded. Marc had seen a woman at a political meeting and he thought it was Kate. 'It was one of those Women's Suffrage meetings,' he wrote.

She made a speech – her accent sounded English – and though she did not
use her own name, I believe it was your
friend. She slipped away before I could
get to her afterwards, but I have a lead
now and—

'What are you reading?'

Gérard's voice spoke from behind me. I
was so startled that I jumped and dropped
the letter, swinging round to face him.

'Gérard – is it really you?' I could hardly
breathe. He was just the same, his eyes as
blue as ever, his skin slightly darker from the
Italian sun. 'You have come home at last.'

'Did you think I never would?' He smiled
as if amused, then bent to retrieve the paper
I had dropped. 'What is this – a love-letter?'
His smile was fading. 'Is this from your
lover? Henriette has told me about him.'

'It is from Marc,' I said and saw the glint
of anger in his eyes. 'But he is not my lover,
Gérard. You must know that? You may read
the letter if you wish.'

He did so but his expression did not
lighten as he returned it to me. 'Who is Kate
Blake?'

'I've talked about her, Gérard. You must
remember? She was my special friend at
school. Her brother came here looking for
her once.'

He nodded, his eyes intent on my face. 'If

you wanted to find her, why did you not ask me? I would have employed professional agents to search for her.'

'I did not know where to start. It was only when Henriette took me to Paris that I discovered she was still in France. I would have asked you then – if you had been here.'

He looked at me then, eyes brooding, angry. 'You hate me for going away. That is why you have found a new lover.'

'No, that's not true!' My head went up, my eyes clashing with his. 'I do not hate you, Gérard. Why do you accuse me of such a thing? You know I could never hate you. Besides, as I have already told you, Marc is not my lover – he is a friend, no more. Please believe me. You know I would not betray you with someone else – you must know it?'

'But you are angry with me. I can see it in your eyes.'

'I hoped you would write to me, Gérard.' I could feel the sting of tears but would not let them fall. 'You have been away so long.'

'Too long, I see.' He glared at me, then turned on his heel and walked away.

I stared after him, unable to believe what had happened. Gérard had come home at last, but we had quarrelled. Tears were running silently down my cheeks, but I made no attempt to wipe them away.

How foolish I had been to allow Marc to

visit me! I cared nothing for him, but Gérard was convinced he was my lover.

When I had my emotions under control, I returned to the house. There was no sign of Gérard. I looked for him everywhere without success. It was later, when I went to collect Charles from the nursery, that I discovered the truth.

'Uncle Gérard came home,' Charles announced, scowling at me. 'Now he has gone away again.'

'Gone away – where?'

'To Paris,' Charles said importantly. 'He told me, but it is a secret. I am not to tell Maman.'

'What are you not to tell me, my love?' Henriette asked, coming in at that moment.

Charles looked at her, his mouth set stubbornly. 'It's a secret.'

'Gérard was here – but he has gone to Paris,' I said, my throat tight with emotion as I struggled to contain my disappointment.

'That wretched boy!' declared Henriette, frowning. 'Béatrix wanted to see him. He spent only five minutes with her. He is so thoughtless. She will have one of her headaches again – and it will be Gérard's fault.'

'Perhaps he will return soon...'

I prayed that he would. This parting was even harder to bear than the last, because we had quarrelled.

'Uncle Gérard promised to bring me a present,' Charles piped up, his bright eyes fixed on me. 'He said he might bring you one too, Jenni – but I'm not to tell you because it is to be a surprise.'

Henriette's gaze narrowed as she looked at me. 'Are you quite well, Jenny? You look flushed.'

'I am well, thank you.' I avoided her penetrating gaze. I did not want to tell her I had quarrelled with Gérard, because I suspected she might have meant it to happen. She and the comtesse were both determined that I should not marry Gérard, it seemed.

I had believed Henriette my friend, and it hurt me to think that she had worked against me. I knew I was not Gérard's equal in birth or fortune, but if we loved each other ... My thoughts came to an abrupt halt.

Did Gérard love me? I had thought so, but now I could not be certain. He had sworn he cared for me, but he had left me for months without a word – and now we had quarrelled.

Charles was demanding that I take him to sail his boat. I gave in to his demands, trying to forget the ache in my heart.

It was foolish to feel so miserable. I had always known that a marriage between us was unlikely. There was no point in weeping. I must try to think about the future –

about what I would do if I left the château and my guardian's protection.

'Laurent has written to me,' Henriette announced a few days later when I came in from the gardens, a basket of cut flowers on my arm. I was planning to arrange the blooms in the main parlour. 'He intends to visit us next week. He says it is time we made plans for your future, Jenny. He has asked for your measurements. New gowns will be made for you at Worth's – and there will be a dance in your honour soon.'

'It is very generous of the comte, but—'

'Laurent considers that he stands in place of a father to you, Jenny. He was your mother's friend for many years, as you know. I dare say he feels obliged to arrange a good marriage for you.' She frowned. 'It seems he does not think Marc Bruge suitable. He asks that you discourage any further visits from that young man.'

'I did not encourage them.'

'No.' Henriette had the grace to look slightly ashamed. 'I admit that was my fault, but I thought ... but no matter! Laurent has made his wishes clear. He will not accept an offer from Marc Bruge. He looks higher for you, Jenny.'

'I am grateful for his concern.'

I did not add that I would prefer to make my own decisions, because the comte's letter had given me hope. He would not allow me to make an unworthy marriage. If he thought so highly of me ... it was just possible that he would give his consent to a match between Gérard and I.

But I was not sure that Gérard wanted to marry me any more.

'Go to Roseanne now, Charles.' I gave him a little push towards his nurse, then turned back towards the rose arbour with a sigh. Why did I always come here when I felt sad?

It was a warm afternoon. I knew I ought to go in and change for the evening, but somehow I sat on, breathing in the soft scents of early summer and dreaming.

'What secrets are you scheming now?'

I turned as I heard Gérard's voice. He was smiling as he came towards me and my pulse raced with excitement. *This* was the man who had captured my foolish heart.

'I was thinking of you,' I said truthfully. 'Wishing you were here with me.'

'Have you forgiven me?'

'Yes, of course – there was nothing to forgive.'

'I quarrelled with you,' he said, eyes bright with mischief. 'I was jealous, my Jenny. I thought you had forgotten me – taken a new lover because I went away.'

'How could you be so foolish?' I gazed up

into his eyes. 'You know I love you – only you.'

'Do you?' He moved closer to me. I felt breathless, my head whirling. I stood up, and then he reached out for me, drawing me into his arms. 'I pray you do, Jenny – because I do not think I could live without you, my love.'

'Oh, Gérard,' I sighed and lifted my face for his kiss.

It was so tender, yet so passionate that I came near to swooning. I clung to him, winding my arms about his neck as I gave myself up to the magic of that moment. All the doubt and misery of the past few months dissolved in the warmth of his embrace, and I knew that I was truly happy.

'I love you, Gérard.'

'And I adore you, my Jenny.' He smiled and touched my cheek with his fingertips. I was surprised at the expression in his eyes, the hunger and tenderness I saw there. 'And now, my love, I have a surprise for you.'

'A surprise?'

He nodded, an air of triumph about him as he stepped away from me and made a signal. I watched in bewilderment, and then, as a woman moved out from the shelter of some bushes, I gasped with shock.

'Kate!' I cried in disbelief. 'Oh, Kate.'

She looked much the same, a little older perhaps, thinner in the face – and her gown was of poor quality material, cheaply made. But what did that matter? She was my friend and she was here! Gérard had found her for me.

She came to join us, an odd, self-conscious expression in her eyes. 'Hello, Jenny. I wasn't sure you would want to see me – but Gérard said you have been looking for me.'

'Oh, Kate!' I said again and went forward, my arms opening to embrace her. 'Of course I want to see you. Of course I do. I am so very pleased you have come.'

'Are you?' She was still uncertain as she returned my hug. 'You might not be when you've heard my story.'

'My mother gave me your letter a few months before she died. I am so sorry I did not know at the time, Kate. I would have helped you then if I could.'

'Your mother was wonderful to me,' Kate said with a sad smile. 'I was very sorry to hear that she had died, Jenny.'

'Yes.' I took her hand as we sat on the wooden bench together, then glanced up at Gérard. He nodded, then turned away, leaving us alone to talk in private. 'I was devastated when it happened – but it doesn't hurt quite as much now. I still miss her – I always shall – but I don't wake up crying now.'

'Poor Jenny.' Kate squeezed my hand. 'I

know how you feel.'

'Yes; you lost your mother just before you came to the school.'

We held hands for a moment in silence.

'I hear you've joined the Women's Suffrage Movement, Kate?'

'You wonder why I have taken up the cause for *féminisme*?'

I shook my head. 'You were always sure of your ideas, your beliefs. It's just that I know so little about it.'

'Women in France were deliberately excluded when the bill which provided for universal manhood suffrage was brought in in the forties, and that provoked a small group of Parisian women into forming a committee for women's rights.'

'Yes, I do recall being taught something of that – but do you think the men of France will ever accept the idea? Women have been excluded from succession to the throne since the late sixteenth century, remember – and in France powerful women have never been liked. You have only to remember Catherine de Medici.'

'And Jeanne d'Arc,' Kate said, grimacing. 'After what she did for France, the way she was treated was disgraceful – but like her we shall not abandon our beliefs, no matter the cost. You have only to read *L'Emancipation de la Femme en Dix Livraisons* to know that the Cause is deeply enshrined in the hearts of women such as Julie-Victorie Daubie.'

'And you have a champion in Hubertine Auclert, do you not?'

'You should read some of our material,' Kate said. 'You should read *La Citoyenne*.'

'Yes, I shall,' I promised her. 'But now – tell me about you, Kate. How did Gérard find you? A friend of mine has been trying for months without success.'

'Because I did not wish for Marc Bruge to find me.' She gave me a rueful look. 'It was through the Movement that Gérard got to me. I am exceedingly careful, but he attended one of our meetings, and was enthusiastic about our cause. He asked questions about me – and my friends thought him so charming, they told him where I would be speaking the next evening.' She smiled, glancing in the direction he had taken. 'I like him, Jenny – much better than the other one. *He* is the kind of man I most dislike.'

'Marc Bruge?' I nodded, understanding why she should feel that. He must remind her of Richard Havers: they had the same over-confident manner, the same way of looking at a woman. 'I do not like him very much either. I did not ask him to find you, Kate – it was his own idea – but I did place a card in a shop window, near the newspaper stand where we almost bumped into each other.'

'I'm sorry I ran away that day,' Kate said, fiddling with a fold in her skirt. 'It was so sudden, seeing you like that. I couldn't face you. I was afraid of what you might say.'

'Because you ran away with Mr Havers?'

'You warned me not to trust him but I wouldn't listen.' Her cheeks were pink. 'It was partly my brother's fault. He forbade me to see Richard again – and that was completely the wrong thing to do. I can never bear to be told what I may or may not do, you know that, Jenny. If Thomas had agreed to an engagement, I might have discovered what a rogue Richard really was before it was too late.'

'You must know I would not condemn you for that? I know you loved Mr Havers.'

'You do not know ... what I was forced to do after he left me.' Kate could not look at me as her fingers moved restlessly on her gown. I took her hand in mine and pressed it. 'He had already sold all my jewellery. I had no money. I was desperate.' She brought her eyes up to meet mine and I saw both pain and shame reflected there. 'You may despise me for it, Jenny – but I went with other men. I picked them up in the street like a whore and was treated like a whore by them. I would probably have been a prostitute for the rest of my life if it hadn't been for Adele. She was an angel. She gave me money, made me feel whole again.'

'I know. She told me what she had done – but not until long afterwards.' I held Kate's hand very tightly. 'I am glad she helped you, but I wish it could have been me. I wish I had been able to talk to you, to tell you that I cared for you – and always shall.'

'You still want to know me – after what I've just told you?'

'Of course. I care for you, Kate. We were friends – almost sisters. I want to be your friend again.'

Kate leaned forward and kissed my cheek. 'Thank you, Jenny. Gérard said you would understand. He persuaded me to come here.'

'He is very persuasive.'

Gérard had done in a few days what Marc had not been able to accomplish in months, but it did not surprise me. There was something about Gérard, an irresistible force that meant he did not allow anything to stand in his way. He wanted to find Kate for me and he had; it could not have been any other way.

'Yes.' Kate laughed. 'You are very lucky to have found him, Jenny. He loves you very much.'

'Yes, I think he does.' I blushed. 'How did he find you? Did Marc tell him where to look?'

'Your lover is very resourceful,' Kate said. 'He came to the meeting where I was speaking, and he persuaded one of the other women to arrange for him to talk to me. I refused and tried to slip out the back way, but he was waiting outside and he insisted on walking me home. It took him three days to talk me into coming here – but as you see, I have.'

'Yes.' I smiled at her fondly. 'I can hardly believe it. I've thought of you so often – wondered if we would ever meet again. Hoped we would be together one day, share our lives.'

'If you really mean that...' I nodded and Kate pleated the material of her skirt again. 'I have a child, Jenny. Her name is Louise. I leave her with a woman I trust when I'm working for the movement, but I'm hoping to spend more time with her when I can.'

'Oh, Kate!' I looked at her in awe. She had been through so much, and yet she had kept her child near her. 'You are so brave.'

'For keeping my daughter? She is all I have, Jenny – all I shall ever have. I could not bear to part with her.'

'You might marry one day.'

She shook her head, her eyes distant and full of memories. There was at that moment a bitter twist to her mouth, and I heard the anger in her voice as she said, 'Gérard told me my brother has been here?'

'Yes; he came before he went out to Italy to take up a post there. He asked me if I knew where you were.'

'You didn't tell him anything?'

'No. He asked if I would write to his solicitors if I discovered your whereabouts. He wants to give you your own money, Kate. He seemed genuinely upset. I told him my first loyalty was to you.'

'Thank you.' Kate's expression was hard, unforgiving. 'I do not want to see him – but I shall take the money. I need it for Louise. If my brother truly wants to help me, he can have the income paid into a bank in Paris.'

'I will write to his lawyers,' I promised, looking at her sadly. 'Can you not forgive him, Kate? I am sure he would accept you and your child.'

'No. Please do not ask it of me, Jenny. I would rather leave the past as the past.'

'As you wish.' I took her hand again. 'I do understand, Kate. I just want you to be happy.'

'Happy?' She met my eyes, then smiled oddly. 'It may seem strange, but in a way I am happy. I have Louise. I am independent. I have my work, which means a great deal to me – and now I have you.' She gave me a shy, hesitant look. 'May I bring Louise to visit you sometimes?'

'Of course. I should love to meet her, Kate.'

Kate's story of what had happened to her after her lover deserted her was shocking. I understood now why she had asked my mother to conceal it from me, why she had not wanted to be found – but it made no difference to the way I felt about her, to my love for her. If anything, it made me respect her more for her strength. She had fallen as far as any woman could, but she had taken the chance Mama had given her, and now she was living her life as she wanted, proud, respectable, standing up for the cause she had always believed in.

Although I did not put my thoughts into words, Kate read them in my face. She smiled and kissed me.

'Thank you,' she said. 'I shall bring Louise soon.'

We both looked up as Gérard approached. 'Henriette has been out into the garden looking for you, Jenny. And I must see Kate safely on her way.'

'I am going to England,' Kate said. 'I have been asked to speak in London.'

'Isn't that dangerous? I've read that the English police are arresting the suffragettes – imprisoning them.'

'I've already been in prison for demonstrating once.' Kate pulled a wry face. 'It was awful. They forced us to eat by means of stuffing tubes down our throats.' She laughed harshly. 'That's another reason I didn't want to be found – I struck a policeman six months ago. They are probably waiting to pounce on me again.'

'You shouldn't go back, Kate.'

'It will probably be for the last time.' She shook her head at my concerned look, a smile on her lips. 'You worry too much, Jenny. I shall be back before you know it. I never leave Louise for long.'

'And you will bring her to see me soon?' I looked at her anxiously. 'You won't change your mind and disappear again?'

'No, I shall not do that. And I will bring Louise to visit you, as soon as I return,' she promised.

'I will see you tomorrow, Jenny,' Gérard said, and the look in his eyes was a caress. 'Stop looking so serious, my love. Kate has told you – she will be fine.'

I watched as they walked away together, laughing, Kate gazing up at him, and I thought how much alike they were – my best friend and the man I loved. Both were reckless, headstrong, heedless of their own safety – and irresistible.

It was little wonder that in their own ways, both had captured my heart.

Twelve

'I hope you meant it when you said you were not interested in Marc Bruge,' Gérard said, a glint of steel in his eyes. 'Because I have told him he will not be welcome here again.'

At that moment, Gérard was very much the young aristocrat, very much the master here.

We had been riding but now we were walking, leading our horses as we talked. The air was warm, sweet with the scents of newly mown grass from the meadow, and high above us a song-thrush trilled its joy of life from the branches of a cherry tree.

'Oh, Gérard,' I said, faintly reproving. 'That was not kind of you.' I laughed as I saw the flash in his eyes. 'But I am glad you did. It is perhaps unkind of me, but I was never comfortable in his company. I do not really like him. His hands are always moist – and he looks at me as if he saw me with no clothes on.'

'Oh, Jenny!' Gérard's eyes lit with a wicked amusement. 'I have always loved your honesty. It can be devastating – and so very English, my love.'

I pulled a face at him. 'Mock me if you will. I have never been back to England since my mother brought me to France – how can I seem English to you?'

'It must be your ancestors coming out in you.' He arched his brows. 'Do you really know nothing of your family – of your father's people?'

'My mother would never speak of them,' I said, frowning. 'I wanted to ask many times, but it always upset her. I think perhaps there must have been a quarrel.' I gazed up at him. 'Perhaps one day I shall go to England and find them.'

'I shall take you there,' he said decisively. 'When we are married. We shall look for your family together.'

'Oh, Gérard,' I whispered as he leaned towards me. My heart was racing and I was waiting for his kiss, which was soft and gentle, his mouth barely touching mine. When I looked at him, he shook his head and looked rueful. 'Gérard?'

'You do not know how you tempt me, my Jenny. I want you so much ... so very much.'

My cheeks were warm but I did not draw my eyes from his. 'I love you,' I whispered, and he understood what I was saying, what I was offering.

'We should be patient for a little longer.'

'How much longer?' I asked. 'Supposing your father will not agree to a marriage between us?'

Gérard hushed me with a kiss, a kiss that left me feeling weak and helpless. 'If he refuses, we shall go away,' he said. 'I shall never give you up, Jenny. Believe me, I shall never give you up ... but for the moment we must be patient. Father will be here soon, and then I shall speak to him.'

'Jenny ... Jenny!' I heard Henriette calling to me the next morning as I walked back from the stream, a basket filled with wild flowers over my arm. 'Where have you been?'

'There's Maman,' Charles cried and ran towards her. 'We've been picking flowers to press in a book and Jenni is going to tell me what they are so we can write the names down...'

Charles stopped as he realised she was not listening. I saw a letter in her hand and sensed that something was wrong.

'What is it? What has happened?'

The letter is from a Monsieur Bartoli. Your old teacher, I think? Before you went to the sisters?'

'Tante Marthe!' I was filled with a name-less fear. 'Her husband cannot write more than his name. She must be ill if he asked Monsieur Bartoli to write to me.'

'It was marked urgent,' Henriette said,

handing me the letter. 'I opened it. I hope you do not mind? They have asked that you go at once. Marthe has had a severe chill and they fear it may have turned to pneumonia. She wants to see you.'

'I shall go immediately.' My throat tightened. 'My poor, dear Marthe. She was always so good to me. I should have gone to see her before this ... soon after Mama died.' I looked around, wanting Gérard, needing him. 'Gérard ... have you told him?'

'He went out early this morning,' she replied. 'To see a friend, I believe.' Her look was disapproving. 'You are not the only one to ask for him, Jenny. His mother is far from well. She needs him here with her.'

'Yes, of course. But you will tell him where I've gone?'

'Naturally. As soon as he comes in. Now go and get ready, Jenny. We shall send you in the carriage,' Henriette said, looking at me with sympathy. 'I would come with you if I could, but –'

'You cannot leave Béatrix, I know.' I managed to smile at her. 'Don't worry. I can go alone.'

'The coachman will look after you. You could take one of the maids if you wish?'

'Marthe's home is just a small farmhouse. A maid would only be in the way when I get there. No, Henriette. I can manage – but I must leave at once.'

I was upset as I went upstairs to prepare for the journey. I wanted Gérard, needed him with me, needed the comfort of his love and support. Marthe was as dear to me as my own mother had been, and if anything happened to her it would break my heart. Gérard's own mother needed him here, however, and I had no right to expect him to desert her for me.

It was a long, fretful journey, and it had been dark for two hours or more before I finally arrived at the farm. Pierre was looking out for us and had the door open the moment I was out of the carriage.

'Oh, Pierre.' I caught his work-roughened hands, gazing at him anxiously. 'I came as soon as your letter reached me. How is she?'

'Asking for you.' His face was creased with worry. 'I wouldn't have troubled you, Jeanette – but she just keeps on repeating your name over and over again.'

'You did right to send for me. I'm sorry, Pierre. I should have come before this.'

His expression was slightly accusing though he made no comment. Obviously he felt that I had neglected Marthe in favour of my new friends.

'It wasn't easy at first...'

Even as I spoke I knew it was a weak excuse. I had been confused and vulnerable at the start when the comte had insisted on taking me to his home, but for many months now I had been free to visit my old friends. Laurent would not have stopped me had I asked his permission. I had stayed on at the château in the hope of Gérard's return, and since then I had thought of no one but him. Now I was stung by remorse and regret.

'Go up and see her, Jeanette. I'll help your coachman to see to his horses and find him somewhere to sleep the night.'

I needed no further bidding. My heart was beating frantically as I ran up the stairs, taking them two at a time in my haste. I loved Marthe so very much. If she died I should never forgive myself for having neglected her all these months.

She was lying with her eyes closed when I entered the bedroom, which was lit only by a shaded lamp on her bedside table. I felt a stab of fear as I saw how weary she looked, but at that moment she opened her eyes, holding out her hand with a smile of welcome as she saw me.

'My precious child,' she said and there was only love in her face, not one hint of reproach or accusation. 'My own lovely girl. I knew you would come to me.'

'Oh, Marthe,' I whispered, a lump in my throat. 'Forgive me for not coming sooner.'

'Hush, child,' she said as my tears spilled over. 'There's nothing to forgive. You've written now and then when you could – it was enough. But I should not want to die without seeing you once more, my love.'

'You won't die! You mustn't! I love you too much.'

I sat on the edge of the bed and held her hand tightly. As I looked down at her beloved face I was filled with a fierce determination. All my life she had cared for me devotedly. She would not die: I would not let her!

Marthe did not die, though she lay close to it for several days. During those dark, terrifying hours when we never knew whether she would see another dawn I would not leave her, except when Pierre took my place for a while.

During this time I hardly thought of Gérard, except to wonder now and then if he was thinking of me. I longed for him, but I knew his mother was ill, and that he would need to be with her as I needed to be with Marthe. Sometimes I wondered if perhaps this parting was a sign, a warning that we were not meant to be together.

And then Marthe began to improve.

I shall never know whether it was my determination to bring her through, our prayers, or Marthe's own courage that worked what everyone declared to be a true miracle. I only know that the day came at last when she began to eat the nourishing broth her neighbours had made for her, sipping a little from the spoon I held to her mouth. Just a little ... then a little more ... swallowing with difficulty. Then she began to ask what was going on outside and who had called to ask after her. Little by little her strength began to return and then, one morning when she sat up and told me I looked worn out and should go to bed, I knew she would be completely well again.

'Oh, Marthe,' I cried, tears of joy stinging my eyes. 'Oh, Marthe, I do love you so.'

'Foolish child,' she chided. 'You've worn yourself out over an old woman.' But she clung to my hand as she slept the first truly peaceful sleep since her illness began.

The next day she was a little stronger, and the day after that the colour began to come back to her face. Soon she began to fret over lying in bed all day.

'I should be up and helping Pierre,' she told me. 'And you should go back to your friends, Jeanette.'

'I'll stay a few more days.' I hushed her with a kiss. 'Pierre can manage. Everyone has been so good, bringing food, helping with the chores. All we want is for you to get really well. The doctor says you must rest for a little longer.'

I smiled as I looked across to the door at Pierre. He had seen how much I loved her and he had forgiven me. The faint air of accusation had left his eyes and we were friends once more.

'You should go out for a while,' he said as I took the water Marthe had used for washing downstairs to empty it in the big stone sink under the kitchen window. 'We don't want you going down with a fever. You've done more than could be expected of anyone.'

'Perhaps I will go for a walk.' I darted a kiss at his cheek and he blushed bright red. 'Marthe is going to come downstairs for a while later, but I shall be back before then.'

'Away with you!' He gave me a little push. 'Take as long as you like. It's too good a day to waste inside.'

I spent an hour or so walking in the fields; there was a shimmering heat haze where they sloped towards the river, sunbeams dancing on water like silver confetti. I wandered past the vineyards, the fresh green of young shoots and red earth a feast of colour that made me stand and stare, then on past the schoolmaster's house. It seemed such a long time ago that Monsieur Bartoli had seen me kissing André Bertrand. I wondered what my life would have been like if he hadn't – would I be married to a local man by now, already expecting my first child perhaps?

My life would have been so different. I should never have gone to the convent school ... never been taken to live at my guardian's château ... never met Gérard.

'Jenny...' I was startled out of my reverie as I heard the man's voice calling to me and spun round in disbelief. 'Jenny! Where have you been? I've been looking for you everywhere.'

'Gérard?' I felt a surge of delight as I saw him walking towards me through the long grass. He had come to me at last, and as I saw him my doubts were all forgotten. 'Oh, Gérard.' I started to run and he spurted to catch me, sweeping me off my feet and swinging me round, making my head whirl, making me laugh. 'I thought you would not be able to come ... How is your mother? Is she better?'

'She is as well as she ever will be,' he said, and there was a strange brooding expression in his eyes. 'You may think her a selfish, demanding woman, Jenny – but you do not know what has made her the way she is.'

'Oh, no.' I denied his accusation because I knew he was hurt. 'I believe she is very unhappy and unhappy people say things they don't mean...'

'My sweet little Jenny – how innocent and forgiving you are.'

I saw that he was distressed by his thoughts and, slipping my hand into his, I asked if he would like to tell me what was on his mind.

'Perhaps it would be best if you understood,' he said. 'Let's sit for a while by the stream, Jenny – and I will tell you.' His face was shadowed by deeply felt grief for his mother, and it drew me to him, making me want to share whatever was causing him pain.

We found a dry spot on the grassy bank of the stream. Gérard took off his coat and spread it on the ground for us to sit on. For a moment he was silent, seeming to watch a mother duck with her brood of young swimming near the reed beds. I waited, sensing that this was difficult for him.

'When my mother was a young woman, a year or so older than you are now,' he said at last, 'she fell in love with a man some years older than her. He was a relative, a distant cousin.'

I looked at him curiously as he hesitated, but said nothing.

'His name was Maurice and he was very handsome, quite wealthy – but wild and dissolute.' Gérard's eyes narrowed, became distant, cold as ice. 'She loved him in silence for some years, refusing offers of marriage from other men. And then at last Maurice noticed her. He seduced her, promised her marriage ... then he lost most of his fortune at the gaming tables and went away without telling her. Her father said she must marry before it was too late – and when the Comte

278

de Arnay asked her, she accepted him.'

'That is a sad story,' I said, looking at Gérard. A little nerve was flicking in his throat and I could see he was feeling some strong emotion. 'So she never loved your father?'

'No, not at first ... that came later.' Gérard's eyes darkened with anger. 'On their wedding night he discovered that she was not a virgin and he was furious. He accused her of being a whore. He threw her from their bed, forced her to her knees and raged at her until she wept and swore that she had never lain with another man before him.'

'And did he believe her?'

'She does not know for certain. He fetched a bible to her and made her swear on it. She had often ridden astride her horse as a young girl and she told him it had made her bleed once, that her hymen had been ruptured, and he accepted her word. Or he pretended to ... but he was suspicious, unkind to her, sometimes not speaking to her for days – and then he would apologise, ask her to forgive him and for a time they would go on together as though nothing had happened. He began to go away for long periods and would return without warning, hoping to catch her with a lover.'

'Oh, how awful that must have been for her,' I said. I pictured the scene, what Béatrix's life must have been like ... and I understood why she had come to hate and fear her husband.

'Despite all his cruelty to her, all his suspicions and moods, she had begun to care for him,' Gérard said. 'And he wanted an heir, and his religion would not allow him to seek a divorce. He visited her bed when he was at the château ... and eventually I was born. After that, he stayed in Paris most of the time, and then, a year or so later, she learned that he had a mistress whom he loved.'

'How that must have hurt her.'

'Yes.' Gérard's expression was sombre. 'She was lonely ... so lonely. And then Maurice came back. He started visiting her at the château, and he brought her gifts, he made her laugh...'

'And she was lonely.' I understood just how she must have felt. Her husband was unkind to her; he had a mistress and he did not love her. Maurice must have seemed like an answer to her prayers.

Gérard nodded. 'She resisted for a long time. She did not want to betray my father. She cared for him ... but Maurice was so charming and in the end she lay with him.'

He paused and I sensed the depth of his emotion as I waited for him to continue his story.

'The comte came home unexpectedly. He found them in bed together.'

'Oh, no!' I stared at Gérard in horror. 'What did he do?'

'He took a whip to her lover, beat him half to death. I think he would have killed him if the servants had not held him off.' Gérard's eyes darkened with pain. 'She thought he would kill her, too, and she wanted to die. But when he came to her later that day, he was utterly cold. He said that he would not divorce her, but that they would never live as man and wife again ... and he told her he would disown me, cut me off without a penny, if she ever went with her lover again. He said that I was not his son.'

'Oh, Gérard.' I felt the ice trickle down my spine and I understood that inner resentment I had sensed in Gérard when the comte was mentioned, the bleak look that sometimes came to his face when he was deep in thought. It was no wonder that he called his father a tyrant. 'That was so cruel.'

'She begged him on her knees to believe that I was his son, promised to do anything he asked of her. He would not listen. And so that night she tried to drown herself in the stream – but he was watching and he dragged her out. He carried her back to the château and he sent for the doctor. She was ill for a long time, and though she recovered, her health was always poor after that.'

'And since then she has lived most of her

281

life in seclusion.' I stared at Gérard in shock, feeling his pain, the pain he carried for his mother's hurt and his father's rejection.

'It would have been better if he had let her live alone, or allowed her to retreat to a nunnery, but he would not – he forced her to entertain his guests when he came to the château, to go on being his wife, if only in name. It was his way of punishing her. She has lived with the dread of his disowning me ... and her suffering has all been for my sake.'

'I am so sorry,' I whispered, taking his hand in mine, raising it to my cheek and holding it there. 'So sorry, my love.'

Gérard seemed to come back from the dark place in which he had been lost for a moment. He sat looking at me, his face full of tenderness and love.

'So now you understand why I do not want to hurt her,' he said. 'She has been against our marriage. She has not told me why, but I have been talking to her, telling her how loving you are – she will come to accept you, Jenny, and to love you. I promise.'

'I would not want to hurt her.'

'Nor I – but you are my love, my heart, my life. Nothing shall part us, I promise you.'

'Oh, Gérard.' My heart caught as I saw the look in his eyes. I saw the love, the need and the hunger, and I began to understand him as I never had before. I had sensed something, but until now I could not have guessed at the terrible shadows that lay hidden in the past. I understood the doubts and the pride, and the resentment – the restlessness inside him. And the hurt that made him throw up a defence of mockery against the world. It was little wonder that he felt the need to rebel against his circumstances, the wonder was that his nature had not become bitter and twisted. 'I love you, want you...'

The shadows in his face were for the moment banished by my words, and his eyes were suddenly alight with wicked laughter as he held me, gazing down at me for a long, heart-stopping moment before drawing me closer and kissing me fiercely.

'My sweet Jenny,' he whispered, holding me crushed against him as if he would never again let me go. 'I love you so!'

I melted against him, feeling the heat of desire wash over me. I had grown up that day on the bank of the stream, and I understood the throbbing need in him, a need reflected in my own body.

'Someone will see us,' I said, glancing over my shoulder as I remembered my first kiss and the trouble it had caused. 'Come, Gérard. I know where we can go to be alone.'

'My beautiful, passionate Jenny.' His tone

was light and teasing but I sensed the passion deep inside him, the intense longing and wanting that matched my own. 'I've thought of you every moment ... every night ... especially at night.'

I took his hand, smiling, leading him to my own secret place in the hayloft, the warm nest I had so often hidden away in as a child. We should be safe there. Pierre would not come. He was in the house with Marthe. No one would disturb us.

I went first up the ladder and Gérard came after. For a moment we stood in the loft gazing into each other's eyes. He seemed to be searching, asking, and the answer was there for him: this feeling between us was too strong to be denied.

As Gérard reached for me I went willingly into his arms, giving myself up to his thirsting desire without fear or reserve. What we were doing might flout the rules and conventions of society, but we were driven by a need that was older than the petty restrictions others would force on us. We loved and saw no wrong in the consummation of that love: it was good, sweet and natural between us.

Our kisses served only to fan the flames of raw desire. Gérard carried me down to a bed of soft, dry hay and lay beside me. His hands caressed and stroked, but we were impatient and eager, swept on by an urgent, aching need. As he thrust himself inside me I gave a cry of pain and for a moment he stilled, looking at me anxiously. I took his head between my hands and kissed him, pushing my tongue inside his mouth. Then we were straining to meet each other, gasping, panting in a frenzy of rushing desire.

Afterwards, we lay still in the hay, holding each other close, whispering of our love. Slowly, desire mounted once more. Gérard made love to me again, taking more time, bringing me to a fluid acceptance of his urgent loving, rousing us both to a new level of pleasure and sweet togetherness.

It was late in the afternoon before we had drunk our fill of each other. Neither of us wanted to leave our love nest, but I knew that Pierre would soon come to fetch hay for the beasts.

'We must go in, Gérard,' I said as he pulled me to my feet and began to pick pieces of hay from my hair. 'They will start to worry if I am not back by dark.'

'I meant to take you home at once,' he said and smiled at me in such a way that my heart began to beat wildly. 'But I think we should stay here another day or so. It will not be so easy to be together like this at the château.'

The burning look he gave me brought the colour to my cheeks. I had not thought beyond the moment when I gave myself in love, but now I was remembering all the obstacles that lay between us.

I had a strong premonition of danger ... of something dark and evil hanging over our lives ... but then I saw the hot glow of my lover's eyes and I forgot everything except this feeling between us.

'Marthe should rest for another day or so...'

'Then you must stay. I can find a room at the inn.'

I nodded, smiling as he climbed down the ladder first and gave me his hand to help me at the bottom.

'Come,' he said. 'Let's go and tell your friends I shall be staying for a while.'

Thirteen

Marthe and Pierre fell instantly under Gérard's spell. He set out to charm them, and when they saw his loving manner towards me, there was no question of their holding back. They were simple people, generous and loving, and very dear to me.

'He is a nice young man, kind and caring,' Marthe told me after he'd left us to seek a bed at the inn for the night. 'And very fond of you, my love. I can see it in his eyes when he looks at you.'

'We are in love,' I said. There was no need to lie to her. She wanted only what was best for me, my happiness. 'Gérard has asked me to marry him – and I've said I will.'

There was just the faintest hint of anxiety in her face as she said, 'Will the comte and comtesse agree to the marriage? Are they aware of your feelings for each other?'

'I don't know if they will agree... perhaps not at first. I do not think the comtesse likes me very much. But Gérard is determined we shall marry, and he usually gets his own way.'

I remembered Gérard's promise, and the passion in his eyes as he vowed nothing would ever part us.

'I should not like to see you hurt, Jenny. Your mother...' Marthe hesitated, shaking her head as I questioned with my eyes. 'No, I can't be sure – it's not for me to say. Adele always went her own way.'

'What do you mean?'

'I think she may have been hoping for something like this when she asked the comte to be your guardian ... for a marriage to someone of his rank. She was forced to work for her living, but she was not born to it. She was determined that your life would be easier than hers.'

I felt a flicker of hope. If my mother had spoken to the comte of her wishes ... Perhaps Gérard's father had intended to encourage the match when he took me to his home. Perhaps all my fears were merely shadows in my mind.

'Mama often spoke of another kind of life for me,' I said, remembering. 'I thought it was just dreams – but now I wonder if this was what she meant.'

'We shall never know just what was in her mind.' Marthe sighed and I saw sadness in her eyes. 'I still miss her, even though her visits were rare these past years. But we shan't dwell on the past, child. As long as you are happy, that's all that matters to me.'

I hugged her, feeling a little guilty at deceiving her about my reasons for staying a few more days. I knew she was well enough to manage now, but I wanted at least one more afternoon alone in the hayloft with Gérard.

We stayed another three days, and each afternoon we sneaked off to our secret place to spend a few stolen, delicious hours in each other's arms. We were not disturbed, but as we left the loft that last afternoon Pierre saw us and I knew we must go.

'Pierre will guess if we stay any longer,' I said. 'We should leave tomorrow, Gérard.'

'Yes, we must go back,' he agreed, looking at me with regret. 'I wish we need never go back to the château at all. Why don't we run away and get married? We could live in Italy...'

There was such passion in his eyes, such a hungry, yearning need.

'Oh, Gérard,' I said and reached up to trace the line of his cheek with my finger-tips. He caught my hand and turned it to kiss the palm. 'I wish we could – but we ought to tell your parents the truth. We should give them the chance to accept the way we feel about each other.'

'You won't let them part us?' His eyes were so intense, such a deep blue, as they dwelled on my face. I sensed that he was experiencing some deep emotion. 'I have this fear ... it is stupid, I know, but ... I'm afraid that I shall lose you.'

'If your parents refuse us their permission we shall elope, just as you said,' I promised. It was odd. I had always felt that Gérard was so strong and sure, but now I was comforting him, giving him courage. 'Nothing will part us, my love. When will you speak to your father?'

'He has arranged a dance for next week,' Gérard said, looking thoughtful. 'We won't say anything to anyone until he comes down for that, then I'll tell him. It will be easier for you if he is there. He has always said that he wants me to settle down and manage the estates, well now I shall – if he gives us his blessing.'

'Oh, Gérard' – I reached up to kiss him – 'surely he will not deny us? It is his wish that I should marry soon.'

'Maman will not be easy to win over,' Gérard said and once again there was a dark, brooding look on his face. 'But in time she will realise that I am not going to change my mind.'

He saw the anxiety in my expression and smiled.

'Don't look like that, Jenny,' he said and touched my hair, drawing it through his fingers and curling the ends over my shoulder. 'No one can stop us marrying. You were twenty on your last birthday, and I have come into my own money. Even if we have to wait for another year –'

'Don't!' I pressed my fingers to his lips as a sudden chill went down my spine. 'We must ask for their blessing – but nothing will stop us being together, because we love each other – don't we?'

'Of course we do. Stop worrying, Jenny.'

His teasing smile was back, the dark shadows banished from his eyes. Once again he was the conquering hero who refused to be denied. He reached out for me, sure and demanding. I responded by letting him take me into his arms to kiss me once more. Yet even as he held me, a little voice in my head was warning of the storms ahead.

'You look wonderful,' Henriette said as I pirouetted for her benefit in my room the evening of our special dance. 'Laurent has such good taste: that gown fits perfectly and is exactly right for you.'

I gazed at my reflection in the long cheval-glass. The dress was pale green and had masses of silk in the full skirts, but the bodice fitted snugly into my waist and the sleeves were short and puffed, a swathe of tulle softening the rather daring dip of the neckline.

Without the tulle it would have been a little too sophisticated for an unmarried girl to wear at her first dance, but as it was it looked young and fresh – quite perfect. Laurent had chosen well.

'It was so kind of Laurent to have it made for me,' I said. 'I think it far more stylish than anything I could have had made locally.'

'You can wear your pendant and bracelet,' Henriette said, giving me a look I found difficult to interpret. 'But you need some earrings. The gold drops Gérard brought you from Italy won't look right. I shall see if I can find something suitable for you to borrow.'

I nodded happily, unconcerned whether or not my earrings matched the pendant. Gérard had given them to me and I intended to wear them whatever Henriette thought.

'Why are you smiling like that?' she asked in an amused tone. 'You've been walking around with your head in the clouds for days. What are you dreaming about, Jenny?'

I was tempted to tell her. I liked her and I'd found it difficult to keep my secret from her, but I knew I must wait a little longer. Laurent had come home that afternoon. Gérard would speak to him soon and then ... everyone would know our intentions.

'I shall tell you soon,' I said. 'It's a secret, Henriette. I can't say more just yet.'

'Jenny?' She looked at me uncertainly.

'You're not – you haven't become involved with Gérard, have you?'

A coldness crept over me as I saw the way she was staring at me in disbelief, even horror. Why? Why was she so shocked by the idea of a love affair between Gérard and I? It might be against his mother's wishes but surely Henriette could not feel the same way?

'Why shouldn't I?' My head went up proudly. 'I know the comtesse doesn't like me, but—'

'That has nothing to do with it. If it were only my cousin's disapproval ... oh, Jenny ... Jenny...' Henriette seemed as if she wanted to say more but decided against it. 'We must go downstairs. The guests will be arriving soon.'

I was puzzled by her manner, but we were only just in time to greet the first of the guests and I had no time to dwell on Henriette's strange look. Before long the château was overflowing with people and the sounds of an orchestra playing sweet music floated through the house.

My dance card was soon filled, but I had saved three spaces for Gérard, and he smiled at me lovingly as he came to claim the first, telling me how beautiful I looked.

'That colour suits you,' he said, looking down at me with pride. 'You are the most beautiful girl in the room.'

'You are prejudiced in my favour,' I replied, laughing. 'I dare say there are a dozen girls prettier than me.'

'Not to me,' Gérard said. 'I want to make love to you, Jenny. I want to take you out into the garden and kiss you right now.'

'You must wait,' I said, teasing him. 'Perhaps later ... after supper.'

'I shall keep you to your promise,' he murmured, a wicked gleam in his eyes.

I smiled and shook my head at him. Our dance was over and he relinquished me reluctantly to my next partner.

It was a little later that Laurent came to claim his own dance.

'You are enjoying yourself, Jenny?'

'Yes, thank you, sir. Very much.'

His smile was warm, caressing, and I felt my cheeks grow hot. He seemed to have a great affection for me, and it worried me. Just why did he look at me that way?

'Is something wrong, Jenny? I have not offended you?'

'No, no, of course not, sir. It was very generous of you to give this dance for me – and to buy me such lovely clothes.'

I could not understand why he was being so kind to me. He had been my mother's friend, but the look in his eyes held a kind of pride – almost of possession – when he looked at me.

I knew from what Gérard had told me that

his father was capable of great anger and great passion. It bothered me that he should seem so interested in me, far more interested than was really necessary for a guardian.

He sensed some reserve in me, and the look he gave me as our dance ended was almost hurt, as if I had let him down somehow.

It puzzled me for a moment, but I had no time to dwell on my thoughts. I danced with so many partners, young men and old, all of them attentive, charming, amusing. It was a brilliant, glittering occasion, the château filled with light and flowers, and the champagne flowing like water. Laurent had indeed been more than generous with his hospitality, and I felt some regret for my coolness towards him.

It was not for me to judge his treatment of his wife. There was wrong on both sides, and I had heard only one. I decided that I would try to be nicer to Laurent in future. After all, he had shown me only kindness – and perhaps he would be my father-in-law one day.

The evening wore on. I was enjoying myself. Time sped by as we danced endlessly, and then the orchestra stopped playing and everyone moved into the supper room, where a sumptuous buffet awaited them.

Gérard came up behind me as I followed

the general exodus, taking my arm and tugging me away, urging me to go with him into the garden. Here too there were lights, strung in the trees and bushes, and along the verandas. Gérard hurried me away from the lights, into the seclusion of the rose arbour, then pulled me into his arms and kissed me. His excitement was obvious.

'What is it?' I asked, gazing up into his eyes. 'Why are you so excited?'

'I've been wanting to give you this all evening.' Gérard took my left hand and slid a ring on to the third finger. It was a large square emerald surrounded by flawless white diamonds and set in yellow gold. 'There – now everyone can see you are mine.'

'Oh, Gérard,' I cried. 'It's beautiful. I love it – I love you.'

He laughed and kissed me again. 'I'm going to find Father now and tell him we are engaged.'

'What about your mother?'

'I shall tell her after I've spoken to my father. She will accept it if he does, Jenny.'

My heart was beating very fast as we went back to the house, and I was conscious of the ring on my finger. Gérard was so excited, so confident, but I was afraid ... afraid of something I did not understand, but which seemed to hang over me like a black cloud.

Gérard left me to go in search of his

father. I went upstairs to freshen my perfume and tidy myself, my heart thumping wildly. What would Laurent say when Gérard told him we were going to be married? It was no use torturing myself like this; I should know soon enough.

Refreshed but still nervous, I was about to leave and return to the ballroom when the door opened and Henriette entered. Her face was white and she looked upset, shocked.

'What is wrong?' I asked. 'What has happened?'

She glanced at my hand, shaking her head as if in sorrow as she saw the ring I was wearing. 'Oh, Jenny ... I tried to warn you. I should have told you the whole truth, but I could not.'

Henriette broke off as we heard heavy footsteps in the hall, then the door of my room was unceremoniously thrust open and Laurent stood on the threshold looking like some demonic god of war. He was so angry! I had never seen him like this. His eyes were so cold, so accusing. I gasped and took a step backwards as he suddenly swooped towards me.

'Laurent!' Henriette read the purpose in his eyes and moved between us. 'You cannot blame Jenny. She did not know – neither did your son. You were at fault, not they.'

'Be quiet!' he said, his voice so harsh that

she was silenced and her face went white, as if he had struck her. She glanced at me and I saw concern for me in her eyes. 'Please leave us alone, Henriette. I wish to speak to my ward in private.' He almost spat the words out, his tone and manner so contemptuous that I shivered.

'Laurent—' His eyes flashed a warning as she attempted to reason with him and she was subdued, sensing as I did that he was barely containing his fury. 'Be careful – do not hurt her or you will answer to me.'

Her courageous defence of me drew a respectful nod of his head, and for one moment I thought there was a flicker of something that might have been humour in his eyes, but in an instant it had been replaced by a bleak, cold expression that chilled me.

Henriette kissed my cheek. 'I shall come to you soon,' she whispered, then with another warning glance at Laurent she went out.

There was silence after she had gone. I felt sick with fright. I had expected some initial opposition to Gérard's announcement that he wished to marry me, but not this cold rage.

'Is it so very wrong?' I asked when I could bear the silent accusation no longer. 'We did not mean to—'

'You will be silent,' he said. 'This idea of a

marriage between you and my son is ridiculous. You will take off the ring he gave you and forget this nonsense at once.'

'But why?' I stared at him in horror. 'Why are you so against it? I thought you liked me.'

'I do like you,' he said, a little nerve twitching in his cheek. His anger seemed to have cooled, but he was still labouring under some deep emotion. 'I have become very fond of you, and I am sorry if this hurts you – but the marriage can never take place.'

'We love each other.' Tears sprang to my eyes. 'You cannot do this ... you cannot. Please; I beg you.'

'My decision is final,' he said. He moved towards me, and for one moment I thought he would take me in his arms. I recoiled instinctively. There was an odd, blind, passionate look in his eyes, as if he hardly knew what he did. He put out his hand to touch my cheek. 'Jenny – do not look at me like that. I do not wish to hurt you, you must believe that. I care for you deeply.'

I was sure he meant to embrace me. I shrank away from him, fear and disgust in my eyes.

'Do not touch me,' I said, retreating until the bed was behind me. 'I hate you. You are cruel. You have ruined my life. Go away ... leave me alone.'

A look of pain came into his eyes, but he did not attempt to touch me again. 'Very well,' he said. 'I shall leave you for the moment. Do not come downstairs again this evening. You are overwrought. I shall tell our guests that you are unwell. Tomorrow, when you are calmer, we shall talk again. There are things I must explain to you ... things I ought to have told you long ago.'

I turned my back on him. I was convinced that he was a jealous, evil man. He wanted me himself, and that was why he had forbidden his son to marry me. I had often been puzzled by the look in his eyes, but now I was sure I knew what it meant – and I hated him for it. He had no right to look at me with lust.

I refused to look at him or answer, and in another moment he went away, leaving me to my tears. I locked the door behind him, not wanting anyone to come in and see me weeping.

All my dreams seemed to be at an end. Laurent had forbidden the marriage, and in such a way that I could see no hope for us. Gérard would surely not dare to defy him now?

'Jenny...' Henriette was at the door. She rattled the handle. 'Are you all right? Jenny, my love, let me in. Please let me talk to you. I must talk to you. It is important.'

'No. Not tonight,' I said. 'Go away. I want

to be alone.'

She rattled the door again. 'Let me speak with you, please. I can comfort you.'

'Tomorrow,' I said wearily. 'I do not want to see anyone this evening. Please, Henriette ... just go and leave me alone!'

I have never been sure how long I lay weeping, but at some time I must have slept, for when I woke the room seemed very dark. The lights in the garden had gone and everything seemed quiet.

As I heard something rattle against my window, I knew what had woken me and I went to look out. Gérard was standing in the garden below, looking up at me. I opened my window and leaned out.

'Come down,' he said and I saw that he had placed a wooden ladder against the wall. 'Don't try to leave through the house. The porter will be waiting for you. He will alert my father. Do not be afraid, my love. I'll come up and get you.'

'I'm not afraid,' I assured him, my spirits lifting. I was suddenly alive again. He had kept his word and come for me as he had said he would if his father refused us permission to marry. 'Wait there and I'll come down.'

But he was already on his way up. He steadied me as I climbed through the window, placing my feet securely on the first rung, and descending one step at a time beneath me so that I could not fall. When we reached the bottom, he helped me to the ground, then took me into his arms, holding me crushed against him.

'Come with me, Jenny,' he said, gazing into my face with a hungry yearning. 'Run away with me tonight. We can go to a house I know – and we'll be married before my father finds us.'

'He was so angry,' I said, trembling as he folded his arms about me. 'He will disown you, Gérard – if we disobey him, you will lose everything.'

'But I shall have you, and that is all I care for.' There was a strange, desperate look in his eyes. 'I cannot give you up, Jenny. I would rather die.'

'No!' I put my fingers to his lips in fright. 'No, Gérard, do not say such wild things. I love you. I shall come with you.'

Once I had thought Kate foolish to run away with the man she loved, but now I understood that there are times when the heart will rule the head. Besides, my case was different: Gérard loved me.

He smiled at me then, such a sweet, loving look that all my doubts fled before it. Nothing else mattered to me that night, nothing but the promise of the happiness I knew I should find with my lover.

And so we stole away into the darkness, where he had our horses waiting. We took nothing with us but the clothes we wore, and neither of us looked back. We both knew in our hearts that we might never return, but at that moment neither of us cared. We loved each other so much, so desperately, that nothing else could matter.

We would defy Laurent. He was autocratic and uncaring, but he could not stop us. Nothing could part us now.

Fourteen

The house to which Gérard took me was a short distance from Paris, very near the palace of Versailles, tucked away in the woods, a building of wood and stone, old, secret and forgotten.

'It's a hunting lodge,' Gérard told me as he unlocked the door and took me inside. 'It has been in my mother's family for generations. No one used it for years, but when I discovered it, I had it renovated. I've often come here with friends since then, but hardly anyone else knows it is here. I doubt if my father is even aware it exists.'

'It's nice.' I was looking around curiously. Although used solely for hunting years ago, it was well furnished with good solid pieces of walnut, and looked as if it had been cleaned recently. 'You say no one comes here?'

'A woman comes when she is sent for,' Gérard said, an odd, shuttered look in his eyes. 'I arranged for everything to be made ready for us, just in case. We should find food and wine in the kitchen. I can cook –

can you?'

'Oh, Gérard...' A little shiver went through me as I realised what we had done: there could be no turning back, no return to our old life. 'Your father will be so angry when he discovers we have eloped.'

'He should not have denied us,' Gérard said, a hard, stubborn set to his mouth. 'He would not even give me an explanation. He said only that I was not ready to marry ... that I should learn to be more responsible before I thought of taking a wife.'

I heard the resentment in his voice and understood why he had decided to elope. Laurent had been unfair, riding roughshod over our feelings, crushing our hopes ruthlessly, giving no good reason – but I believed I knew why he would not let us marry and I shuddered.

'Is something wrong?' Gérard asked. He looked at me anxiously. 'You are not regretting this?'

'No,' I said and smiled at him. 'Of course not. I love you so much, Gérard. When can we be married?'

'I thought we would marry in England. We'll stay here, hidden away, until my father has given up looking for us. He is sure to send agents to the ports, but we shall be here, where he cannot find us, and then we shall go to England.'

'Oh yes, Gérard.' I smiled as I went into

his arms. 'I should like that so much.'

'And when we are married, we will find your family,' he promised. 'We might even make our home in England.'

'But you will want to come back – to visit your mother.'

'Perhaps.' His eyes darkened and I knew he believed he might never see his mother again. 'I left a letter for her – she will understand.'

I went to him then and leaned my head against his chest. In our hearts, we both knew there was no going back.

It was a strange existence in that secluded hunting lodge. We were cocooned in our own little world, seeing no one but the woman who came to the house to clean and bring us food – but we were happy. We went for long walks in the woods, often silent, our hands entwined, lost in each other, living only for our love.

Once we visited the grounds of Versailles. There were other people walking about in the sunshine, but they took no notice of us, merely dismissing us as just two more lovers. And Versailles was a place for lovers.

The palace itself was a huge, costly clutter of buildings with magnificent staterooms, outhouses, an orangery, kitchen gardens, kennels and stables, all vast, all expensive, to say nothing of its miles of drains which had never been properly finished. But the parks and gardens were magnificent: fountains, secret courts, delightful landscaping, and of course the Trianon. It was this that fascinated me most, because of its history.

'Built by a king for the woman he loved,' Gérard teased as he saw my interest. 'How would you have liked to be one of Louis' mistresses?'

'I should not.' I frowned at him.

'You would have outshone them all,' Gérard said, still bent on teasing me. 'La Valliére, Madame de Montespan...'

'Even Madame de Maintenon?' I asked, brows arched.

Gérard laughed. 'Especially Madame de Maintenon.' She had been the love of the king in his later years, known less for her beauty by then than her solid worth. 'Did you know Louis called her "Votre Solidité"?'

'How unkind of him,' I said, laughing up at him. 'Tell me more.'

Gérard told me how Francoise d' Aubigne had come to France almost penniless and was taken in out of charity by Madame de Neuillant, mother of the Maréchal-Duchess de Navailles, and was eventually brought to Paris. She had youth, charm and wit but no fortune.

'She was brought to the attention of the poet Scarron,' Gérard told me. 'He was

307

teased into marrying her. It was a brilliant partnership and their combined wit brought the most distinguished of Parisian society to their drawing room – and then he died.'

'What happened to her then, before she came to court?'

'She passed from one household to another, treated almost as a kind of superior servant in some. But she still had influential friends and at last she was asked to become governess to the king's children by Madame de Montespan...'

'And in the end she married him. It was quite a rise in her circumstances.'

'She was a very clever woman.'

We laughed together in the sunshine. Versailles was a magic place to be on that warm summer day, and we were young and very much in love.

For several days we continued in our happiness. Sometimes Gérard took me to quiet inns, where we dined alone in the host's private parlour. But at other times, we packed picnic baskets filled with delicious cold chicken, pies and fresh bread, eating with our fingers and drinking wine cooled in a stream, or we cooked our own food at the lodge, laughing at each other's efforts.

Gérard could conjure up the lightest, tastiest omelettes but little else. Remembering Marthe's delicious stews and soups, I tried to emulate them, but not always with success. Yet it did not matter if we dined on bread and cheese, for we hardly knew what we ate.

Our nights were spent together in the huge, four-poster bed, and it was there we found our heaven. Such happiness as we knew during those golden days is offered to only the fortunate few. If only it could have gone on like that for ever – but it was bound to end. I think we both knew it in our hearts. Nothing as perfect as those few precious days could last for long.

I had sensed it almost from the beginning. Perhaps Gérard believed in all his promises, or perhaps he was just snatching at happiness while he could. I shall never know for sure.

We had come back to the lodge that evening – the evening I shall never forget, that will haunt my dreams for as long as I live – after taking supper at a pleasant inn by the river, walking through the woods, our hands clasped, listening to the sounds made by tiny night creatures snuffling in the under-growth. Neither of us spoke very much. We were content just to be together.

Once inside the house, Gérard lit the lamps, then turned to take me into his arms, drawing me close, his lips moving against my hair.

'Shall we go to bed, my love?'

I was about to answer when I heard something, an indrawn breath perhaps or the sighing of the wind. I turned slowly, feeling a tingling at the nape of my neck, a sign of impending disaster, and then I saw him, standing in the doorway of the adjoining room, staring at us. I gave a little cry of alarm, and Gérard pushed me behind him, as if to protect me from the anger we could both see in the comte's face.

'What have you done?' Laurent's eyes were intent on his son, cold, colder than the northern wind. 'I am ashamed of you, Gérard. I never thought to see this day. Have you no sense of decency – no honour?'

'How did you find us?' Gérard's face was ashen but he made no attempt to defend himself from Laurent's accusations.

'Do you imagine I do not know your haunts?' Laurent's lip curled in scorn. 'To bring her here! A place like this – the scene of your orgies with your friends and their women. Is that what you think of Jenny? Is she just another of your conquests – or did you do this to spite me?'

'I love Jenny. We are going to be married despite you. We came here to hide until you had given up the search.'

'You are a fool as well as a wastrel,' Laurent said, then his scornful gaze turned on me. 'I might have expected this of Gérard –

but I am disappointed in *you*. I thought better of you.'

My cheeks flushed beneath the sting of his bitter scorn, but I lifted my head and looked at him proudly. 'I have done nothing shameful. We love each other. We are to be married.'

'No! I cannot permit it.'

'You cannot stop us,' I said, facing him defiantly. 'If you force me to return to the château with you, I shall run away again – and if you lock me in my room, I shall wait until I am no longer in your power and then I shall—'

'In my power? Good grief!' Laurent looked startled. 'Do you imagine I wish to use my authority over you in some evil manner? What nonsense is this? Am I a monster? Have I ever done anything to harm you? I care for you, Jenny, perhaps more than you know. I care about what happens to you.'

'Why?' My eyes met his in a fierce challenge. 'If you care for me as you claim – why have you forbidden me to marry the man I love? Why do you want to break my heart?'

Laurent had gone very pale. I could see he was in some distress. He looked at me for some seconds in silence, then at Gérard. The atmosphere was very tense, and a trickle of ice began to work its way from the nape of my neck to the base of my spine.

311

Laurent seemed to shudder, then squared his shoulders as if what he was about to say was very painful for him. 'Your mother has sworn on her bible that you are my son, Gérard, and though I doubted it once, I must accept it as the truth now.' His gaze turned to me, seeming sorrowful but also accusing. 'I had hoped you would discover this for yourself, Jenny, but it seems I must tell you myself. I believe that you are my daughter.'

'Your daughter?' Gérard was staring at him, a look of horror in his eyes. 'How can ... you mean Jenny's mother was *her* ... the woman you loved ... your mistress for so many years?'

'Yes, Adele was my mistress.' Laurent's eyes sought mine in a plea for forgiveness. 'I loved her very much, and I believe she loved me. She always knew we could never marry, that I could not divorce Béatrix. I was honest with her from the beginning.'

'But ... you cannot be my father.' My throat was dry. I had begun to tremble. 'She told me ... she told me ... my father was an English gentleman. He died in France, leaving her alone – and we went to live with Marthe at her family home...'

'Marthe was in my employ. She became your mother's maid after Adele brought you to France – to the house I bought for her in Paris. You were born in England, in my

312

house in London.' Laurent's expression was grave. 'My name may not be on your birth documents – Adele insisted it should not be, though I begged her to allow me the privilege of giving you my name. She said it would not be fair to Béatrix, and that we must never hurt her, must always be discreet – and she did not want you to know, because she did not want to hurt you. She preferred to be known as Madame Heron, but it was her maiden name, her family name – she was never married.'

'Never married...'

My head was whirling in confusion. I could not believe what he was telling me. It meant that my whole life had been a lie ... everything I had believed in was false and ugly, like the tangled threads on the reverse side of a pretty tapestry.

Even the story about living with Marthe's family was not true. She must have known – or at least suspected – that my mother was the comte's mistress, but she had never told me. This last betrayal was almost more than I could bear.

I looked at Gérard, pleading with him to help me, but he seemed stunned, unable to take in what his father had just told us.

'I don't know ... I cannot believe this ... Gérard?'

He seemed suddenly to wake as from a bad dream, but the horror was still there in his eyes. Clearly he had not realised that my mother was the mistress Laurent had loved for so many years – the woman who had caused his mother so much pain – and it disturbed him.

'Do not believe him,' he said at last, an angry, bitter twist to his mouth. 'Why should your mother lie to you, Jenny? He has no proof. She may have been his mistress, but he is *not* your father. He just wants to destroy us ... me. You must see that.'

'I cannot be certain,' Laurent said, and there was both pain and pride in his face. 'But I believe it to be true. Adele allowed me to believe it. With her dying breath she begged me to take care of our child – our daughter. In view of that, I could not just turn away and allow this situation to continue. You must see why –'

'No!' I backed away from him. My eyes went from one to the other as I tried to shut out the horror of Laurent's words. A terrible sickness began to build inside me. I could feel a scream rising to my lips and knew that I was close to losing control. 'No! I won't believe this. I won't!'

If Laurent was my father, Gérard was my half-brother. A relationship such as we had shared these past few days was forbidden by the laws of God and man.

Giving a little sob of despair, I turned and

ran into the bedroom, closing and locking the door behind me. How could I bear what Laurent had just told me? Despair swept over me in a great wave and I wished God would strike me down. The emptiness of a life without Gérard was so terrible to contemplate that I did not know how to face it.

Laurent my father ... No, no, no! It could not be, must not be true. The realisation of all it would mean swamped me, as I sank to my knees, covering my face with my hands as the bitter sobs broke from me.

Gérard was outside the door, hammering against it, demanding to be let in. 'Do not believe his filthy lies, Jenny,' he pleaded. 'He has done this to spite me, to have his revenge for my mother's betrayal of him. He is a vengeful, bitter man ... do not let him win. Do not let him destroy us. Open the door. We shall go away. He cannot stop us. I'll take you to England. We'll find your family ... we'll discover the truth.'

I almost opened the door to him then. *Oh, God, why did I not listen to him? Why did I not let him take me away? What did anything matter but the love we felt for each other?*

I almost opened the door, but Laurent's words had worked their poison in me. I was remembering things my mother had said ... the pendant she had told me was given her by my father, and the matching bracelet

Laurent had given me. I had thought the look in his eyes was lust, but it could just as easily have been the pride a possessive, passionate man might find in the child of his one true love.

'Let me in, Jenny. I beg you. I beg you ... if you love me. Come away with me now.'

'I cannot,' I whispered, my throat tight with emotion. 'Please, Gérard, leave me alone. I need to be alone ... I need to think.'

'Jenny!' He thundered against the door with his fists. 'God damn him for this! God damn his soul to hell!'

I sensed him standing there, and I felt his pain, his despair, because it was my own, and then I knew he had gone.

I lay on the floor sobbing, feeling as if my life were draining out of me. Gérard was my love, my life, my heart. I wanted to die. I prayed for death to take me, to sink into the oblivion of the grave and let the grass grow over me. If I could not have Gérard, then I did not want to live.

I slept little that night, pacing the floor restlessly, gazing out every now and then at the woods, which lay mostly in shadow despite a pale moon. Once, towards the dawn, I thought I saw Gérard's pale face staring at my window, haunted desperation in his eyes. I longed to run to him, to beg him to sweep me up in his arms and take me away, but I knew I dare not. We might count the world well lost for love in our present madness – for I had felt his desperation and knew he suffered as I did – but one day we would wake and the weight of our sins would have grown too heavy. Besides, there might be children.

'Oh, dear God!' I whispered as the thought entered my mind. *There might be a child already growing in my womb.*

The union of close cousins was frowned upon by many because too much inter-breeding amongst families might cause physical or mental defects; how much worse then was the sexual union of a brother with his sister?

I recalled Marthe talking of the union of close cousins once and the memory of her words sent shivers through me.

'That latest child of Matilde's is not right in the head,' she had told Pierre when she came in from visiting the family. 'But what can you expect? Her mother married her cousin and so did she ... they've done it for generations for the sake of the land, and this isn't the first of them to be born an idiot.'

If I gave birth to the child of my half-brother ... a shudder of horror gripped me. My sin might destroy the life of such a child.

I prayed then that our stolen moments of passion would not bring harm to an inno-cent babe.

'Anything but that,' I babbled feverishly. 'I promise I won't give way to my wickedness again ... please, please don't punish me like that.'

Surely God could not be that cruel? The love I felt for Gérard was sinful but I had not known it when I lay in his arms. Neither of us had known what we were doing.

It was soon after the sun came stealing into my room that I opened the door and went through to the living room. Laurent was sitting in a chair with his eyes closed, but he opened them almost at once, as if sensing my presence.

'Jenny,' he said, and his face was grey with tiredness, as though he too had spent the night without sleep. 'Forgive me ... I never meant to hurt you.' He stood up, taking a few steps towards me until I held up my hand to ward him off, and then he halted. There was pain in his eyes, and a plea for forgiveness, for understanding. 'I had to tell you ... I could not let you remain in ignorance. You hate me now, and I cannot blame you – but one day you will see that it was for your sake.'

'Please,' I said, my lips stiff. 'I would rather not speak about it. Where is Gérard?'

'He went off last night,' Laurent said, a bleak expression in his eyes. 'Things passed between us ... things that were better never said. He would not stay here while I stayed, and I could not leave you.'

'Why did you not tell me at the beginning?' I asked, and I heard the bitterness in my own voice. 'I could have accepted it then – and none of this need ever have happened.'

'You do not wish it more than I,' Laurent said, his voice hoarse with anguish. 'If I could go back ... but I was consumed with grief, Jenny. I did not know how to bear her loss. I should have told you when I brought you to the château, but I thought you would open her box, that she would have left documents, a letter.'

I bowed my head, closing my eyes. I too had been at fault. Why had I not enquired more closely? Why had I not gone through my mother's papers? Looking back, I saw that the signs had been there if I had bothered to look – but perhaps I had not wanted to, preferring to live with the fairy-tale I had invented for myself as a child.

'Let me take you back to the château,' Laurent said. 'You cannot stay here.'

'I want to see Gérard,' I said. 'I need to talk to him – you will not deny us that, at least?'

'You think so ill of me,' he said sadly. 'It was because I wanted to spare you both pain that I tried to keep this from you on the night of the dance. But you are right to blame me, Jenny. I have not acted as a father. I should have insisted on your being told years ago.'

I shook my head wearily. What was the point in all this now? It was too late ... far too late.

Fifteen

When we arrived at the château I went straight to my room and locked my door. I did not want to see anyone and I lay on my bed, looking at the ceiling and weeping.

Henriette came to my door once, but I asked her to leave me alone and she went away again. I was waiting ... waiting for Gérard to return. It could not end like this. We had to talk ... to say the things that must be said.

The day passed away and was followed by another restless night.

My eyes were sore with weeping. Wearied by emotion, I lay down at last, sleeping fitfully for an hour or so. When I woke again, I had reached my decision. It would be better if I left almost at once. I could stay with Madame Leconte in Paris until arrangements could be made for me to travel to England.

What little I knew of that country had been gained from drawings and photographs in newspapers. It was the land of my mother's birth, but she had seldom spoken of her life there. I should be a stranger in my own country, for I had not left the shores of France since I came here and was in my heart reluctant to do so now. With Gérard it would have been exciting ... like an adventure ... but alone, and with a broken heart? The prospect was daunting.

My alternative was to stay in France, in Paris ... I squashed the faint hope that came immediately to my mind. If I stayed in France there would always be the chance of meeting Gérard or Laurent. And that would be painful for us all.

No; I must see Gérard once more to say goodbye, and then never again.

When I had dressed and washed the tearstains from my cheeks, I went in search of Henriette. She was in her own private parlour and opened the door to me as soon as I knocked.

'Jenny!' she cried and tried to embrace me. I moved away and she looked saddened by my rejection. 'I'm so sorry, my dear. So very sorry.'

I stood proudly, my manner keeping her at bay. I was not angry with her, but neither was I an innocent child to be comforted by hugs and sweet words as I had been after my mother died. In a few short hours, I had become a woman, wiser and harder.

'You knew my mother and ... *he* ... were lovers, didn't you?' She nodded, watching, uncertain now. 'Why didn't you tell me?'

'Laurent wanted to tell you himself. We did not realise – of course we were wrong. We should have seen the danger.'

'You knew that he was my father?' I stared at her in horror.

Henriette looked uncomfortable. 'I was not sure … I suspected something, but I did not think even Laurent knew for certain.'

'He never told you?'

'No.' She hesitated, then met my accusing gaze frankly. 'I did see you soon after you were born, Jenny. My parents had taken me to London and we were visiting Laurent at his house there. I was not supposed to go into the nursery – but I did. Your mother came in while I was there. She let me hold you. Laurent called her Madame Heron. I did not know she was his mistress then … Only later, in Paris, when she began to make gowns for me did I discover the truth. At the time, I imagined that she had lost her husband and you were his child … I truly believed that, until Laurent brought you to live here, and then I began to wonder.'

'Why did you never tell me?'

'How could I? It was not my business to tell you – and I was not certain. But I did try to warn you not to fall in love with Gérard. He can be so wild … so restless … I thought you would do better to marry someone else, someone more steady, older. I know you think I tried to throw you at Marc Bruge, but I only wanted to make you see that there were other young men – to make you forget Gérard. I have always been your friend, Jenny. Please believe that.'

Tears stung my eyes. She was right: there was a wild, unbalanced streak in Gérard at times. I remembered the way he had beat so desperately against the door I had locked, how he had pleaded with me to open it to him. The look in his eyes when he had told me he would rather die than live without me...

'My poor Gérard,' I whispered, half to myself. 'Has he come back? Has he asked for me?'

'No.' Henriette looked grave. 'Laurent told me he rushed out of the lodge like a madman, refusing to discuss the ... situation. It does not surprise me. He was always thus when thwarted ... a little wild, head-strong ... often ungovernable as a child. Much as my own darling Charles was until you came.' A sigh or a sob escaped her as she looked at my determined face. 'Now I suppose you will leave us?'

'I could not stay here now. I shall leave for Paris today – and for England as soon as it can be arranged.'

Something flickered in her eyes. I could not be sure whether it was relief or regret; perhaps it was a mixture of both.

'I shall miss you. So will Charles.' She laid her hand on my arm. 'But you must do as you think fit, Jenny. Laurent was perhaps wrong to bring you here. He forced Béatrix to accept you – though she has no idea that you are his—'

'His daughter by his mistress?' I asked bitterly. 'She did know that my mother was his mistress though, didn't she?'

'Yes. She had known for years,' Henriette said quietly. 'She accepted Laurent's need for someone. I believe she was glad of it in her own way.'

'Yet she resented my being here.'

'Can you blame her?'

'If I were her I should not have allowed it.'

'Laurent is master here. There was a time when she resisted ... I remember frequent quarrels between them years ago, but that finished long before I came to live here. I believe she hates him. He ... he treats her with respect but sometimes, when he is unaware of being observed, I have seen such loathing in his eyes. It is as if he can hardly bear to see her or speak to her. As if he has to force himself to behave as he ought to the woman he married.'

'And yet he has never sought to divorce her?'

'It would not be possible. With all his faults, Laurent is a strict Catholic. They should never have married, of course. They

325

were not suited, and—'

'She did not love him. Gérard told me her story. It must have been terrible for her all these years. Laurent has much to answer for – to all of us.'

Henriette looked away, and I knew she loved him despite his faults.

'You should try to forgive him, Jenny. I believe he too has suffered – and I know he cares for you. I did wonder for a while ... but I was mistaken. If he is your father it is natural he should love you. Laurent is a stern man at times, a passionate man – he would need to protect his daughter, to guard her.'

I felt the anger rise inside me.

'He should have told me at the start. I can never forgive him,' I told her. 'He has ruined my life.'

Henriette looked at me sadly. 'No real harm has been done. Laurent found you in time, before you could marry. You are so young. You will love again.'

So he had not told her the whole. He had kept our secret. And I knew that I must keep it too.

Henriette must not be told the truth of what had happened between Gérard and I, the sin that we had committed through ignorance and the neglect of others. She would never ... must never know the dark secrets I carried in my heart. I could not speak of my shame or hurt to anyone.

'Will you help me?' I asked. 'I want to leave soon. I don't want to see Laurent, though I shall have to before I leave – but I would like to speak to Gérard, if he should return.'

I felt in my heart that he would not. He had tried to talk to me that night at the lodge, but I had locked my door against him. He must have thought it was useless, that I had turned against him – and so he had ridden off into the night in anger.

'Do you think it wise?' Henriette asked, still doubtful. 'Must you go, Jenny? Could you not stay here for a while – at least until you are feeling calmer?'

'I cannot stay. It is impossible. If Béatrix were to discover the truth ... you must see how this would hurt her. Has she not suffered enough?'

'Yes.' Henriette agreed to this at once. 'Perhaps it is best you go at once. You need take only a few clothes with you. The rest of your things can be sent to Paris – or straight to England if you prefer.'

'I am not sure ... Perhaps when I am settled. I think I may decide to stay in England, but I cannot be certain yet.'

'Oh, do not say so,' she cried in genuine distress. 'I shall miss you, Jenny. When you are – calmer, perhaps you will come back to visit Charles and I?'

'No,' I said. 'No, I shall not come back.' I lifted my head and looked into her eyes. 'I shall never return to the château – never.'

When I told Laurent I wanted to go away, he was silent for a moment, then he inclined his head. He turned away, walked over to the window and stood looking out, his back towards me.

'Yes, perhaps you should go right away,' he said. 'I have a house in London. I will have my solicitors transfer the deeds into your name. And I shall have an allowance paid into a bank for you each month. You will never want for money, Jenny. I promise you that.'

It was in my heart to refuse him, but even as I hesitated, he turned and gave me such a defeated, pleading look that I remained silent.

'Let me do this, at least,' he said.

'Thank you.' I blinked away my tears. 'I accept your generosity – but I cannot find it in my heart to forgive you.'

I turned and walked away from him.

'You look so tired and pale,' Madame Leconte greeted me as I came downstairs that morning some three days following my unannounced arrival, when without question, she had taken me in from her doorstep, wrapping her arms about me in a warm

328

embrace. 'Did you not sleep well, my dear?'

I had told her only a part of the story – just that I had fallen in love with the comte's son, that he had forbidden the marriage, and I was to go and live in London with his blessing.

'Not very,' I replied hesitantly. 'I keep thinking about Mama, wondering why she did not tell me.'

The truth was that I did not dare sleep because my dreams were terrible, tortured nightmares in which I saw Gérard standing in a mist calling to me, begging me to come to him; restless dreams from which I woke sobbing. 'If only she had told me! If only I had known – '

'That she was the Comte de Arnay's mistress?' Madame Leconte sighed. 'I warned her that you would find out one day. I thought he would speak of it himself when ... I'm sorry, Jeanette. I should have said something after Adele died. I wanted to when you came here to ask about finding work that day, but I thought she might have told you in the letter she left for you amongst her things.'

'She left a letter for me?'

'Did you not find it? I packed it in her trunk, though I think you will find various documents that may be useful to you in her writing-box. The record of your birth ... and other things. I did not pry but I believed you would find the truth amongst her letters.'

'I have not yet touched Mama's trunk – or her writing-box.'

Had Laurent known the letter was there? I recalled the moment when he'd asked if I would like the trunk carried up to my room. If I had said yes then ... would I have saved myself much of the pain I was feeling now?

I could not be sure. The attraction between Gérard and I had been instantaneous. From the moment we had met there had been a strong feeling between us. Would it have become the passionate love it had if we had known the truth? It was impossible to know now ... and far too late.

Laurent should have told me when he fetched me home from school! It was his fault. I should never forgive him for what he had done to us.

'I have sent your note to Marie as you asked,' Madame Leconte said, breaking into my thoughts. She reached for the pretty pink porcelain chocolate pot and poured herself another cup. 'She has been working for her present employer for several months, but I am not sure she is happy with the position. I think she might be willing to go to London with you.'

Madame Leconte had already promised to travel with me to London and see me safely installed in my new home, but she could not remain with me for more than a few weeks.

330

I would have to find a companion of some kind, for it would not look right if I were to live alone.

'With Marie and a companion you will have respectability,' she had told me when I spoke of my intention to live in London. 'I will help you to find someone – an older woman, sensible, reliable.'

I would have preferred to live alone, but I would not upset my kind friend by refusing her help. Once she had returned to France I could please myself.

'Marie was so loyal to my mother,' I said. 'I hope she will consider coming with me, because—'

I broke off as we heard the doorbell jangle, and then there was the sound of footsteps and a man's voice in the hall. My heart stood still as the door of the salon was thrown open and he came in. 'Laurent...'

I jumped to my feet as if to flee his presence but something in his face held me rooted to the ground. There was such grief in those eyes, such pain! I had noticed that he was dressed in severest black, just as he had been for my mother's funeral, and I felt sick, already beginning to guess why he had come.

'What has happened?' I asked as he stood there looking at me. A cold dread clutched at my heart and suddenly I knew. I understood the meaning of the dreams that had

331

kept me sleepless all night. 'Is – is it Gérard?'

'I had to tell you myself,' Laurent said in a hoarse, rasping voice. 'He ... Gérard is dead. He came home the day after you left. When he discovered you had gone – he was beside himself with grief. He stormed out of the house, would not listen to either Henriette or me. He was riding wildly ... like a mad thing, they say ... and he fell. His neck was broken and he died instantly. They tell me he could have known no pain.'

'No pain...' I stared at him dully as the terrible agony swept over me. Gérard dead. Gérard dead! No, no, it could not be true – and yet the look in Laurent's eyes told me that it was. 'How dare you say he felt no pain? How dare you! When you know ... you know the pain you inflicted on us both.'

'Jenny,' he begged brokenly. 'Please, Jenny. Forgive me. I never meant ... I never wanted this to happen. How can you believe I would willingly have caused either of you such pain? I have blamed myself a thousand times, wished I had done things differently.'

In my terrible grief, I hated him. Nothing he could do or say would have softened my heart towards him at that moment.

'Don't touch me!' I cried, holding out a shaking hand to ward him off. 'Don't come one step nearer. I hate you. I never want to see you again. Never.'

'You won't have to see me,' he said and there was such sorrow and grief in his face then that I might have felt pity for him had he not been a murderer. But by his careless, selfish behaviour he had ruined my life and taken that of his own son. 'Forgive me, Jenny – and believe that I shall pay for what I have done. I shall suffer. I promise you.'

'Please go.'

His suffering was nothing to me. My heart felt as if it were turned to stone.

'Everything is arranged ... the house ... an account at my bank in London ... If there is anything else you need, you have only to ask.' He gave me one last despairing glance before he turned to leave. At the door he looked back. 'Try to forgive me,' he said and then he was gone.

I stood staring after him for a few moments and then, as the room seemed to whirl faster and faster around me, I fell down in a swoon.

When I came to myself again I was lying on the sofa, watched over by Madame Leconte and Marie. How had she come here? I gave a small, strangled sigh and tried to sit up, only to fall back again as the dizziness washed over me.

'Are you in terrible pain, my dear?' Madame Leconte touched my cheek anxiously. 'You hit your head when you fell. It was fortunate that Marie arrived when she did, for I was in a dreadful state and did not know what to do.'

'I was coming to see you in answer to your letter,' Marie said. 'I thought you would not want a doctor? It was simply a faint. Nothing to worry about.'

'And a knock on the head,' Madame Leconte reminded her with a hint of reproach. 'I was worried – but Marie said you would come round in a moment and so you have.'

Madame Leconte hovered anxiously. My vision was clearing. I could see the painted fire-screen, the prints of dancing girls on the walls and my friend's work-box lying on the floor, where it had tumbled in her fright at Laurent's entry. I was aware of a fly buzzing against the window-pane – and of the strange emptiness inside me.

'Yes. I am better now.' I sat up cautiously. My head ached and I still felt a little dizzy, but that cleared after a moment or two. 'How foolish of me to faint like that. I can't remember what happened...'

'It was the shock,' Madame Leconte said. 'How could he be so cruel as to tell you like that? It was brutal. Wicked!'

With her words, the awful reality came flooding back. Gérard was dead! I should never see him again, never hear his voice, never touch his hand. Even though I had known I must not give in to my longing for him, the shock of hearing that he had been killed had been too much for me. It had been painful enough to accept that we must never be together again, but this ... Grief and despair welled up in me. I bowed my head, covering my face with my hands as the tears flowed.

'Oh, my dear...' Madame Leconte fluttered uncomfortably at my side. 'This is terrible ... terrible.'

'Would you leave us, madame – just for a while?'

I heard Marie speak and my friend answered, but I was not really aware of what was happening. At that moment I wanted only to dic. I envied Gérard: in death he would find peace. He would not know the torment I was enduring.

'Stop crying, Jenny. It won't change anything and you'll only make yourself ill.' Marie spoke sharply as the door closed behind Madame Leconte. 'You can't bring him back. You have to think of yourself now – and your child.'

'My child?' The shock stopped my tears. I looked up at her. 'What are you saying?'

'Am I wrong?' she asked. 'Forgive me if I have misjudged you. I thought perhaps...'

'I'm not sure.' I bit my lip as the colour burned my cheeks. 'My monthly flow is a few days late, but...'

'There is a chance that you might be

carrying Gérard de Arnay's child?' I nodded
and Marie frowned. 'I thought as much. You
did not say in your letter, but I guessed ... I
wondered if you had been lovers. I thought
that was perhaps why you wanted to go
away.'

Neither she nor Madame Leconte was
aware of my true relationship with Laurent.
They knew that he was my guardian, that he
had forbidden the marriage between Gérard
and I – and they knew that my mother had
been his mistress for years. They had known
of her association with him all the time, of
course, and they believed it was the reason
for his refusal to allow the marriage. It was
best that way.

'You will think me very foolish?'

'It would have been better if it had not
happened,' Marie said. 'But it is not for me
to judge. Love makes fools of us all. I was
Adele's friend as well as her maid. I shall be
yours – if you wish?'

'I do – of course I do.' I smiled at her. 'I
was hoping you would come to London
with me – will you?'

'You will need someone to take care of
you,' Marie said, nodding to herself thoughtfully. 'Especially if ... but we must hope you
are not pregnant. We must say nothing to
Madame Leconte ... unless you wish her to
know?'

'No, no, I do not,' I said quickly. 'Nor my

guardian. Particularly him! If I am carrying Gérard's child, I do not want any of my friends or family to know.'

The shame overwhelmed me. I could not bear the thought of telling Marthe or Pierre ... of seeing disappointment in their faces, or hearing their condemnation of Gérard. They had liked him but they would think he had let me down – and I could never, never tell them the truth of my birth. It was too shocking, too terrible.

'It will be our secret,' Marie promised, looking at me with an odd expression. 'You may want –' She hesitated uncertainly. 'You may not wish to have the child.'

Her suggestion stunned me. It had not occurred to me until that moment that I could get rid of the child.

I hesitated, not looking at her as I said, 'I'm not sure. I had not really thought about it properly.'

I had prayed that I was not carrying my lover's child, but now I was not certain how I felt. I ought to feel revulsion at the very idea ... and yet a child would be something of my own, a part of Gérard.

But if Laurent was my father, it was the child of an incestuous relationship.

The thoughts went round and round in my head, chasing themselves endlessly. There was the possibility that the child could be deformed or subnormal in other ways … but who could say that for certain? It might be perfectly healthy. How could I take the life of my own child? Would that not be an even more terrible sin than the one I had committed unknowingly?

'So we shall wait and see,' said Marie with an understanding nod. 'Whatever you decide I shall help you. I shall take care of you as I did of your maman.'

'Thank you, Marie. Thank you.' I held my hand out to her. 'I really do not know how I should have borne all this without Mama's friends to help me.'

I thought then that if it had not been for Marie I should not have been able to cope with my life. It would have been easier to give into the grief and pain, to retreat into my own little world and let reality drift away, to let go my hold on life itself.

Sixteen

The very next day Kate came to see me. When Madame Leconte brought her into the parlour, I rushed straight into her arms. For a moment she held me as I wept, her hand stroking my hair as if I were a child and she my mother.

'I am so sorry,' she whispered. 'So very sorry, Jenny. I had no idea until Henriette told me.'

'Henriette told you?' I drew away from her as the storm of grief subsided, accepting her kerchief to wipe my face. 'You have met her? When?'

'I went to the château to visit you two days ago,' she said. 'Henriette told me that your ... guardian ... had forbidden the marriage, and she told me where to find you. She is very concerned for you, Jenny.'

'Did she tell you why he forbade us to marry? And ... that Gérard was killed in a riding accident?'

Kate nodded, her expression sombre. 'It must be very hard to bear,' she said. 'To lose the man you love twice...'

'I am not sure I can bear it,' I said. 'I loved him so much, Kate.'

'Yes, I know. He loved you too. At least you had that – you had his love, Jenny. No one can take that from you.'

I was thoughtful as I looked at her. She was right. Gérard had loved me. Our love had been beautiful, and the memory of those days at the lodge, before it had all become tarnished, was something no one could take from me.

'I hear you are going to England?'

I nodded. 'Yes – and Laurent has given me a house.' I looked up at her then. 'I am luckier than you were, Kate. I shall have somewhere to live and money. I would rather not take his money – but I don't think I have a choice.'

'I would have taken money if I had been offered it. Don't be too proud, Jenny; it isn't worth it.' Kate looked thoughtful. 'Henriette asked me if I would like to take care of Charles for her. He misses you, Jenny.'

'Will you go – to the château, I mean?'

'Perhaps. There is a decent woman living in a cottage nearby who would take care of Louise. I could see her often, and it would be better for both of us in the country.'

'It is a chance for you, Kate.'

'Yes; perhaps my luck has turned.'

'I am happy for you.'

Her eyes were sad as they dwelt on my

face. 'You *were* lucky, Jenny,' she said softly. 'Always cling to that. To be truly loved is a blessing.'

'Yes,' I said, and for the first time in days I felt calmer. 'Thank you for coming to me.'

She smiled at me. 'Of course I came – and I brought Louise ... if you can bear to see her?'

'Yes; I should like that.'

I wiped away all signs of my tears as Kate went to fetch her child. She returned holding the little girl by the hand, a look of pride in her eyes. Louise was like a little doll, her hair dressed in ringlets, her gown made of soft wool and a much better quality than her mother's.

'Oh, Kate, she is lovely,' I said. 'So beautiful -- and so very like you.'

'Yes, I think she is,' Kate said softly. 'I thank God every day for her, Jenny.'

She brought the child to me, telling her to say hello to 'Aunt Jenny'. Louise put her hand shyly into mine, then climbed on to my lap as I held out my arms to her. She settled her head against my breast and I could smell the fresh, baby scent of her hair and body. Somehow it was healing.

I smiled at Kate above her head. 'Thank you,' I said. 'Thank you for giving me this, Kate.'

I woke that night from a restless sleep,

knowing that I had dreamed of Gérard. My face was stained with tears and I could still see his face, still feel the touch of his lips on mine.

'I love you, Jenny,' he had whispered as he held me close. 'Our love was no sin. Believe me, my darling. You must live. You must be strong ... strong for our child ... strong for our child...'

'Oh, Gérard,' I whispered as I tried to hold on to the image in my head, to the feeling of being near to him, in his arms. 'I love you so much ... so much.'

How could I bear to live without him? We had known and loved each other for such a short time and yet it seemed I had lived a lifetime. I had grown up and become old in the space of a few weeks. The future seemed so empty ... so lonely. Must I really go on living for years with this aching despair inside me?

'You must be strong for our child, Jenny.'

Gérard's presence was so real then that I felt him near me. I cried out, begging him to come back to me, but in my heart I knew he could not. Only in my dreams would I feel the touch of his lips on mine.

I had his child growing inside me, however, and I knew then that I must be strong.

My mother's trunk arrived at Madame Leconte's house. I opened it; inside it was lined in a faded pink silk and the smell of her perfume was very strong. It brought a lump to my throat, but I knew I must not be put off this time. I spent some time searching for the letter my friend said she had packed in the trunk, taking out my mother's clothes and possessions piece by piece. There was no sign of the letter.

In Maman's writing-box I found papers relating to my birth, which were just as Laurent had told me. Something had been entered where the form asked for the name of the child's father, but had later been crossed through and through in black ink, obliterating all trace of his identity.

There was also a pile of love-letters from Laurent tied up with blue ribbon. I opened one and then thrust them aside, because I could not bear to read it. They revealed a very private relationship, and a very different man from the one I had known.

Several other documents and letters were in the box, including one from Kate to my mother – but there was nothing from her to me.

'I cannot think where it could have gone,' Madame Leconte said, looking upset when I told her I had been unable to find it amongst Mama's things. 'I know it was there, Jenny. I packed it just inside, right on the top.'

'Then someone must have taken it,' I said,

and my heart hardened against the man I believed responsible. 'Why would he have done such a thing?'

I hated Laurent then. It must have been he who had taken the letter. He was the only one to have had the key to the trunk – other than myself.

Why would he do such a thing – unless he had wanted to destroy the evidence? Evidence that he had lied to us.

Yet why should he do such a cruel, unnecessary thing? In the one corner of my mind that still retained the ability to think sensibly, I knew it was unlikely. Laurent would never have done what he had if he did not believe himself my father.

I was clutching at straws, hoping to ease the burden of guilt and shame.

'This is terrible!' Madame Leconte glanced up from her letter as I entered the parlour some days later. 'My brother's wife has written to say he is very ill. She begs me to go to him at once.'

'I am so sorry, madame. Of course you must go.'

'But ... we are due to leave for England in two days' time.' She was overcome with dismay. 'How can I ask you to delay your journey – with your passage booked? Oh dear! What are we to do?'

'I shall go with Marie as planned. No,

no...' I held up my hand as she began to protest. 'Marie will look after me. You know how capable she is. There is no reason for you to upset yourself.'

'But a young woman travelling alone ... unmarried. It is not proper. You cannot –'

'I could call myself Madame Heron,' I said. 'Marie can go and buy me a ring. I am in mourning – why should I not let people think I am a widow? What harm can it do?'

'It would be wrong.' She looked unhappy. 'But I suppose it might be better than ... If you really think you should?'

'Please do not distress yourself further.' I crossed the parlour to kiss her cheek. She had been a good friend to me, but was inclined to panic at the least thing. 'I have been thinking I might present myself as a widow in London. I do not intend to seek an entry into society – nor should I be welcome if I did. I am determined to live quietly in seclusion – to choose my own friends.'

'I can see you have been thinking of this before this morning.' Madame Leconte was reflective, a faint suspicion in her eyes. Then she smiled at me. 'If you are certain it is what you want to do, I believe it might serve.'

'It will be easier,' I said. 'And you must go to see your brother. He obviously needs you.'

'Poor Henri was always an invalid as a child. His wife must be at her wits' end to send for me – and he is the only family I have left.'

'Stop worrying,' I told her. 'You can always come and stay with me when he is well again.'

'Yes, I can.' She was clearly relieved. 'And Marie is so sensible. You will be quite safe with her to take care of you. Adele always relied on her completely.'

Marie smiled when I conveyed the news to her later that day. She handed me the gold wedding ring she had bought earlier.

'It is as well we had decided to be prepared.'

'I am three weeks late, Marie. As a widow I can have my child and remain respectable in the eyes of the world ... as my mother did.'

'Your mother had a wealthy protector,' Marie said with a slight frown. 'Whatever the comte has done to hurt you, Jenny, he was good to her. She always knew that he could never marry her—'

'Please, do not speak of him. I do not wish to hear his name.'

'Very well,' she replied, still frowning. 'But it does not suit you to be hard, Jenny. You are not the first woman to be in this situation. Besides, you feel as if you are a widow – don't you?'

'Yes, I do. I loved Gérard. If it had been possible—' I turned from her as the emotion tightened my throat. I could not speak.

'I took the necklace and bangle you gave me to the jeweller's,' Marie said. 'The price they offered was ridiculous so I did not sell. It will be better to wait until we are in London. I shall find an honest dealer given time.'

She was placing the pieces in my dressing-case as she spoke. I nodded but made no reply. I had wanted only to be rid of Laurent's gifts, but Marie was practical. We should need money. Laurent had provided for me at his bank but I was not sure how much money I would have. If I had been able I would have refused his help entirely, but I had no choice. My education was not suited to any trade; I had been taught to be a gentlewoman and I should find it difficult to earn a living. I had once spoken of becoming a governess but things were altered now, especially if there was to be a child.

I was still not certain I was with child but it seemed more likely as each day passed without my monthly flow. Marie had promised to help me if I decided to have something done. My mind shied away from the details. I was vaguely aware that girls in trouble sometimes went to places ... horrible, dirty little houses in back streets where things were done to bring on a miscarriage. It was dangerous and the very idea made me shudder with horror. To kill my unborn child seemed a terrible sin. Sister Isobel would certainly deem it so. I did not think I could do it, whatever the consequences.

Besides, since holding Kate's daughter in my arms I had felt myself grow stronger. And I had dreamed several times of my lover. In every dream he had told me I must be strong for our child. I felt that he was trying to tell me to keep the baby and in my heart I knew it was what I wanted.

I had reached a decision, albeit unspoken: if I was carrying Gérard's child I would brazen it out. No one in London would know me. No one would have any reason to suspect that I was not a widow.

I stared out of the bedroom window at the sunlit streets. The chestnut trees were just beginning to blossom. Soon I would be leaving France for ever. I was going to a new country and a new life.

It was while I was packing some of my things that I came across the sketches the street artist had made of Mama and I that day in Paris. I stared at them for several minutes, tears in my eyes, and I wondered again if the man who had paid the artist to take our likenesses had been Philip Allington.

Had he wanted the sketches to take back to England for someone? Perhaps a member of my mother's family? A woman ... the woman he had spoken of when I saw him at my mother's house?

Why had she wanted to see me? And why had my mother been so much against it? I had found nothing amongst Mama's things to unravel the mystery of Mr Allington's visit – but I remembered very clearly that he had made her unhappy.

I knew that Laurent must have Mr Allington's address, but I did not want to ask him for anything. I did not want to see or speak to him again. For the moment I was confused, unsure of what the future held for me. When I was ready, I would make enquiries about my mother's family, but not yet.

I needed time to be alone. Time to heal.

Kate came to see me off the day we left Paris. She embraced me, and I saw tears in her eyes.

'Take care of yourself, Jenny,' she said. 'Write to me – promise?'

'Yes, of course.'

She looked into my eyes. 'You are having Gérard's child – aren't you? And you intend to keep it.'

I nodded silently, my cheeks warm, unable to look at her. She reached for my hand, held it.

'You won't tell Henriette – or Laurent?'

'You know I shan't.'

'We didn't know, Kate...'

'That Laurent was your father?' She smiled at me. 'No, of course not. Do not look so ashamed; you have no need.'

'But—'

Kate touched her fingers to my lips. 'You do not know for sure,' she said. 'Even Laurent is not certain. I think that is why he is torturing himself now. He is living at the château now. He hardly sees anyone. I think he is punishing himself for what happened to you – and Gérard.'

'Is he?' My voice hardened, my expression becoming distant, unforgiving. I felt as if my heart were made of jade, that hardest of stones. 'Is he really suffering?'

'I think you know that,' she said and kissed me. Her eyes were bright and full of love for me. I was reminded of the day when I had thought how alike she and Gérard were, and for a moment I smiled at the memory.

'Go to England, Jenny,' she told me. 'Find your family, discover the truth about your mother's life and yourself.'

'Yes,' I said. 'Yes, I have to know, Kate. I have to know the truth.'